Newlywed Dead

NANCY J. PARRA

BERKLEY PRIME CRIME, NEW YORK

An imprint of Penguin Random House LLC
375 Hudson Street, New York, New York 10014

NEWLYWED DEAD

A Berkley Prime Crime Book / published by arrangement with the author

ISBN: 978-0-425-27037-0

PUBLISHING HISTORY
Berkley Prime Crime mass-market edition / May 2016

PRINTED IN THE UNITED STATES OF AMERICA

10 9 8 7 6 5 4 3 2 1

Cover illustration by Ben Perini.
Cover design by Sandra Chiu.
Interior text design by Laura K. Corless.

This book is for Jeanette Hait Blanco.
Thank you for your unconditional friendship, wisdom and joy,
and for sharing adventures with me.

Acknowledgments

It takes a village to create a book. Special thanks to my editor, Michelle; her assistant, Bethany; and all the copyeditors, production folks, and proofreaders at Berkley Prime Crime. Thanks, too, to my agent, Paige Wheeler, who keeps me on track and helps me make a living doing what I love. Finally, thanks to the readers who keep buying my books, sharing my stories, and allowing me to be a part of their lives. You all ROCK.

Chapter 1

"Get ready," I called to the wedding party and the rest of our family and friends outside the church. The bridesmaids and groomsmen lined either side of the church stairs.

We waited patiently for the photographer to finish taking pictures and for Felicity and Warren to come out of the church. I passed out small bags of rice and birdseed along with bubbles. The rice was a nod to my parents who insisted that only rice was a sign of good luck. I argued that birdseed was better because rice was bad for the birds. Felicity had tried to solve the problem by asking for bubbles to be blown when they came out of the church. Somehow we ended up with all three.

I had paid the altar boys twenty dollars each to sweep up the stairs after we left. That way no birds would be harmed.

1

"Here they come!" George Grayson, Warren's best man, shouted.

Everyone cheered as Felicity and Warren stepped out hand in hand. We tossed the seeds and rice and blew bubbles as they stopped at the top of the steps and kissed. Their shiny new rings caught the evening light. Felicity's veil fluttered in the wind and they pulled back, ducking from our pelting, and ran to the waiting limo. The rest of the bridal party jumped into waiting cars and chased them through town, honking and waving.

I sat in the back of George's Lexus next to Warren's sister, Whitney, and her boyfriend, Carlton, while George's girlfriend, Kelli, sat in the passenger seat. I felt like a fifth wheel without a date. My new boyfriend Gage's mother had fallen this morning and broken her ankle. He'd been so sorry to miss the wedding, I told him I completely understood. Besides, George was supposed to be my "date" for the night. It was weird how they always matched the best man and maid of honor even though they were rarely a couple in real life. Tradition, I guess.

"That was the most beautiful wedding I've ever attended," Whitney said.

"And she's attended a lot," Kelli said with laughter in her eyes.

"Wait for the reception," I said. "Our families went all out."

"Wedding traditions are so much fun," Whitney said, and looked at Carlton with love in her eyes. "Don't you think so?"

"Sure," he said, and patted her hand. "Especially the open bar."

"And the garter toss," George added.

Kelli smacked his arm.

"What?" George said, and everybody laughed.

My parents had asked if I wanted to ride with them, but I really wanted to be around the cool kids for once. When else could I do that except when I was part of my little sister's wedding party? It didn't matter that Warren and his friends were all trust-fund kids while my dad was a plumber and my mom taught piano lessons. We were all a cobbled-together family now.

"Kelli, Pepper's the one I was telling you about," Whitney said with a wink.

"Oh, the one with the business?" Kelli asked.

I frowned, not sure what they were trying to say. "Are you talking about Perfect—"

"Yes," Whitney said, cutting me off and touching my arm with a second wink. "Kelli and I are really interested in that thing that you do."

"You mean plan pro—"

"Parties," Whitney cut me off again. Her blue eyes twinkled.

"Really? What kind of parties?" Carlton asked.

"The kind of parties girls like," Whitney said.

"Oh, you mean like lingerie parties?" Carlton's expression perked up.

"No," I said as I felt my cheeks turn pink.

"Princess parties," Whitney said. "Felicity told me you did a little mermaid one recently."

"Oh," I said. "Yes, yes, I did." This time I nodded. I wasn't sure why they were not simply stating what I really did—plan wedding proposals—but I went along anyway.

"Is there delicious cake?" George asked. "I like delicious cake."

I could see his blue gaze in the rearview mirror. "Yes," I said. George was Warren's best friend, and since Warren helped me start my business I knew that George knew what I did. It didn't take much deduction to understand that Carlton was the only one not in on the full conversation.

"Well," Carlton said. "I'm for any party with delicious cake."

"So am I," Whitney said, and patted Carlton's hand. "We'll talk more later. Kelli has a friend who needs a princess party."

"Sounds perfect," I said, and smiled.

It's tradition to drive around town with your "Just Married" decorated cars and honk and wave at the locals. We drove around for a good half hour. Long enough for the rest of the guests to arrive at the swanky country club Warren's parents had insisted we use as the reception venue. My parents had argued over it for a full month. There was no way they could afford the country club, and my father's pride was not going to let Warren's family pay. It was the bride's family who paid for the wedding.

I tried to tell my father that times had changed. But there was no getting around his devotion to tradition. Finally

Warren and Felicity had brought both families together and announced that they were paying for the wedding. Period. At that moment I saw relief on my mother's face and a wide smile and nod on Warren's mother's face. Meanwhile my father's face turned red. I held my breath. I thought for sure he was going to have a stroke.

Felicity, in her gentle way, took my dad by the hand and pulled him into a corner and spoke to him one-on-one. Finally, my father relented and the wedding was on. The compromise had been that Felicity and Warren would get married in the big old church where my parents and grandparents had gotten married.

My family was nothing if not traditional.

We pulled up to the front of the club and valets rushed out to take the car. Doors were opened for us and we gathered our coats around us as we stepped out into the cool Chicago night. My sister was born under a lucky star. Not only did she meet and marry a millionaire, but the winter weather had stayed away for her special day. It was relatively warm for early December at 50 degrees. Still, I could smell snow in the air as I stepped toward the double doors of the club.

"Hurry in," Whitney said. "The bride and groom are right behind us."

I followed as the rest of the wedding party laughed their way inside. We shucked our winter dress coats, handing them off to the coat check girls. Then we gathered at the mouth of the ballroom, which was brightly lit with twinkle lights and candles. There was a three-piece orchestra playing in what would later become the dance floor.

Warren's mother had hired a wedding planner with big plans. Luckily Felicity loved the woman. The planner was brilliant. She took my sister's ideas and turned them up ten notches. I stepped farther into the ballroom to see my mom and dad already standing near the head table with champagne in their hands.

"Here they are," the wedding planner, Donna, said as Warren and Felicity slipped into the foyer. Warren wore a black wool dress coat over his tux. His dark hair was cut close with a seemingly effortless look of prep and class. His black shoes shone in the twinkle lights that covered the entrance to the country club.

Felicity wore a pearl cashmere coat with ermine fur trim and white kid gloves that came up to her wrists. Her blond hair was done in a French twist. For the reception, she had changed into a shorter veil. She took off her coat and handed it to the coat check girl. Her dress was a lovely abalone-colored silk that shimmered in the lightest of blues and pinks and whites. The top was a delicate pale bluish white lace that covered the strapless part of the pearl silk and formed a portrait collar and three-quarter-length sleeve. The gown narrowed at the waist then flared slightly, falling to the ground.

The skirt was in two parts: an overlay of satin and lace that fell at a diagonal to reveal a panel of white embroidered flowers on silk. The same flowers were embroidered on the bottom of the long train. Donna hurried behind Felicity to button the train up. The buttons were designed to create a shorter bustle effect that allowed the bride to sit and dance without dragging the train behind her.

"Okay," Donna said with a smile. "Here we go, folks. Bridesmaids and groomsmen first, then best man and maid of honor, then the bride and groom." She gave a sign to the orchestra and they paused. The DJ stepped up and made the announcement as we entered the ballroom.

Everything was perfect, from the food to the dancing to the traditions of cutting the cake and tossing the garter.

It was tradition in my family for the bride and groom to leave the wedding reception first. They were supposed to sneak away for their big night, but usually the sneaking was seen by everyone and they were followed out by catcalls, whistles, and congratulations. After Felicity and Warren had left, my dad took his tux coat off and undid his tie. Mom still sparkled with joy and tears. The orchestra had been replaced by the DJ, who currently played slow songs as couples danced.

Having nothing much to do but watch others dance, I offered to get Whitney a drink from the bar.

"Sure, a Cosmo, please," she said.

"I'll come with you," George said. "Kelli's in the little girls' room and I know she'll want something when she gets back." George was handsome in his custom tux. His hair was cut in a neat preppy style that was longer on top and shorter near his neck and ears. Even though it was winter in Chicago, George, Kelli, and Whitney looked golden with tans that didn't come out of a spray booth.

Everyone in the bridal party had flown to St. Bart's the week before to rest up before the big event.

I had begged off. First of all, I didn't have the money to spend a week on a tropical island. Secondly, I had a new business to nurture. Perfect Proposals had had a slow but steady stream of clients. Planning proposals and engagement parties was a lot of fun and hard work. This kind of business needed consistent word of mouth, and that meant I had to find every opportunity to work. So I had stayed home.

I knew that I practically glowed in the dark in comparison to the rest of the wedding party. After all, I had redhead skin, which was pale to begin with, but winter pale was blinding. Luckily I sort of sparkled in the low twinkle lights the room was decorated in.

"Hey, George, how's it going?" A man who looked to be in his early fifties came up and shook George's hand. He was dressed in a black tux cut to fit his mid-sized frame. He had short black hair with gray at the temples. "Is this your new girlfriend?"

"Hello, Judge Abernethy, good to see you," George said smoothly. "No, I'm still with Kelli. This is Pepper Pomeroy. Pepper, let me introduce Judge Winston Abernethy."

"Nice to meet you," I said, and shook his hand.

"Part of the bridal party," the judge said, his dark blue eyes sparkling. "Oh, yes, you are the maid of honor. Are you related to the bride or the groom?"

"Felicity is my sister," I said.

"Beauty runs in the family," the judge said, and stepped closer.

"It does," George said smoothly, and put his arm around me, gently moving me forward in the line. "How's your wife and kids?"

Judge Abernethy chuckled. "Anne's fine. Beatrice's at Brown University and Joe's at MIT."

"Sounds like you have bright children," I said.

"They're good kids. They have their heads on straight," the judge said.

"Excuse me, dear," a thin, older woman said to catch my attention. "Are you Pepper Pomeroy?"

"Yes," I said.

"Mrs. Fulcrum," she said and held out her hand. I shook it on instinct. Her handshake was firm and in charge. "I understand you planned Warren and Felicity's proposal event."

"Yes," I said. "Besides being Felicity's sister—"

"And maid of honor," George added.

"And maid of honor," I said and sent him a sidelong look to tell him I thought he was being silly. "I'm the owner of Perfect Proposals. It's a high-end proposal planning business."

"Good," she said and ran her hand over her perfect hair, flashing a massive diamond encrusted wedding ring set. "Do you have a card? I am looking for someone like you to plan a proposal."

"Yes," I said and dug a business card out of my clutch. "Is this for yourself or a friend."

"Oh, dear no," she said with a well-practiced laugh. "It's for my son." She took my card and slipped it in her Dior clutch. "I'll call you next week."

"I look forward to it," I said.

She turned and waved at another woman who was also very thin and dressed in a designer outfit.

"Oh, Mrs. Fulcrum," George whispered near my ear. "You're in the big money now."

"What can I get you?" the female bartender asked. She was about five foot four and scary skinny. Her black slacks and white shirt hung on her frame. She wore simple makeup, but compared to the other female bartender beside her, she looked as if she'd lived a rough life. In fact, she seemed just a little out of place for waitstaff at a wedding.

"We'd like a scotch neat, a Cosmo, a glass of white wine, and . . ." George paused and looked at me.

"I'll take white wine, too," I said. Ever since I'd broken up with my longtime boyfriend Bobby, I'd tried to remember that there was more to adult beverages than beer. So far I had ventured into the wine territory and sort of stuck there. Wine was a safe choice. I felt it made me appear sophisticated, hiding my ignorance of alcoholic drinks, and I liked it most of the time.

I watched in fascination as the bartender—her name tag said Ashley—created the Cosmo. She poured from two bottles at the same time into a shaker, adding cranberry juice and a fresh-squeezed lime, and shook the concoction for thirty seconds before straining it into an elegant martini glass. I made a mental note to think about 1950s cocktails for the next engagement party I planned.

The bartender handed me the two white wines while George took the Cosmo and scotch, and we said good-bye to Judge Abernathy and threaded our way back through the growing crowd.

"Here's your wine," I said, and sat the drink down next to Kelli, who had returned to sit next to Whitney. "George has your Cosmo."

"Oh, yum!" Whitney said, and took the drink from George and sipped.

"How is it?" I asked, sipping my wine. I didn't want to sit down. The music had picked up to a fast happy dance.

"Cosmos are great!" Whitney said. "Haven't you ever had one?"

"No," I said with a short shake of my head.

"You poor thing," Kelli said. "We need to educate you."

"Speaking of educating," Whitney said, "Kelli's got a friend who wants to propose to her boyfriend."

"Really?" I turned to Kelli.

"I know it's sort of different," Kelli said, "but my friend has been dating this guy for five years and he's clueless about how and when to propose."

"Have they talked about getting married?" I asked, worried. The last thing I wanted to do was plan a proposal for a couple that wasn't all in. Toby—my friend and onetime oblivious client—had taught me to be cautious. Poor Toby had assumed that marriage was like a business merger, and all he had to do was propose and a smart woman would say yes because he was a billionaire. Luckily, I had been able to show him that romance was a huge factor in the proposal business.

"Oh, yes, in fact, my friend is pregnant," Kelli said. "She

thinks it would be great to propose and then let him know she is in the family way."

"We couldn't talk about this in the car because of Carlton," Whitney said. "All this wedding talk makes him nervous. We've only been dating a year and I don't want him to think I'm pressuring him."

"Okay, it all makes sense now," I said, and dug my card out of my clutch. "Here's my card. Have your friend call me to set up an initial appointment. You can come, too, Kelli, if that will make her feel more comfortable."

"Is this friend someone I know?" George asked.

Kelli laughed. "No, she's a girlfriend from the aid society downtown where I volunteer."

"Whew," George said with a twinkle in his eye. "You had me worried for a moment there."

Kelli smacked his arm. "What are you saying?"

"I'm saying I want to be the one who does the proposing," George said. "Even if you are knocked up."

"Stop," Kelli said. "We'll have this discussion another time."

George grinned and reached down, planting a kiss on her lips. "I'm simply letting you know I want to do the guy thing when the time comes. Okay?"

"Okay," Kelli said. She turned to me with concern in her eyes. "It's not crazy for a girl to propose, right?"

"No," I said. "I just pulled off a successful proposal for a girl who wanted to surprise her man."

"See, I told you," Kelli said.

"Seriously, call me on Monday and we'll set up a time to meet and talk about some of the things I've done."

"Great!" Whitney said. "I told you Pepper could help."

Carlton approached the table. "What's great?"

"That you are here," Whitney said, and stood. She took one more sip of her drink. "Come on, dance with me."

"Okay," Carlton said as Whitney took his hand and pulled him out to the dance floor. George and Kelli went out to dance as well. I wandered over to the bar to see if the bartender made any other cocktails I could use at one of my engagement parties.

Mom stopped me on the way.

"Your dad's gone to get our coats," Mom said. "We're going to take Aunt Betty home. It's been a long day."

Aunt Betty was my father's sister. She was ten years older than my father and lived in a nearby suburb. My mom's family was much larger. She had six brothers and sisters scattered all over the United States. Warren had offered to fly them all in and put them up at the W Hotel downtown so that Felicity had a good showing of family on their special day. When you have a family as large as mine, there are the inevitable family feuds. That said, we all come together when there is a family crisis or a wedding. My aunt Sarah had come with her husband, Bill, and their three teenagers. Then there was Uncle Tom and his wife, Chrissy. Their two kids were ten years older than me and hadn't come. Aunt Karen brought her partner, Sue. Uncle Alan brought his wife, Emma, who he had met and married

in the UK. Uncle Joseph came alone because Aunt Lilly
had left him for a doctor. Finally, Uncle Lee was a confirmed bachelor. My uncles left within fifteen minutes of
Felicity and Warren leaving. Aunt Karen and Sue were
in the far corner talking with some friends of Warren's
family. They loved to talk politics, and from what I could
see they found people who agreed with their political
views.

"Where are Aunt Sarah and Uncle Bill?" I asked, looking around.

"Sarah and Bill left right after Felicity," Mom said.

"Oh, I'm sorry I didn't get to say good-bye."

"They'll be at the house tomorrow for brunch," Mom
said. "You'll see them then."

Dad walked up with Mom's coat in his hands. His own
coat was thrown over his rented tux. "Ready?"

"Where's Aunt Betty?" I asked looking around him.

"She's waiting at the door. The music is getting to her,"
Dad said as he helped Mom into her coat.

"It was a wonderful wedding," I said, and gave my parents a hug and a kiss. "Felicity looked so happy."

Dad ran his hand over his bristled hair. "Who would
have figured we would be part of high society?"

"I think we fit in just fine," Mom said, and patted Dad's
hand. "Did you say good-bye to the Evanses?"

"Yes," Dad said. "They want us to come for dinner in two
weeks."

"Wonderful, I'll talk to Emily tomorrow. You did

NEWLYWED DEAD

remind them we are having a brunch tomorrow at the house, didn't you?"

"Yes, they said they wouldn't miss it."

"Perfect," Mom said, and turned to me. "Well, honey, we'll see you in the morning. Are you bringing Gage?"

"I've asked him," I said. "But his mom just got out of the hospital, so I don't know if he'll make it or not."

"That's right, poor thing. Terrible to break your ankle so badly you need surgery." Mom hugged me and kissed my cheek. "Tell him hi for us."

"I will."

Dad gave me a bear hug. "See that you get home safe."

"I will." I hugged Dad back. He was a solidly built man, and at five feet ten inches, he was just two inches taller than me.

"Text when you get home," Mom said over her shoulder as they left.

"You'll be asleep," I called after her.

"Text anyway." She waved at me.

I shook my head and glanced at the time on my phone. It was only ten P.M. There were still two hours of party left. I was not old or dead. I needed to try to mingle some more. But first I wanted to text Gage and see how he was.

I made my way back to the bar area. There was only Ashley tending the bar. There were two guys ahead of me. I pulled my phone from my clutch and did a quick check. Gage had texted at eight P.M. to say he hoped I was having a good time. I texted back. "Wish you were here."

"Hey, lonely lady," Ashley said. "Can I get you something?"

"What?" I said, and looked up at her.

"You look like you could use a drink, and here I am, a bartender with lots of free booze. Can I get you something to drink?"

"Oh." I put my phone away, embarrassed to be caught texting at a wedding reception. "I don't know," I said with a sad shake of my head. "Do you know any good 1950s cocktails?"

"Well, that's an interesting question," she said, and leaned her elbows on the counter. "Are you looking for a martini? Or something classic?"

"I'm sorry, that was vague," I said and held out my hand. "I'm Pepper, the bride's sister."

"And maid of honor," Ashley said, and eyed my bridesmaid's gown.

"Oh, right," I said. "You're very observant."

"It's part of being a bartender," she said. "I'm Ashley Klein, by the way. Now, martini or something classic?"

"Surprise me," I said. "I don't know anything about cocktails. I've been sort of stuck in beer for most of my life."

She eyed me knowingly. "Well, then, let me fix you something better than beer." Ashley pulled out a shaker and filled it with crushed ice, gin, cherry brandy, lemon juice, and club soda She shook it and strained it into a martini glass, then pushed the glass toward me.

"This is a Singapore Sling."

I picked it up and took a sip. "Wow!" I said as I let the

tartness tingle my taste buds a second time. "This is awesome."

"Thanks," Ashley said with pride. As I sipped my newfound favorite drink, I noticed that she looked to be in her mid- to late thirties, but when I talked to her she seemed as if she might be in her mid-twenties like me. Maybe she seemed older because of how scary skinny she was.

"Do you bartend at weddings often?" I had to ask. She really didn't seem the type that was hired for such events. Her stained teeth and the lines in her lips gave away that she was a heavy smoker. Her hair was dull blond and thinning, but her eyes were bright.

"I've done a few weddings. Some higher end ones, but this is my first gig here," Ashley admitted. "I usually bartend at the Elks Lodge or when someone gets married at the fire station. When this opportunity came up, I had to take it. Christmas is coming up."

"I know," I said, and sipped my drink. "A girl has to work."

"That's right," Ashley said. She glanced around to ensure the other bartender was gone and leaned against the bar. "What do you do for a living, Pepper?" she asked me. "Or is that a bad question. I mean, considering the crowd." She waved her hand. "You don't seem like a trust-fund girl."

I laughed. "What gave it away? The hair or the shoes?"

Ashley laughed. "You're the only one here all night who talked to me like a person."

"I'm sure it's not that bad. I mean, they are my family, and we're not trust-fund people."

17

"Oh, gee, now I've gone and offended you," she said and straightened. "I'm sorry. It's just that most of these people don't seem as nice as you."

"It's all right. It's a wedding. Most people get nuts at weddings," I said. "Right?"

"There's truth in that," Ashley said, and leaned on the bar. "So your sister married into society?"

"Warren's a great guy," I said, not sure why I felt the need to defend him. "He actually got me started in my business. I'm an event planner. I plan engagements and engagement parties." I pulled out one of my cards and handed it to her. "Perfect Proposals." I sipped my drink.

"Huh. People plan proposals?" Ashley said. "You mean like flash mobs and airplane banners and such?" She looked up and something seemed to catch her eye. She paused a moment. "What was I saying?" Then suddenly she gripped the bar and closed her eyes. "Whoa."

"Are you okay?" I asked. "You look like you're about to pass out." I set my drink aside. "Maybe you should sit down."

"It's nothing," Ashley said with her eyes closed as she rubbed her left temple. "Just a minor spell. I get them sometimes. You see, I had a head injury once. Sometimes flashbacks come up when I see a certain color or even smell something. My doctors said they were triggers and I shouldn't worry."

"Was it a bad injury? What happened?"

"I don't really remember," Ashley said. She slowly opened her eyes and breathed in through her nose and out through her mouth. "I woke up in the hospital. The last thing I remembered was riding in a homecoming parade—"

"Wait, homecoming parade," I said. "How old are you?"

"I'm twenty-five," Ashley said, and tried to smile but it didn't reach her eyes. "I know people think I look older."

"So you were at college riding in the homecoming parade and what happened?" I asked, trying not to let her see that I thought she was older, too.

"Apparently, sometime between the parade and when I woke up, I was attacked. Shot, actually." She lifted her lank hair and showed me a thumbprint-sized scar just above her temple. "My best friend was killed that night. They tell me we were together. I survived and she didn't."

"I'm so sorry to hear that."

She shrugged. "It was a couple of years ago and I can't remember what happened. It's usually no biggie except when I have one of these spells. It hurts like a lightning bolt went off in my head."

"Like just now."

"Yes," she nodded. "Weird, but it's the third time it's happened in the last hour. It usually doesn't do that." Ashley scanned the crowd as if she were looking for someone.

Maybe she was looking for the trigger for her flashbacks.

"Is it someone who's here that's causing it?" I asked. "Or a smell, maybe? Maybe it's the dance floor lighting."

Ashley merely winced, clearly preoccupied with whatever was going on in her head. A young guy and a girl made their way to the bar and I stepped back to let them order their drinks. I slipped two dollars into Ashley's tip jar. She seemed to really need the cash.

The guy was really young, but very wealthy. I noticed he had a preppy haircut and was wearing a Valentino tux. His shoes were highly polished soft leather, surely from Italy. If I knew anything, I knew my designers. I sighed at the fact that someone so young could dress so well. Clearly they came from Warren's side of the family.

"I'll take a martini," he said with a snicker. His blue gaze was rowdy, his mouth pulling into a sneer. "Shaken, not stirred."

"Stop it, Clark," the girl with him said, and frowned. "He wants a Coke."

"No, I want a martini." He ran his hands down his lapels. "I'm wearing a tux. I should get to drink a martini."

"You know I can't serve you," Ashley said. "You aren't old enough to drink, so stop coming over here and pretending that I should serve you."

"Aw, come on, one martini is not going to hurt me," Clark said.

"It can hurt you," Ashley said sternly. "It kills brain cells."

"It kills brain cells," Clark mocked. He turned to Ashley and narrowed his eyes. "I'm going to tell my mother that you talked back to me and refused to serve me. She's a Fulcrum. Everyone knows you don't mess with a Fulcrum. You're going to find your butt out the door faster than you can down a shot of whiskey." Clark stormed off.

The girl stayed. "Don't mind him," she said. "I'll take that Coke."

Ashley poured cola over ice and the girl sipped it from a straw, chatting with Ashley. The music had turned from a slow waltz to a fast swing beat, and I couldn't really tell what they were talking about, but it seemed like Ashley knew the girl and the boy who had stomped off.

I perused the room, but saw that there was no opportunity to mingle. I checked my phone but Gage hadn't answered my text. Sighing, I pulled my attention back to Ashley. The young girl had left and we were alone again. "I thought you said you hadn't served here before," I shouted over the loud music. "But you seemed to know those two." I nodded my head in the direction of the table where Clark had flung himself into a chair next to a woman who looked like she was in her early fifties.

"Oh, yeah, no," Ashley said. "This is my first time here. I met Samantha Lyn and Clark when I was bartending Clark's cousin's wedding in October." Ashley grabbed a bar towel and wiped down the bar. "Samantha Lyn was bored and came over for a cola then and we struck up a conversation—sort of how you and I are talking now. I have a sense for people, and Samantha Lyn has her head on straight. She's a nice kid."

"Oh," I said, and sipped my drink. "Funny how you saw them at two weddings in a few months' span."

"It's a small world," Ashley said. "With a country club scene this expensive, it's a little inbred, if you know what I mean."

"No," I said, and shook my head. "I don't understand."

"There are only so many people in the area who can

21

afford the fees. That means that whenever you attend one of these functions you tend to see the same people over and over again. It's sort of like attending a small college. After a while everyone knows everyone else."

"Huh," I said. "Sounds like you attended a small college."

"I did," she said, "but before you ask, I didn't graduate." She pointed to her head. "Graduating sort of got blown away." She tried to make light of her injury but she failed and could tell I saw through her. "Really," Ashley said. "Bartending weddings brings in good money, and the people aren't all bad. Take Samantha Lyn—" She pointed toward the dance floor where the young girl was dancing with a reluctant Clark. "It's too bad that she's mixed up with Clark. He's trouble—a real momma's boy. I don't know what she's doing with him. If you ask me, she's out of his league." Ashley shrugged.

Ashley took the half-full glass out of my hand and mixed me another drink. "This is called a Moscow Mule. It was created in the 1950s and uses vodka, lime juice, ginger beer, and a few drops of bitters. Try it."

I took a sip and it was good. "I like the ginger," I said. "But there's no way I can drink all this on top of the last drink you made me."

She winked and poured half of my drink into a glass of her own.

"Wait, should you be drinking?" I asked.

"Don't worry. No one here notices. To us," she said, and raised her glass and clinked hers to mine. "May we both find what we're looking for."

That was something I agreed with, so I lifted my glass and said, "To us."

Ashley tossed down the half a drink and then pressed her fingers to her head again and bit her lips. "Ugh. Excuse me for a minute," she said, and headed toward a nearby door. As if on cue, the second bartender with a name tag that said Tracy came out of the hallway and took her place near the bar.

"Hi," Tracy said. "Do you need anything?"

"No, I'm fine, thanks," I said, and turned to watch the dancers. My cousin Bethany, Aunt Sarah's girl, came up to me.

"Come on, wallflower," Bethany said, and took my hand. "You won't get anywhere holding up the wall."

"I wasn't holding up the wall," I protested.

"No, you were holding up the bar," Bethany said. "I was being nice. Come on, the maid of honor should spend the night dancing."

"Oh, right," I said, and let her drag me toward the dance floor. After all, the night was young and my sister had just married one of the richest men in the country. I should dance to that, right?

Chapter 2

"Okay, so I'm really drunk." A tall blond girl came up to me and dragged her equally soused boyfriend with her. "But you're like that proposal planner, right?"

"Yes," I said. It was nearly the end of the reception and I sat two tables back from the dance floor where only a few die-hards slow danced.

"Cool," the blonde said, and grabbed a chair to sit extremely close to me. "This is Brad Hurst and I'm Jennifer McCutchen."

"Hi, Brad," I said with a small wave. I wasn't about to mention how weird it was for a couple to be Jennifer and Brad given a certain celebrity couple who had broken up while I was in junior high.

"Hi," Brad said, and grinned down at me. He had a high-ball glass in his hand. His tux was undone. His suit coat was on a chair somewhere, I imagined. The shirtsleeves were rolled up, and his bow tie was untied and wrapped causally around his neck. He had brown eyes and well-styled shoulder-length hair. He flashed perfectly straight white teeth.

"So, Brad wants to use your services," Jennifer said, and leaned tipsily toward me. Her breath was a cloud of alcohol vapor.

"He does?" I asked, and crossed my arms.

"I do," Brad said, and gave a short nod. "Jen says so." He waved at the blonde.

"Okay," I said, and looked confused. "Why do you say so, Jennifer? Does he want to propose to a friend of yours?"

"Oh, no, silly," Jennifer said, and slapped my knee. Her martini glass with pink liquid sloshed and threatened to spill on my dress. I moved a few inches back. "He wants to propose to me, but I keep ruining it. I always find out, you see. Isn't that right, sweetie?"

Brad merely motioned with a dip of his head and a swirl of his hand that she was right. He sipped his drink and I sighed.

"Okay, so how is engaging my services going to help not ruin the surprise?" I had to ask. The whole thing was a bit crazy. Especially with the state Jennifer was in.

"Oh, that's the great part. If anyone can surprise me, it's you," she said, and tossed down the remains of her drink. "You see, I want a really grand proposal with all the bells and whistles. Isn't that right, Brad?" She looked at Brad who just nodded. "I heard you were like the best at this engagement planning thing."

"You did?" I asked. "That's nice. Who referred you?"

"Well, you set up Warren and Felicity, right?"

"Yes, I did."

"They were engaged on a jet, right? There were lots of mementos and great decorations and such. Then you did that sparkly mermaid one, right?" Jennifer wobbled a little. "Now you're going to do something completely over the top for me. Right? And you can make it a complete surprise. Right?"

"Certainly," I said, and shook my head because I knew I was most likely lying. She was drunk and probably wouldn't even remember talking to me in the morning.

"Good. Brad, give the lady your card." Jennifer motioned for Brad to hurry up.

The gentleman dug a wallet out of his back pocket and pulled out a beautiful linen embossed card and handed it to me. "Call me on Tuesday."

"Okay," I said, and took the card, trying not to read it. I slipped it into my clutch. "Anything I should know to start planning?"

"Oh, yes," Jennifer said, and leaned toward me. "I want Brad to propose in the most romantic way with all sorts of bells and whistles. I want it to be over the top." She leaned back and waved her arm over her head. "And I want the entire thing videotaped. I want to be a YouTube sensation and the envy of all my friends. I want tears in my eyes."

"Okay," I said, and tried not to shake my head. "What sorts of things do you find romantic?"

"The normal stuff, you know, like candles and roses and playing our song on a big boom box and ice skating . . . yes, ice skating like in that movie, with flowers raining down on us."

"Um, okay," I said, and glanced at Brad, who merely grinned at me and winked.

"Here's the thing, though," Jennifer said. "I have to be completely surprised. I can't suspect in the least what you are about to do."

"What?"

"Yes, I have to be completely surprised or the whole thing is off." Jennifer sat back and flopped her left hand on her lap and waved her right hand holding the empty martini glass. "If I'm not surprised, the whole thing is off."

"What?"

"Brad has tried four times? Was it four or five?" she asked him.

"Six, actually," he said, and leaned against the chair. "She figured me out each time."

"That's why we need you," Jennifer said, and turned toward me. "I want to be surprised and Brad hasn't been able to pull that off. It's my biggest wish—to be surprised. So, no surprise, no engagement." She tilted her head and studied me. "Understood?"

"Okay," I said, and looked from one to the other. They were completely serious. "You have to be surprised even though you are hiring me to plan your proposal and will be watching every moment waiting for it to happen."

"Yes," Jennifer said, with a nod and a smile. "If I figure it out, I'll tell you to try again." She crossed her arms. "And you will."

"I don't know . . ."

"I'll pay you double," Brad said. "Come on. Think of the word of mouth you can get for your business if you can pull this off."

I scratched my head. "Okay."

"Perfect." Jennifer held out her hand toward Brad. "Come on, dear, I'm tired. It's time we went home."

"Yes, dear," Brad said, and took her hand, helping her up. They left their drinks on the table beside me. "Call me on Tuesday."

"I will," I said. I watched them walk out to get their coats and noticed there were a few die-hards still dancing. I glanced over to see Ashley back at the bar and went over to talk to her some more.

"Hello, there, my proposal-planning friend," she said with a wane smile. "You and I seem to be the only two non–country club types left. Does that make us social heavies and not socialites?" She laughed, her chuckle deep and thick like a heavy smoker.

I looked around. "Huh, I think you're right. We are the only two women left who might actually work for a living. Does that happen often?"

"Yes, actually," she replied, suddenly sober. "When you have to work you usually go to bed earlier and try to get some rest. Socialites stay at parties because that's how they work. Networking for family and friends. For them it's all about who they know, not what they do."

"That's an interesting observation," I said, and put my elbows on the bar. "Lucky for me tomorrow is my day off."

"Cool," she said. "Do you want me to mix you up another exotic cocktail?"

"Sure," I said. "I can't promise I'll drink it all."

"The drinks are already paid for," she explained. "You might as well use the free booze to expand your cocktail knowledge. You like the fifties, right?"

"Yes, I'm thinking it might be a cute theme for a proposal, especially with all the midcentury modern architecture in the area."

"Well, then, let me make you a classic martini." She poured gin and vermouth into a shaker and added ice. Then she shook it and poured it through a drink strainer into a martini glass. "This is a gin martini. Classically served with olives or cocktail onions." She pushed the drink toward me.

I took a sip. "Strong," I said.

She chuckled. "Lounge music and cocktail hour became popular in the fifties as a way to relax. The world had just come out of the war and a strong drink in hand was thought to be cool."

"*Cool* meaning *drunk*?" I teased.

She took the drink from where I put it on the bar and tossed down a good half. I made a sound in protest and she shrugged. "Night's almost over. Don't worry, I'm taking the bus home. I don't own a car. Now, also popular in the

1950s and something great to serve at a proposal party is the champagne cocktail." She pulled out a champagne glass. "You take a sugar cube and drop some bitters on it." She held the cube between her fingers and carefully placed four drops of bitters on top. "Then you put it in the bottom of a champagne glass like so." She dropped the cube into the glass. "Then you cover that with cognac."

"Oh, that's going to be very sweet," I observed.

"That's why you include the bitters," she said, and winked at me. She poured the cognac until it covered the sugar cube and put the liquor bottle down. "Finish it off with champagne." She pulled out an open bottle and looked at the label. "This is a very good year," she teased, and then poured the champagne into the glass so carefully that the cognac didn't mix, but remained in the bottom of the glass. "And there you have it." She put the champagne bottle down and pushed the glass toward me. "Go on, try it."

"Cheers," I said, and toasted her with the glass before I took a long swig. I got mostly champagne with a touch of cognac. The sugar cube had just started to dissolve at the bottom as I set the glass down. "I think that's more for show than for drinking."

"It's clearly a dessert," she said.

I noticed that she was weaving a bit and clung to the bar for a moment.

"Are you all right?" I asked. "Is it your headache? Maybe you shouldn't be drinking."

"I haven't had that much," she said. "It's this darn headache. I can't shake it."

"Thank you for teaching me about cocktails," I said. "I really appreciate it. Especially since you aren't feeling well."

She waved off my comment. "I consider you a friend now. Anytime you want more information, just give me a call." We exchange cards so that we had each other's names and phone numbers. "I'm always up for work. I could use the money."

"Got it," I said, and put the card in my purse. "Maybe you should have some coffee. The caffeine is good for a headache."

"You're right," she said. "Can I pour you a cup?"

"No, thanks," I said. "I'm going to make a trip to the ladies' room." I stepped away and then turned back. Ashley was pouring coffee into a white mug. "Listen . . ."

She looked up.

"I feel like we really bonded. Do you want to meet for lunch or dinner sometime? On me? One hardworking woman to another?"

Her smile was genuine. "I'd like that."

"Okay," I said. "I've got your number. Don't forget, my name is—"

"Pepper," she said. "I never forget a friend. Besides, you gave me your card, remember?"

"Oh, right." I felt a blush rush over my face. "Sorry if I'm a little heavy-handed on the networking."

"No worries," she said and sipped her coffee. "You're doing all right."

"Thanks. You are, too." I walked to the ladies' room thinking what a great night it had been. Felicity looked so happy when she and Warren left, I'd seen some relatives I hadn't talked to in years, and I'd made a new friend. It didn't get much better than that. My phone buzzed and I looked down. Gage texted me back sending love and warm thoughts. I smiled.

As I stepped out of the restroom, the lights went up and the DJ turned off the last song.

"Hey, Pepper, we're going into town to do some club hopping. Want to come?" Whitney asked. She and Kelli came over to where I sat. I noticed that the guys had gone to get their coats.

"No, I think I've had enough partying for tonight," I said with a smile and stood. "You go without me."

"But we were your ride," Kelli said with a faint scowl.

"No worries, I'll catch a cab," I said. "Besides, you guys live in the city. I live in the suburbs. It's best I get a cab anyway."

"Are you sure?" George asked as he helped Kelli into her coat.

"I'm sure," I said.

Someone screamed. We all turned to the sound as one of the waitresses stumbled out from the back kitchen. She looked very pale and her expression was one of horror. Before I knew what I was doing, I was running toward her. "What's wrong?" I asked, and touched her. She didn't really see me. I think she was in shock.

"It's that bartender . . ." the waitress said, and pointed.

That's when I saw Ashley in the hall leading to the back kitchen, crumpled on the floor. I raced to her. She was too pale. I felt for a pulse and didn't find one. Leaning down,

I listened for breathing. She wasn't. "Someone call 911," I shouted. I hit her chest and started CPR. Thankfully I was certified a few months earlier. When your adrenaline is going and you're actually working on a real person, it's very different than the dummy. I tried to remember to hinge from the hips and use the heels of my hands. I was so worried I was breaking her ribs. She was so small and so thin. But the voice of my instructor kept ringing through my head. Push hard!

Ashley remained pale. People gathered around. George pushed through the crowd with a plastic kit in his hands. He knelt down and felt for a pulse.

"She wasn't breathing," I said as I counted out pulses.

"She's still not," he said, and sat back on his heels. He tore open the kit and pulled out a face mask with a rubber bag attached. "I'm going to try to push air into her lungs in between your counts."

I nodded. He put the mask over her nose and mouth and squeezed two breaths. Then I continued with compressions.

After what seemed like an hour the EMTs showed up. "You can stop now," a blond EMT said as he maneuvered in beside me. I raised my hands in the air and then scooted out of the way as they took her vital signs.

"No response," I heard the blond guy say.

There were two other guys in full gear. A guy with brown hair and blue eyes took over from George while a guy with black hair broke out a defibrillator.

I was startled by a hand on my shoulder. "Come on,

you've done what you could." It was Whitney. Her face was pale and her eyes large. I let her help me up and away from the men working.

"Here," George said as he put his coat around my shoulders. "You're shivering."

Whitney and Kelli helped me over to a chair out of sight of the men at work. The lights were all up full blast in the hall and the remaining people gathered in little clumps talking in hushed tones.

"I was just talking to her," I said. Tears flowed down my cheeks and I wiped them away. "She seemed like a nice person. You know?"

"Here." Kelli brought me a handful of tissues. "It's okay."

"The police are here," George said. "Thank goodness Warren and Felicity are long gone. What a bummer to learn someone died at your reception."

"She died?" I looked up at George.

His mouth tightened and he looked away.

"I just heard the EMTs say they couldn't revive her," Kelli said. She looked tired under the bright lights. I imagine we all looked a little worse for wear. "You did the best you could, Pepper. The best anyone could do."

"The police want to talk to everyone before we can leave," Carlton said. His expression appeared tired, his mouth a tight line. "You girls might as well take your coats off. We could be here awhile."

Whitney and Kelli took off their coats and put them on the backs of chairs. George went in search of bottled water. I wiped my eyes but couldn't stop the tears. "I feel terrible.

She seemed so nice," I said to Whitney. Then I remembered her headaches. "You know, she did say she was having headaches. I wonder if she had an aneurysm or something."

"If that's the case there's nothing you could have done," Whitney said, and patted my shoulder.

A nearby group of people talked in low tones about how horrible it was. I noticed that Clark and an older woman were the first ones to the police when the cops turned to the crowd. "It's too bad about that girl," I heard the woman say. "But you can't keep us here." She had her hands on Clark's shoulders. "My husband Douglas is outside in the car waiting. We didn't see anything."

"Who is that woman?" I asked Whitney. "I think I've met her. Is she one of your invitees?" I drew my eyebrows together.

"Oh, that's Mrs. Fulcrum. She and her husband Douglas have been benefactors to my mother's pet nonprofit project for years. They are huge in the country club set."

"That's her son, Clark?"

"Yes," Whitney said, with a shake of her head. "That boy is trouble. He's one of those who just slides by because his parents have money and he thinks he doesn't have to do anything." Whitney sighed. "The worst part is that his mother lets him. You know? I mean, we have money but my parents made sure that we knew how to be responsible adults."

"He tried to get Ashley to serve him a martini and she refused."

"Good for her," Whitney said. "My mom likes the Fulcrums, but frankly I think they're a little too high and mighty. And I completely disagree with any parent who lets their kids coast through life. A parent should never spend more time covering for their child than parenting them."

I nodded my agreement. "My parents believed in consequences. It wasn't always fun but it helped me understand the world better."

I noticed how Clark had a smirk on his face, as if seeing Ashley dead was just another game. He had his hands in his pockets and craned his neck to see around the first responders. Mrs. Fulcrum wore her fur coat and kept her hands on her son's shoulders. I could no longer hear what she was saying, but it was pretty clear she was giving the police the business about being held up from leaving.

With a calm expression on his face, one officer took notes and then let Mrs. Fulcrum and Clark leave. The next ones in line were Samantha Lyn and her parents, Mr. and Mrs. Thomson. They also seemed to be in a big hurry to leave. Mrs. Thomson looked impatient, as if she wanted to leave with the Fulcrums and the short delay to ask questions was putting her and her family out.

"That girl, I think her name is Samantha Lyn," I said and nodded toward them. "She's dating Clark, right?"

"Yes," Whitney said with a shake of her head. "They are so young. I sometimes see them hanging out at the club with their moms. Not that *I* hang around with their moms, but we attend a lot of the same functions. You know, fund-raisers, luncheons, golf and tennis tournaments, that sort of thing."

"Sure," I said, completely out of my element but willing to trust Whitney on the subject.

"Samantha Lyn is such a nice girl. Clark, on the other hand, is a piece of work. He's been known to treat the staff poorly. I've seen him spill things on purpose just to make a staff member get down and clean it up. Talk about a bad kid. One time he even hit on me. As if I would ever think about doing anything with a kid ten years younger than me. None of us knows what she's doing with Clark."

"Except her mom, Mrs. Thomson, is an obvious social climber and doesn't care who knows it. That woman is over the moon that a Fulcrum is dating her daughter," Kelli said. "It's crazy in this day and age to be proud that your daughter is dating someone from a certain family. I mean, shouldn't she be proud her daughter is majoring in economics? Poor Samantha Lyn, her entire identity's wrapped up in who she's dating."

"Like I said, she's young. Everything your parents say or do is so important at that age. Some kids want to do nothing but please their folks, while others rebel and do everything to upset them," Whitney said. "Samantha Lyn seems smart. I'm sure she'll figure it out."

Next up for questioning were Brad and Jen. It was clear that Jen was too tipsy to know what was really going on. Brad sort of held her upright with an apologetic look on his face. The police officers in charge let them through without a second glance. The hall cleared out steadily as there were only about twenty or so people left at the end of the reception.

"I'm so sorry." Donna, the wedding planner, rushed over to me and Whitney. "I told them not to keep the guests any longer than necessary. Please, go next. The waitstaff will be questioned last. I will see to the cleanup and such. I promise. It's part of my duties."

"As an event planner, I know there was nothing you did to cause this," I said, and patted her hand.

"I certainly hope this doesn't affect your review of my services," she said, and chewed on her bottom lip.

"We'll ensure you're reviewed on your work, not this incident," Whitney said, and patted the poor woman's shoulder.

I stood when it was our turn and gave George back his coat.

"You were the one giving the victim CPR," the policeman said as we approached the area where they were doing the interviews.

"Yes," I said. "I'm Pepper Pomeroy. This was my sister's wedding reception."

The cop looked around. "Are you part of the family who hired her?"

"No," I said, and shook my head. "My family and the Evanses hired a wedding planner." I pointed to where Donna stood talking to the country club's catering manager. "Donna took care of all the details."

"So you didn't know the deceased," he said as he looked up from his notes.

"I just met her tonight," I said with a sigh. "She seemed like a nice person."

"You spoke to her?"

"Yes," I said, and drew my eyebrows together. "I did spend some time with her after my sister left."

"Don't you think it's odd for the maid of honor to spend time with a bartender at a wedding?"

I shrugged and gave a small smile. "I'm a proposal planner and she was making these interesting cocktails."

"So you were talking shop."

"Yes," I said, and nodded. Carlton came over and handed me my coat. "Thanks," I said as I took the coat and folded it over my arm.

"Is everything okay?" he asked me. Carlton had his arm protectively around Whitney's waist.

"This will only take another minute," the police officer said to Carlton. Carlton and Whitney took a step back. "Now, you were telling me that you talked about cocktails with the bartender."

"Yes," I said, and blew out a long breath. At least the tears had stopped flowing. I could imagine how red and splotchy my face was. There were makeup and mascara stains on the tissue in my hand.

"How did she seem?" he asked.

"She seemed fine. I was asking her about different cocktail ideas I thought I might be able to use for one of my events."

"So she didn't seem drunk or disorderly?"

"No," I said, and shook my head. I remembered her sharing some of my drinks and weaving. "Wait, she did take some sips of alcohol," I said, "but not enough to make her

39

pass out or quit breathing. We just spoke for a while and then she was having coffee."

"Did she say anything to you that might cause you to suspect she would end up dead?"

"That's a strange question," I said. "What do you mean?"

"Did she seem at all suicidal? Or scared someone here would hurt her?"

"What? No," I said with an emphatic shake of my head. "I would have done something if she seemed suicidal. I wouldn't let something like that slip." I paused. "Although she did say she had a terrible headache all night. She seemed to think it had something to do with an old injury to her head."

"I see." The police officer gave me his card. "Listen, if you think of anything else, give me a call."

"Okay," I said, and let Kelli and Whitney pull me toward the door where George waited. I glanced over to see the police talking with the paramedics. I had the terrible feeling that there was something they weren't telling us.

"I've called you a cab," George said, and helped me into my coat. "We're going to head home."

"Yeah," Whitney said. "I think we've all had enough excitement for one day. Let's just hope that Warren and Felicity don't hear about this until they come back from their honeymoon."

I felt my eyes widen. "Oh, I certainly hope so. I'd hate for them to not go on their trip."

"Don't worry," George said. "Their flight leaves pretty early tomorrow morning. As long as they don't listen to the news, they'll be fine."

"I doubt there is anything much to report," Carlton said. "Besides that a woman collapsed and died at the country club."

"Gosh, I hope they don't say it like that," I said. "I'd hate for Felicity to worry."

"I'm sure Warren and Felicity will be too busy to listen to the news," Whitney said. "I know I'd be." She looked at Carlton, who smiled at her knowingly.

We stepped out into the cold clear air and George opened the door to the taxi. "Text Whitney when you get home safe, okay?"

"Okay," I said as I got into the cab. George closed the door and I waved as the cab pulled out toward my home. I pulled out my phone and thought about texting Gage but it was really late and I didn't want to wake him. Besides, I figured you shouldn't talk about something as horrible as death in something as playful as texts. I put my phone away. It would keep until I saw him the next day.

Chapter 3

♂

"Mom, how many people did you invite to brunch?" I asked as I squeezed my way through family, friends, and some people I didn't even know. Mom and Dad had folding chairs set up everywhere. In the corner of the living room was what appeared to be a coffee and tea bar. The dining room table was laden with platters of bacon and ham, heated serving vessels full of scrambled eggs, poached eggs with sauce for eggs Benedict, and Mom's famous egg scramble casserole. There was even a plate of mini skirt steaks. The buffet was covered with platters of donuts, muffins, Danish, English muffins, and pancakes. There was a side table set up with bowls of fresh fruit salad and plates of oranges and grapes and strawberries. Then there was a table set up with expensive paper plates, silverware, coffee cups, and juice cups.

"Hi, dear," Mom said as she lifted a pan full of breakfast sausages over the heads of the crowd that flowed into the kitchen. "Can you put this on the dining room table?"

I carefully took the dish from Mom. Luckily I was four inches taller than she was and able to lift the dish above the crowd more easily and squeeze into the room to put the platter on the end of the already overflowing table. The noise was loud. A glance through the dining room windows told me that the crowd had flowed out to the backyard. Music played through the windows that were open an inch. Even though it was cold enough to need coats outside, there were so many people inside my parents' small home that they needed the windows open to keep the air moving.

"Hi, Pepper," Aunt Sarah said as she wormed her way toward the table with a plate in each hand. "How are you this morning?"

"I'm good. Where's Uncle Bill?"

"He's outside with the kids," Aunt Sarah said. "He's not too big on crowds."

"Isn't it cold out there?" I asked.

"Oh no," my mom's friend Doris said from the other side of me as she spooned eggs on her plate. "Your parents have set up a big tent with tables and chairs and they have those really cool, tall outdoor heaters like you see in Las Vegas. It's quite comfortable."

"Huh," I said. "You've been to Las Vegas?"

"Oh, yes. Last year for a wild girls' weekend." She winked at me and moved into the crowd. Doris was five feet tall and sixty years old. She had a middle-aged figure with a bit of heft around her waist. Today she wore jeans and a sweatshirt embroidered with cardinals across the bodice. I stood for a moment trying to imagine Doris or my mom in Vegas for a girls' weekend. Then I was bumped and pushed toward the dining room, so I went with the flow of the crowd.

I had to hand it to Mom. I didn't think the brunch would be that big of a deal. Right now it looked like there were more people at brunch than at the wedding reception. I grabbed a plate for myself and snagged a couple of donuts and a cup of coffee and wound my way back through the kitchen. Mom was nowhere to be seen, so I assumed she was outside.

I assumed right. The tent was practically the size of the backyard. Dad had set up speakers and was playing his favorite records on the old turntable he kept in the basement. At one point my father had thought he'd be a disc jockey and bought a complete set with two turntables, a microphone, and four giant speakers.

I had to laugh. I bet he'd waited longer than Felicity's twenty-four years to play for a crowd of family and friends. He was currently grooving to some seventies oldies. Mom was in the far corner of the tent flitting from person to person, asking if they were comfortable and thanking them for coming.

"Hey, Pepper." Aunt Karen called me over to sit at a table with her and Sue.

"Hi, Aunt Karen," I said, and pressed a kiss on her cheek. "Hi, Aunt Sue," I said, and kissed Sue's cheek as well. Then I sat down at the round table next to them. The chairs were all folding chairs and the tables were covered in white plastic tablecloths. It was a classic neighborhood party. The only thing missing was the keg. Usually if a party happened anytime near noon there was a keg of beer tapped in a corner somewhere. "There are a lot of people here," I said.

"I think your mom invited the entire neighborhood plus all her old students," Aunt Karen said. Aunt Karen was a lovely redhead. Like me, she was tall and thin with a smattering of freckles and a wide smile. Unlike me, her red hair was cut short and the curls managed with gel. Her blue eyes sparkled. Aunt Sue was also tall, but she had wide shoulders, a broad face, short salt and pepper hair, and happy green eyes. Aunt Sue was quiet while Aunt Karen was vivacious and outgoing. "By the way, this is our friend, Laura." Aunt Karen pointed at a lovely brunette beside Aunt Sue.

"Hi, Laura," I said. Putting my donuts down on the table, I reached out and shook Laura's hand. "Welcome to the madness that is our family."

Just as I said that, Aunt Sarah's two teenage boys came racing through the tables chasing each other. "Watch out!" someone called. One of the boys pushed the other into the side of the tent. My dad was fast. He grabbed both boys by the backs of their shirts and had them out into the cold before we could even understand what happened.

"Wow, that man is good," Laura said.

"That's my dad," I said proudly. "He didn't have any

sons, so he volunteers as a coach for the intramural lacrosse and hockey teams. He knows his way around rambunctious boys."

"Yeah, your dad's one of the good guys," Sue said with a soft smile.

"Thanks," I said, and swigged my coffee. "It's too bad Felicity isn't here to see this," I said.

"I was surprised the happy couple didn't make a showing," Aunt Karen said.

"Felicity wanted to," I said, "but their cruise starts at noon today and Mom and Dad said that the brunch was just going to be a small thing for the family members from out of town." I glanced around. "That's sort of gotten out of hand."

"You think?" Karen said with a twinkle in her eye. "I see even Warren's parents came."

I followed her gaze to see the wealthy Evanses in the corner talking with my mother. They were dressed for a country club brunch. Mrs. Evans wore a deep purple sheath dress and Christian Louboutin pumps. She had a cream pashmina with purple violets embroidered on it wrapped around her shoulders. Mr. Evans was an older version of Warren. He had a full head of hair with gray at the temples, cut short on the sides and long on top in that preppy way. He wore a gray suit coat, black slacks, and a pale blue shirt with a blue and red striped tie. They looked perfectly comfortable outside under a tent, eating off of paper plates with plastic silverware. I shook my head. Warren's family never ceased to amaze me.

"Yeah, Warren's family is great—unlike some of their friends," I said, and shook my head.

"So is it true?" Aunt Karen asked.

"Is what true?"

"Did a girl die last night at the reception?" Aunt Karen said in a stage whisper.

"Yes," I said, and wrapped my hands around my coffee cup. "I tried CPR until the paramedics came but they couldn't revive her. It makes me really glad that Felicity and Warren are on their honeymoon. I hope they don't find out until they get back."

"Oops, looks like they haven't left yet," Aunt Sue said, and pointed toward the door to the tent.

I turned to see my sister and Warren making an appearance. They both glowed with happiness. "Don't tell them, okay?" I said, and stood to intercept them.

I hurried to her and gave her a hug and a kiss. "Hi, I thought you guys would be long gone."

Felicity blushed. "Warren's going to helicopter us out to the ship."

"We didn't want to miss the brunch," Warren said. "Look at all the work your mom went to for the family. The least we could do is come."

At that moment my father played a rock guitar version of "Here Comes the Bride" on his turntables. "Ladies and gentlemen, let me introduce Mr. and Mrs. Warren Evans," my dad said into the microphone. The entire tent erupted into clapping and cheering. My mom rushed over and gave them both hugs and kisses.

47

"You are missing your honeymoon," she scolded, but it was clear she was pleased as punch that they had come anyway.

"We couldn't miss it," Warren said. "The place looks fantastic."

"Thanks," Mom said, and blushed.

"I get my event planning genes from Mom," I said. Dad came over and gave them both hugs as well and then I was pushed aside as a line formed. Everyone was here because of Warren and Felicity and wanted to celebrate them. I made my way back to my half-eaten donuts and cold coffee and sat down at the table. Aunt Karen and Sue had left to greet the happy couple, so I sat closer to Laura.

"So, Laura," I said. "Tell me about yourself."

"What do you want to know?"

"What do you do for a living?" I narrowed down my choices.

"I'm a pharmacist," she said. "In other words, I count pills all day."

"Sounds glamourous."

"It is," she said, and winked at me. "I hear you plan elaborate proposals."

"And engagement parties," I said. "I got my start with Warren and Felicity."

"Good start," she said, and sipped her coffee. "So, would you be interested in helping me plan to ask my partner to marry me?"

"Sure," I said, all business. "What are you thinking about?"

"I want something low-key. The ability to get married is pretty new and I know that she's been thinking about it ever since they passed the same-sex marriage bill in Illinois. But I don't want anything huge and definitely not on YouTube."

"I can understand that," I said. "What do you like to do together? Is there anything special? A memory you want to evoke? A first date? The first time you knew you were in love with her?"

Laura sat back and chewed on her bottom lip. "Sure. There's a lot of things."

"Tell me how you met."

"I knocked on her door looking to borrow some sugar. I know, it sounds like a cliché, but it really happened. When Monica answered the door I was speechless . . . just speechless. She noticed the empty sugar bowl in my hands, smiled, and asked if I needed sugar. I nodded like a deaf mute and she invited me in for coffee." She shrugged. "One thing led to another and we've been together ever since."

"How long have you been dating?"

"Eight years next month."

"Wow, that is fabulous. Here's my card," I said, and dug it out of my clutch purse. Normally I put my purse on the kitchen counter at my mom's house, but with the number of people wandering in and out today, I had decided to keep it with me. "Call me on Monday and we'll go over my fees and get more details to figure out what you are looking for in your event. Okay?"

"Yes," Laura said with a nod and a shy smile. "Thank you."

"Hey, Pepper, there you are!"

I glanced up to see my new boyfriend Gage walking toward me. My spirits always lifted at the sight of him. He had short, dark brown hair, a chiseled jawline, and blue eyes with thick black lashes that any redhead would envy. Today he'd dressed for brunch in a pale blue dress shirt and dark brown slacks with brown shoes. He had his coat thrown over his arm, so he must have come straight from his car.

"Gage!" I rushed over and gave him a hug and a kiss. "I didn't expect you. How's your mother?"

"She's good. She's home and in her favorite chair with a blanket, a pitcher of water, and a stack of cozy mystery novels." Gage hugged me hard. "She said I should come, and so here I am."

"I'm so glad. This place is a madhouse."

He laughed and looked around. "Yes, it is."

"And yet, I missed you." I brushed another kiss on his cheek. "Do you want something to eat?"

"Maybe in a bit," he said. "First let me go congratulate Felicity and Warren."

"Oh, yes, of course," I said. We wormed our way through the thinning crowd around the happy couple.

"Gage!" Felicity said, and hugged my boyfriend. "I'm glad you came. How's your mom?"

"She's good. She told me to come, so don't think I ditched her or anything," Gage said.

Felicity smiled. My sister was a gorgeous blonde, petite and curvy in all the right places. When she smiled the entire room lit up.

"Good to see you, Gage," Warren said, and clasped Gage's hand. "Good to hear your mom is on the mend."

"Thanks," Gage said. "Congratulations, you two. I thought you were headed off to a cruise this morning."

"Warren got us a helicopter to the ship so that we could come and say a proper good-bye to everyone," Felicity said. She clearly had stars in her eyes.

"That's great," Gage said. "It's good to see you. Sorry I missed yesterday."

"Oh, a lot of people missed the good stuff," Uncle Bill said, approaching us. "If they didn't stay to the end." He nodded solemnly.

"Why, what happened?" Felicity asked. "Did Aunt Sarah get drunk?" She winked at my aunt.

"Nothing important happened," I said, and gave my uncle the stink eye. "One of the bartenders passed out."

"Are they okay?" Felicity asked. I noticed the shadows that passed through her bright eyes.

"Actually—" My uncle started to tell Felicity the truth.

"They're fine." I cut him off and gave him a serious glare. "Aren't they, Uncle Bill?"

Aunt Sarah had her hand on his back and I noticed the slight wince before he said, "Sure, sure, nothing to worry about."

"Oh, good," Felicity said, and put her hand on her heart. "I've felt like from the time I got engaged bad things have happened. If I were superstitious I would be very worried. I'm glad everyone is okay."

"Everyone's great," I said with a shake of my head. I

glanced at my watch. "Wow, you two need to get going. It's almost eleven thirty. You don't want to miss your cruise."

"Oh, yes," Felicity said. "We might have a helicopter on standby, but we do want to get to our honeymoon." She stood up and gave my aunt and uncle hugs and kisses. Then she gave me a hug. I hugged her tight.

"Congratulations, Fel," I said into her ear. "I'm so happy for you. Go and enjoy your honeymoon. Don't worry about anything. I'll make sure Mom and Dad don't overdo it."

Felicity laughed and let me go. "I think it's a bit too late for that." She waved her hands to illustrate the crowd and the tent and the giant trash bins full of empty paper plates.

"I plan on stopping by tomorrow when they crash to bring them some dinner," I said. "How's that?"

"Perfect." She gave me a kiss and another hug. I hugged Warren and they headed out the door.

Gage waited until they were out of the tent before he turned to me. "What really happened last night? Your texts were vague."

"It's a story," I said. "I'm not sure Mom and Dad even know, but one of the bartenders collapsed and died." Tears welled up in my eyes. "Sorry," I said.

Gage, ever the gentleman, pulled a clean tissue out of his pocket and handed it to me. "Was it someone you knew?"

"Not really," I said, and wiped my eyes then blew my nose in an attempt to pull myself together. "I'd just been talking to her throughout the night. She seemed like a nice person who was down on her luck. I asked her about making

1950s cocktails and she showed me a few. We seemed to get along really well and I was going to meet up with her another day." I dabbed at my eyes. "Then when I came out of the restroom, I learned she had collapsed. I tried CPR until the paramedics got there, but it didn't matter. They couldn't save her."

"Oh, sweetheart." Gage pulled me into his arms and held me tight. I rested my head on his shoulder and wallowed in the comfort. "You should have called me."

"It was, like, midnight, and what could you have done?"

"I could have been there for you," he said, and lifted my chin so that I looked him in the eye. "I want to always be there for you. What time did you get home?"

"Two A.M.," I said, and rested my head against his chest again. There was something comforting about his warmth and the sound of his heartbeat against my cheek. "George called a cab for me."

"You should have let me know," he said. "Mom was sleeping. I could have come and gotten you."

"Hey, what's with the PDA?" my teenage cousin Alex called from across the room. "Are you two next? Hmmm?"

I stepped away from Gage. "Alex, why don't you go help my dad with the music, huh?" I called back.

"Oh, cool!" Alex said, and rushed over to the empty DJ area. Dad was busy walking Felicity and Warren out and had left the music to die.

"Good call," Gage said, and took my hand. "You've had a bit of a rough twenty-four hours. Do you need to stay?"

I looked around at my rowdy family and my mom and

dad's friends. "Not really," I said. "I've spoken to most everyone between yesterday and today. But I need to check with Mom. I want to make sure she has help with the cleanup."

"I get it," Gage said. "Let's go find your mom and see what we can do to help."

Alex started playing heavy metal music as loud as the speakers would go. Gage took my hand and pulled me from the tent. After we got to the side yard, the music levels lowered dramatically. I guessed that one of my aunts or uncles had grabbed Alex and made him knock it off.

With a family as big and as crazy as mine there was no telling what would happen next. I just really hoped that everyone else kept Felicity blissfully unaware that a girl had died at her wedding reception.

Chapter 4

Later that evening Gage and I sat in the warm, mint-green-painted living room of the little house I rented. It was my first house. I had lived in an apartment ever since I moved out of my college dorm, but I knew it was time to change my life when I realized that I had rented my apartment based on my ex-boyfriend Bobby's favorite bar. The Naked Truth had been right across the street from my old apartment so that he didn't have to go far to see me.

I lucked into the house. I happened to be talking to the local homicide detective, Brian Murphy, when I started my house hunting. He mentioned that his mom was moving to Florida and wanted to rent out her house. It was a cute 1920s bungalow with three bedrooms and a finished basement. I negotiated a real deal on the rent. Well, to be honest, it was

Detective Murphy who offered me the deal. He felt having someone in the house was better than letting it sit empty. I didn't mind living in an older cop neighborhood. It was pretty safe. Generations of police officers and firemen had lived in this neighborhood and built families.

It did come with a few strange neighbors. Mrs. Crivitz next door had a tendency to peer out her windows whenever I walked outside. Mrs. C was in her seventies. She liked to hang around in floral housecoats and brightly colored muumuus. She had a daughter who was in her late forties who lived with her. The two were harmless but nosy to a fault. It made me very aware of how much time Gage spent at my place. I knew Mrs. Crivitz was judging me. I tried to tell her it was 2014 and grown women could live alone and have boyfriends who sometimes slept over. She wasn't buying it.

Then there was Mr. Mead across the street. He was a walking cliché. He loved to sit on his front porch and yell at the neighborhood kids to stay off his lawn. He had No Trespassing signs on the edges of his lawn along with signs of dogs pooping with a circle and a line through them. One day I saw him chase a dog owner off with a shovel. It was kind of funny since Mr. Mead was a forty-year veteran of the police department before he retired.

Of course, with all the perks of low rent and a great house, there were other disadvantages besides the neighbors. Detective Murphy had made it a habit of stopping by once a week to check on the house and see if everything was working well. Everything was always working because the house was close to perfect. I didn't mind his visits most of the time. He was a nice guy who liked to talk about his daughter, who was my age and in a not-so-great relationship. Not that I had any good advice for him. I'd been with Bobby far too long.

"What is this cocktail?" Gage asked as he raised the highball glass I had handed him.

"It's a Tom Collins," I said, and sipped the tart drink containing gin. "I'm trying different cocktails. I think it would be nice to add signature drinks to my engagement parties. I got the idea from the bartender at Felicity's reception."

"Not the same one who ended up dead, is it?" He tasted the cocktail and raised his eyebrows, curved his mouth down, and nodded. "This is good, by the way."

"Thanks," I said, and snuggled in beside him. We had a fire in the fireplace and there was soft music playing from the iPhone holder. "Unfortunately, yes, it was Ashley who gave me the idea. She was making Cosmos and other cocktails. She made me one that was just wonderful and I thought that I needed to expand my horizons beyond beer and wine."

"What, you don't like the wine I bring?" Gage seemed hurt.

I turned toward him. "What? No, I didn't mean that."

He grinned at me and kissed me quick. "Just checking," he said, and lifted his glass. "I like this."

"Thanks," I said, and leaned my head against his broad shoulder. "I think Felicity and Warren will be happy together."

"They seem like a great couple."

"It's too bad that there were so many deaths around their wedding," I said, and sat up to count them off on my fingers.

"First there was the dead man at the scene of their proposal. Then the dead woman at the bridal shop, and now Ashley." I sighed. "I'm glad that we were able to get Felicity off to her honeymoon before she found out about Ashley."

"So tell me what happened." Gage said.

I studied him for a moment. He had always been interested in what happened to me. Bobby had only cared if it had something to do with him. "I talked to her a couple of times last night," I said, and sipped my drink. "She was nice. She seemed to know some of the people at the wedding who were friends of Warren's family. She told me she had bartended at a few of the high-society weddings and had a bit of a rapport going with at least one of the guests."

"Sounds interesting. I can imagine that if you do enough of those events, you can get to learn a lot about the upper crust in Chicago."

"I got that feeling," I said. "The weird part is she didn't really fit the usual society bartender look. She was really skinny and looked a bit worn out."

"What happened to her?"

"She passed out in the back hallway. One of the wait-staff came running out screaming. I was the first one to her. She wasn't breathing and she didn't have a pulse, but I wasn't going to witness another death. So I shouted for someone to call 911 and started CPR. George got one of those kits with the breathing mask and air bag and he started pumping oxygen to her while I did compressions. The EMTs got there after what seemed like forever, but they weren't able to revive her."

"Oh, man," Gage said, and put his drink down on the coffee table. He drew me in close and held me tight. "You were brave to do the CPR."

"I didn't even think about it, really. It was instinct. I went through safety and CPR training before the scuba proposal. I thought it might not hurt to be able to help out should there be an accident at one of my proposals. I never figured I'd have to use it at Felicity's reception."

"But you did," Gage said, and took my drink and put it beside his. Then he pulled me into his arms and brushed the wayward hair out of my face. "There's a big difference between training in CPR and actually doing it. You were very brave."

Tears welled up in my eyes. He got it. "It was hard. I was afraid I was breaking her bones, I had to pump so hard, and it was all for nothing."

"Some things you can't fix, Pepper," Gage said, and kissed me soft and slow. "But I'm so lucky to know a woman like you—someone who tries no matter how scary. Most people would look the other way, or worse, they would run the other way. But not you. You step up and try to help."

"Thanks," I said. It felt so right being with Gage here in my living room in front a crackling fire. I didn't want the time to end.

The doorbell rang suddenly and we broke apart.

"Are you expecting someone?" Gage asked.

"No," I said, and looked at the clock. It was eight P.M. I straightened my blouse and got up. The doorbell rang again followed by a knock. "I'm coming," I said to the door. I took a moment to look out the peephole before opening the door. The neighborhood might be safe but it was still a good idea to check the door before opening it. "It's Detective Murphy."

I opened the door to find my friend and landlord standing there with the collar of his winter coat raised up against the chill. "Hello, Detective," I said. "I wasn't expecting you."

"Can I come in a moment?" he asked.

I glanced out into the night and thought I saw faint snow-flakes on the air. "Sure." I waved him inside and closed the door against the cold.

He wiped his feet on my entrance rug. Not because I asked him to, but most likely out of habit. This was, after all, his mother's house. He looked up and spotted Gage standing near the couch. "Oh, you have company."

"Yes," I said. "Detective Murphy, you remember my boyfriend, Gage," I said, and waved toward Gage, who had a smear of lipstick on his jaw.

"Yes," Detective Murphy said as the two men shook hands. "Good to see you." He turned toward me. "I'm sorry to interrupt."

"Let me take your coat," I said. "Can I get you something to drink? Coffee? A cocktail? I'm trying new cocktail recipes for future proposal events."

"No, no," Detective Murphy said, and waved off my suggestion. His hound-dog face seemed troubled. He wore a fedora covering his thinning gray hair. His blue eyes held both interest and sadness. His expression always looked like that of a man who had seen too much and cared too much. "I was stopping by to check on you. I understand you performed CPR on a young lady last night."

"Yes, the bartender at Felicity's reception," I said. "It was tragic."

Detective Murphy drew his mouth into a firm tight line. "Yes, it was."

"Do you know what she died of?" I had to ask.

"It's too early to tell," he said with a shrug. "Autopsy's scheduled for Monday afternoon."

"I can't imagine it was natural causes," I said, and hugged myself. "She seemed too young for that."

"It's standard procedure to check things out when there's an unexplained death," he said. "And you're right, she was young."

"How young?" Gage asked.

"She was twenty-five," Detective Murphy answered.

"That's what she told me," I said. "I was surprised because she looked a lot older."

"The life she had was tough," he said. "I was surprised to see that you were involved in another death."

"She wasn't involved," Gage said, and put his hand on my shoulder and squeezed it comfortingly. "She was at her sister's wedding reception and tried to save a girl's life. She did CPR until the EMTs got there."

"That's courageous," Detective Murphy said. "You are a good person, Pepper."

"Thanks," I said.

"Anyway, I won't stay," he said, and eyed Gage's protective stance. "We'll talk later. You two have a nice night."

"Thanks," I said. "Stay safe." I closed the door behind him and turned to Gage. "What do you think that was all about?"

"I don't know," he said, and took my hand and led me to the couch. "We were in the middle of something . . ."

I let him draw me down next to him. "I'm worried." I said, and wrapped my arms around my waist. "I've got a bad feeling that Ashley didn't die of natural causes." I looked into Gage's deep blue eyes. "That means that my family is involved—however indirectly—in another murder."

"It's beginning to become a thing," Gage agreed.

"Maybe I can figure something out before Felicity and Warren get back from their month-long cruise."

Gage drew me against him and planted a kiss on my forehead. "If anyone can do it, you can, Pepper."

"Then maybe Ashley can rest in peace and Felicity won't worry about what happened and how she could have prevented it." I reached up and wiped the smudge of lipstick off his jaw with my thumb. "I like happy endings."

"I know," he said. "Let's hope we can give Ashley one."

Chapter 5

My phone rang at nine A.M. the next morning. "Perfect Proposals, this is Pepper, how can I help you?"

"Hi, is this Pepper Pomeroy?"

"Yes," I said. "How can I help you?"

"Hi, I'm Sherry, Kelli's friend? She mentioned that you said I should call this morning."

"Okay," I said, then sat down and opened my event planning notebook.

"I'm not sure if you remember, but I'm the one who is pregnant and I wanted to propose to my boyfriend, William, and then tell him I'm pregnant."

I sat back. "Yes, I remember," I said, and made a note of her name and her boyfriend's name. "Sherry, can I have your last name?"

"Oh, sure, it's Burlingham, and my boyfriend is William Herald the Third."

"How long have you been dating?"

"Oh, gosh, for at least three years."

"And you're sure he isn't planning on asking you to marry him? Have you talked about it?"

"Oh, yes, we've talked about it," she said. "But he joined the Air National Guard and then got called up into active duty. He flies jets. Anyway, I think he was thinking that we'd wait until after his tour of duty is up to get married. But then he came home two months ago on leave and one thing led to another . . ."

"Okay," I said, with a smile and a nod. "These are just questions I ask right at the start. I need to get a good sense of the couple and their situation. I like to make sure that both parties are happy with where they are in their relationship and ready to take it to the next level."

"I'm certain we're ready," she said. "I think he'll be ecstatic to know I'm pregnant. He comes home this weekend and I think it would be great to welcome him with a surprise engagement. Don't you?"

My thoughts went to all the welcome home ceremonies I saw on television. "Yes, I think it will be." I explained my fees and she reassured me that they could afford it and I was to spare no expense.

"Will didn't go into the service for the money or the college tuition," she said. "His father and grandfather are huge supporters of the military and Will wanted to earn their respect. It's sort of a rite of passage with the Herald men."

"Great. Do you have an idea or venue in mind?"

"Yes, Will is a big tough guy who is a kid at heart. I thought it would be fun to do it at F.A.O. Schwarz."

"Oh, the one in Macy's downtown?"

"Yes," she said emphatically. "I know the store manager, Eric Moore."

"That sounds promising. Can we meet with Eric?"

"Yes," she said. "He's willing to meet this afternoon, if you are. Can we meet at two P.M.?"

"I can do it," I said, and wrote down the details. "This will be a lot of fun."

"That's my hope," she said. "I'll see you downtown."

I hung up and went online to research the store and what kind of fun things we could do with the engagement. With less than a week to plan it, I might have to skip the engagement party after. I needed to find out more from Sherry about where their families were located and what kind of engagement party she might be interested in. I noted that Macy's had a tearoom on the top floor. I made a quick phone call to see if it might be available. It was as long as we used them to cater and the party wasn't more than fifty people.

A quick search of the Herald family told me that the party might be a bit bigger than fifty people. The Heralds had been rubbing elbows with Chicago elite since the Worth family dominated the social scene. I scoured the surrounding area and put in several phone calls for venues. The biggest part of proposal planning was the short amount of time you had to pull the event together. It was a challenge I liked.

My phone rang again at eleven A.M.

"Hi, Pepper, it's Laura Emmerson. We talked yesterday at your parents' brunch."

"Oh, yes, Laura, hi," I said, and snagged a pen and my event notebook. "How are you?"

"I'm well," Laura said. "You said to call and make an appointment to talk about what you could do to help me propose to Monica."

"Yes, of course," I said. "I have free time this evening. Can you meet?"

"How about five P.M.?" she asked. "I'll leave work a little early and we can beat the dinner crowds."

"Great, where do you work?"

"I work in Des Plaines. Can you meet me at Rosa's? It's close by and they have booths. Early evening means the lunch crowd should be long gone and the dinner crowd won't start for at least another hour. We should have plenty of privacy."

"Sounds perfect," I said, and made a note in my calendar as she hung up. I started a business file on Laura, with notes about what we had already talked about and possible ideas for her proposal. I did some basic research on Laura and Monica. Monica's Facebook page showed a happy woman with a genuine smile. There were a couple pictures of the two of them together. They looked very happy.

After a quick glance at the time I knew I had to get going. Researching people and venues and party ideas online always seemed to suck the time away. I ran a brush through my wild curly red hair and piled it in a loose knot on the top of my head. Then I put mascara on my lashes to make it look like I had some and finished off the look with a pop of red lip color. I wore a black turtleneck sweater, a navy miniskirt with black tights, and knee-high boots. I grabbed my navy wool coat, wrapped a long multicolored scarf my mother had knitted me around my neck, grabbed my purse and tablet, and headed out.

Downtown traffic was always interesting, and it would take time to find a place to park.

My phone rang as I drove. I hit the button that connected it to the Bluetooth earpiece I wore. My car was a big old Buick I'd inherited from my grandmother. I loved Old Blue, but it was a bit of a boat. Which meant it was great in winter weather but a bear to park on the street. "Perfect Proposals, this is Pepper. How can I help you?"

"Pepper, Brad Hurst. I gave you my card on Saturday."

I made a face as I wove through traffic on the Kennedy Expressway. "Hi, Brad. Yes, I remember. I thought I was supposed to call you. How did you get my number?"

"I asked Whitney. Look, I'm sure Jen made an impression on you," he said with a laugh. "She doesn't usually drink so much, but she's had a bit of a tough go lately. Listen, I was wondering if we could set up a meeting tomorrow."

"Sure," I said, and grabbed my bag and dug out my notebook and pen as I slowed down in the inevitable bumper-to-bumper traffic that seemed to be perpetually going into or coming out of downtown. "I'm driving, but I have my appointment book open. What time works for you?"

"Jen and I are free to talk at two," he said.

I wrote with my right hand and drove with my left. I slammed on the brakes when I glanced up and saw I was a bit close to the guy in front of me. "Okay, I've got a free spot at two P.M. Wait—you and Jen?"

"Yes, Jen insists on being a part of the planning."

"But she wants to be surprised," I said, and managed to weave Old Blue out of my lane and into the express lane. "How can she be surprised if she's part of the planning?"

Brad chuckled. "That's what I asked, but she insists you can figure out a way to make this happen."

Great. "Okay," I said, wondering why I was doing this. Any sane woman would say no and let them go find someone else. But no, not me. I liked to drive in the crazy lane. "Where would you like to meet?"

"Let's meet at McGee's Pub and Grill in Arlington Heights. Do you know where that is?"

"Sure," I said. I lied, of course, but I could Google it later. "We'll meet tomorrow at McGee's in Arlington Heights. So, anything you can share with me about Jen's likes and dislikes before we meet tomorrow?"

"Um, what do you need to know?"

"I don't know, things like her favorite book or singer or movie."

"Oh, well, she sort of likes that old movie *Serendipity*."

"Seriously?"

"Yeah, she likes the idea that things are meant to be. Sort of like how we are meant to be—that is, if I can figure out a way to propose without her knowing. See?"

"Sort of," I said, and tried not to sigh out loud.

"Great. Bring your ideas for over-the-top, viral video fun." He hung up. I felt the weight of inevitable failure heavy on my shoulders.

"Crazy people's money is just as good as non–crazy people's money," I muttered to myself. "Just charge them double. It's clear they can afford it." I made a final note in my notebook about figuring out where McGee's was, then exited off the highway to my favorite parking garage. It cost $17 an hour to park there, but they had spaces big enough for Old Blue and I could catch a taxi to Macy's.

* * *

Sherry was a petite woman with thick dark hair that was scooped up into a high ponytail. She wore a red designer dress and six-inch heels, which meant she came up to my shoulder. She spotted me as I crossed in front of the giant stuffed gorilla. "Pepper?"

"Yes, hi, Sherry," I said, and gave her a hug. She sent me air kisses on each cheek. "Thank you so much for meeting me on such short notice."

"Short notice is what proposal planning is all about," I said. "This is an interesting venue. What made you pick it?"

F.A.O. Schwarz occupied two floors in the Macy's store. We currently stood in the stuffed toy section. It was December and there were kids and harried parents everywhere. It had a kind of playful, frenetic energy.

"They have this great section full of those green army men you see in the *Toy Story* movies," she said. "Will loves those little guys." She took my hand and pulled me through the stuffed toys to the section she had mentioned. There were little boys running and yelling and shooting at each other with green foam guns. "Isn't it great?"

"It's interesting," I said, and looked around. "You know it will be quite original."

"That's what I thought," she said. "Will won't see it coming. Oh, here's Eric." A young man came over dressed in a white dress shirt, Macy's red tie, and black slacks. He had dirty blond hair that was well-styled and thick, black horn-rimmed glasses. "Eric," she greeted him with the same enthusiasm and air kisses, then pulled him toward me. "This is Pepper. She's the proposal planner who is going to put this whole thing together for me."

"Hi," I said, and shook Eric's hand.

"Hi, Pepper. I'm looking forward to your ideas." At that moment he was hit in the side of the head by a foam puff. "What?" He turned to the boys. "Hey!"

"Sorry, mister," one of the boys said with a sassy shrug.

Eric shook his head good-naturedly. "We're going to have to figure out a time where Sherry can propose without getting shot at with a foam bullet."

"When do you close?" I asked.

"With this being the holiday season, we close at ten P.M.," Eric said.

"How about when you open?" I asked

"We open at eight A.M.," Eric said.

I turned to Sherry. "What about a morning proposal? He won't expect it. You can bring him shopping and stop in here. Eric could close this section for ten minutes while you propose," I suggested. "Afterward, you can take his hand and run under the gun arch to the baby toys section where you will announce the pregnancy. I can get it all on video."

"I like it!" Sherry said.

"Eric, will that work? I can get it on the morning news show," I said, hoping it would be a good incentive.

"I'm pretty sure that would work," Eric said with a smile.

"Then, Sherry, I usually have an engagement party planned right after the proposal. I've got a few venues within walking distance or the tearoom upstairs. We could do a themed morning brunch with diamonds, Green toy soldiers, and storks."

"Oh, wonderful!" Sherry clapped.

"Let's go iron out the details," I suggested, and we went to the snack bar area. Sherry got a table and I bought us all coffees. It didn't take long to get all the particulars down. It was going to be quick, but it would be something Will and Sherry would always remember.

Chapter 6

Satisfied that Sherry's proposal was well under way, I headed back to Old Blue. My thoughts turned to Brad and Jen. I had no idea how I was supposed to surprise Jennifer when she was the one who wanted to set up the engagement. She would know something was up the minute I showed up. She might even stalk me just to catch me setting stuff up. I bit my lip. The key to a true surprise was to not be planning her engagement. What I needed was an accomplice. Maybe Toby could help. He'd enjoyed helping me put together the last two proposals. Maybe he would help me out with this one, too.

Toby was a genius, independently wealthy, and a bit of a geeky romantic. He could do whatever he wanted, and he often did. The problem was that Toby had decided it was time he got married. He thought he could go about marriage the same way he went about a business merger. He'd do some background research, match financials, and ask the woman to marry him. What he didn't get was that women wanted to be courted and, more importantly, loved for themselves, not for their fertility or financial status. The expression of that love and respect is what went into my proposals. Each was not necessarily glitzy, but rather very personal and well thought out. When I met Toby he had wanted me to set up a proposal to a woman he'd researched and decided was the girl for him, even though they had never dated. While I didn't accept Toby's money and he'd offered me quite a bit—I instead asked him to accompany me on two of my proposals so he could understand what it meant to be in love and ask a woman to marry him.

For my Perfect Proposals business I wanted to cater to people who were in love and who had already begun to build a life together. That's why my first inclination was always to ask if a couple had talked about marriage and if they were both ready.

I could tell that Brad and Jennifer were in love. The hard part was that Jennifer wanted to be surprised. I had a feeling it was a game for her. That meant she'd be watching me like a hawk. I got to thinking that a way around that might be to get Toby to carry out some of the details. I might even have to set up a false trail of clues for Jennifer. If she wasn't surprised, then they wouldn't pay me. I didn't think that was quite fair. I'd talked it over with Gage. He agreed that I needed to insist on a retainer and that all vendor costs be paid whether she was surprised or not. That was what I needed to talk to Brad about. I had hoped to talk to him alone, but it wasn't looking like that was going to be possible. In fact, I thought of leading Brad down the false path as well. That way he couldn't give anything away when it was actually happening. Hmmm, I'd think about that.

My cell phone rang as I got into Old Blue. I put on my Bluetooth earpiece and answered. "Perfect Proposals, this is Pepper speaking, how can I help you?"

"Pepper, this is Sugar Fulcrum, Clark's mom. We met at your sister's wedding. How are you?"

"I'm well. What can I do for you, Mrs. Fulcrum?"

"Please, call me Sugar," she said. "Clark and Samantha Lyn are such a cute couple, don't you think?"

"Perhaps," I hedged. "But they are very young."

"Not so young," Sugar said. "I got married at eighteen and Samantha Lyn is twenty. Anyway, Clark says she's the one for him. Our families are really close and Samantha Lyn's mother, Josie, and I were talking. We want to hire you to plan a really cute and glitzy proposal for Clark to ask Samantha Lyn to marry him. We want it to be so incredible it makes more than the society papers. We want it to make the morning shows. You know, like one of those viral video things. I'm sure you have an idea what I mean."

"I think so," I said.

"Yes, well, money is no object. I don't mean to be vulgar, but I know you are a businesswoman and you need to know that there really won't be a budget. Clark has a huge trust fund and his father is on the Forbes list. So, as you can see, we have to make this huge. Think reality-show huge. I want a press release to go out and I want reporters invited. I want diamonds and gold and sparkles. I want romantic settings and only the top-shelf chef to cater. I'm certain you have resources that can make this happen."

"Okay, well, we will have to set up an initial meeting where I flesh out ideas for the proposal. When would you like to meet? I'd like Clark there as well. I want to find out what he and Samantha Lyn like to do, some of the dates they went on, how they met, et cetera. It really helps to plan a very personal event. Then I'll also need at least a semblance of a budget. I charge a nonrefundable retainer of 50 percent of that budget the day we sign the contract." I chewed on my bottom lip thinking that nonrefundable and 50 percent of an unlimited budget would make her stop and think about this crazy idea.

"Perfect," Sugar said, completely unfazed by my outrageous proposal. "I can meet tomorrow. Does that work for you?"

"That works," I said, and scribbled it into my date book. "Where would you like to meet?"

"Oh, how about the Pavilion tearoom on Wabash. We can have tea and discuss all the details."

"Okay, great. I'll make reservations for you and Clark."

"Add Josie as well," Sugar Fulcrum said. "She'll want to be a part of the planning, and no one knows Samantha Lyn like her mother."

"Great, I'll get a table for four tomorrow at noon at the Pavilion on Wabash."

"Perfect," Sugar trilled. "This is so exciting. See you then."

I hung up the phone and frowned. Samantha Lyn seemed like such a nice girl, but so very young. I was worried for her. It seemed as if her parents were more excited about matching her with the sullen Clark than Samantha Lyn was. I frowned. If I were a good businessperson, I'd suck it up and plan the proposal. This was clearly going to be a big-ticket event.

I started Old Blue and drove her out of the parking structure. I frowned as I inched my way out onto the road. A fat bank account was nice, but I wanted my reputation as a proposal planner to be impeccable. Which meant that I wanted all of my proposals to generate a true yes. And for the marriage to last as long as possible . . . I suppose that was asking a lot in today's day and age of massive weddings and quickie divorces.

I honked at a taxi that tried to cut me off and ignored the insulting gesture that followed as I took the exit back onto the Kennedy Expressway. If money wasn't a stumbling block to this proposal, maybe talking would be. I chewed on my bottom lip and picked up my phone. While crawling along in bumper-to-bumper traffic, I Googled the Pavilion. When the number came up I hit the link to dial it and sent the call to my earpiece.

"The Pavilion tearoom."

"Yes, I'd like to make a reservation for four tomorrow at noon."

There was a pause. "I'm sorry but we have no openings at that time."

Huh. "Okay, well, I'm making the reservation for Mrs. Sugar Fulcrum and Mrs. Josie Thomson. Should I have Mrs. Fulcrum's secretary call you?"

"Mrs. Sugar Fulcrum? No, no, we always have a table for Mrs. Fulcrum. You want a table for four?"

That's what I thought. "Yes, please," I said. "You can put the reservation under Pepper Pomeroy for Mrs. Sugar Fulcrum."

"Perfect, we will see you then."

I hung up and shook my head. I wished I didn't have to resort to name dropping, but if Sugar Fulcrum wanted to meet at the Pavilion, then I needed to use her name to make that happen.

The traffic started to clear up the closer we got to the O'Hare Airport interchange. The sky was a brilliant blue with a weak light due to the time of year. The cold made the sky haze free and really gorgeous. But there wasn't a lot of light in a Chicago winter. It had snowed last night and we had three inches on the ground. The plows had come through early and hit the side roads, leaving a foot of mounded snow near the sidewalk, but the rest was soft, perfect snow that frosted the neighborhood in a blanket of fresh white.

I got off the highway and made my way home, thinking about the Pavilion tearoom. It was downtown and not one of the places I usually met people to discuss business. But then I had a feeling this particular account was going to be far different than any of my proposals so far. I mean, a press release? Really? Maybe I should look into a film crew following Clark and Samantha Lyn around. Ridiculous, right? Or maybe it was smart. Think of the publicity if this turned out to be the engagement of the century. Samantha Lyn deserved it . . . but not with Clark. Maybe that was an opinion that Ashley had given me. I really didn't know Clark or his parents. Maybe there was more to the boy than I got from my first impression.

Or maybe he was the prankster and lazy troublemaker that Ashley had hinted at that night.

I decided that the thing to do was to call Samantha before this got too far. I pulled into my driveway and used my smartphone to do some sleuthing. Gathering up my things, I got out of the car, waved at Mrs. Crivitz, who peered out her dining room window, and unlocked my back porch door. The curtains fell shut as I entered the house and closed the door behind me. I dropped my things on the small dinette table near the back door, took off my coat and hung it up. I unwrapped my scarf from around my neck and tossed it up on a hook on the wall.

I left my boots by the door and contacted Whitney for Samantha's cell phone number. Once I had her number, I typed a brief text message into my phone. "Hi, Samantha Lyn, this is Pepper Pomeroy from the wedding Saturday night. Can we talk?"

"Okay," came a texted reply.

I made myself coffee, dialed the number, and Samantha picked up. "Hi." Her voice sounded wobbly.

"Hi, Samantha."

"Hi, Pepper." She sounded as if she were crying.

"Are you okay?" I asked.

"No," she said, her voice watery. "I just . . . I can't believe Ashley died."

"Oh, honey, I'm sorry. I saw you talking to Ashley that night. Did you know her well?"

Samantha sniffed. "Yeah, we met at a different wedding. She was nice. She took a lot of Clark's crap without being mean about it. You know?"

"Yes, I know."

"It's just so weird. I've never known anyone who died. I mean, one minute she was there and the next she was dead."

"You've never known anyone who died? Not even, like, your grandparents?"

"Yes." Samantha hiccupped a quiet sad sob. "But they died when I was little. My parents never let me go to the funeral or anything. Pepper, I don't know what to do. I mean, is there a funeral for Ashley? Should I go? What do you wear? What about like a visitation and stuff? I Googled funerals and it all seems so weird. There's a protocol, right? Why don't they teach you about these things at school?"

"Oh, honey, it's okay. I've been to a few funerals," I said. "I have family in the area and my parents have older friends and such. People die. It's not hard to go to a funeral."

"Can you help me? I . . . I just want to do the right thing for Ashley, you know?"

"Sure, honey," I said. "I can help."

"Can you meet me tomorrow afternoon?" she asked. "I'd like to see you in person."

"Sure," I said. I bit my bottom lip. I wanted to ask her more about her conversation with Ashley but she was so broken up, now was simply not the time. I set up a time to meet her at a local coffee shop.

"Wait, why did you call me?" she asked.

"Can we talk about it when we meet?"

"Sure," she said. "See you soon, okay?"

"Okay."

It was too bad I didn't find out a bit more. It would have been nice to be able to tell Detective Murphy about Samantha Lyn's connection with Ashley. But right now there was nothing to go on but the fact that they had talked and that Samantha Lyn was pretty broken up over it.

Chapter 7

"Thanks for stopping by the station," Detective Murphy said as I stepped into his tiny office space. Detective Murphy had a big old wooden desk stuck in the farthest corner of the police station. There was a bookshelf behind him, stuffed with notebooks of cases and law books and other reference materials. His phone system was old and plastic beige. A bulky computer screen took up half the space on the desk, along with a keyboard and a mouse that battled for the rest of the space with papers, Post-it notes, and other office supplies. He had a dirty mug half full of forgotten coffee and another mug filled with pens and pencils and highlighters.

The air in his cramped office smelled of old, burnt coffee and bad aftershave.

Detective Murphy and I had developed a sort of father-daughter friendship over the last few months. He said I reminded him of his daughter, Emily, a bright young woman with a problem boyfriend. I'd done my best to hear his complaints and try to keep him from driving his daughter into defending the boyfriend. He wasn't happy with the wait-and-see game plan, but I reassured him it was best.

"Sure, no problem. You wanted to talk to me?" I settled back and studied the man. He was in his mid-fifties and had a hound-dog face with intelligent eyes. Today he wore a dress shirt with the collar open and the sleeves rolled up. His navy suit coat draped across the back of his old creaky chair.

"How are things with you?" he asked. "I see you have a new boyfriend."

I felt the heat of a blush. "Gage, yes, I've known him since high school."

"Since high school? Did he know your ex?"

"Yes." My blush deepened. "They were best friends. When I broke up with Bobby, Gage got up the courage to ask me out."

"So you went from one guy to another?"

"Wait." I sat up straight. "I wasn't seeing them both. Bobby and I were broken up. Gage was a friend first. It sort of morphed into something else."

He chuckled and raised his hand in a sign to stop. "Okay, okay, I wasn't making any judgment. I was thinking of Emily. Maybe there's another guy waiting for her loser of a boyfriend to fall out of favor."

"How's that going?" I asked. "You didn't say anything, did you?"

"No, no," he said, and sat back. "I've taken your advice and simply been a sympathetic ear."

"Sympathetic? Does that mean there is trouble in paradise?"

"Let's just say things are getting rocky." He picked up his pencil and tapped the end on his desk. "I'm taking your advice and not saying anything. It's tough though. I want to tell her to kick that lazy bum out of her house."

"You do that and she'll hold on tighter," I warned.

"I know, I know," he said.

"How was your visit? Wasn't she just at your house for a week?"

"The visit was good," he said with a smile. "She admitted that she misses me. That's how I got the feeling that there is something going on. You'll be proud of me, though. I didn't tell her to move back. I asked how she liked her job and the area. She said that the job was okay, but she could get a job like that anywhere."

"Anywhere . . . as in Chicago?" I asked.

"I didn't push my luck," he said. "I merely mentioned that things were picking up in the area and that I had heard her best friend Kendra had gotten a job downtown and that she was really happy."

"Nice," I said. "Did Emily take the bait?"

"The next day when I was on the couch watching the game, she plopped down beside me, put her head on my shoulder, and said that she wanted to move back," he said, and his eyes sparkled. "I said, 'Oh?'" He smiled, stretching his droopy jowls tight. "She leaned against me and acted all casual. 'Yes,' she said, 'but I'm afraid.'"

"She's afraid?"

"Yes," he said, and waved his hand. "She said she was worried I'd try to control her life if she moved back."

"Would you?" I asked, and leaned forward. "Don't answer right away," I said, and raised my hand to cut him off. "Think about it hard. Would you want to stop by at random times like you do to me?"

"I don't stop by at random times," he protested.

"What was last night?" I asked, and sat back.

"I wanted to talk about Ashley."

"You could have called," I said, making my point. "We're friends, right?"

"Yes," he said. "You know I consider you a daughter like Emily."

"Then you need to think carefully," I said. "If Emily moves back, you need to respect boundaries."

"Like?"

"Like calling before you show up at her door," I said. "Like giving her space and not expecting to see her every other day."

"I wouldn't," he protested.

"Or even once a week."

That shut him up. His mouth worked but no words came out. "Not even Sunday dinner?"

"Talk to her, ask her what amount of involvement would

make her comfortable," I said. "Be patient and let her include you in her life."

"This stinks," he said, and put down the pencil. "All I'm supposed to do is stand back and let Emily run the show?"

"Yes," I said, and nodded. "My parents and I have worked out a nice system. They call if they need anything, but mostly I call and it works out well. You'd be surprised how often I call."

"I suppose this is your way of telling me that you want me to call before I show up at your door."

I smiled. "It wouldn't hurt."

"Fine," he said. Then he straightened up. "Listen, I didn't ask you here to only talk about Emily."

"What's up?"

"I want to talk to you again about Ashley Klein," he said, his dark eyes concerned. "You were the first to respond. You tried CPR on her, right?"

"Yes, I did, but it didn't work."

"Why?" he asked.

"I'm sorry?"

"Why did you step up to do CPR? There were twenty people there."

"I don't know," I said, and shrugged. "It seemed like the right thing to do. I talked to her earlier that night and I felt like I knew her. I couldn't just not try to save her."

"You talked to her?"

"Yes, I sort of hung out at the bar. She seemed like a nice person, very intuitive."

"The preliminary lab results came back. It looks like she died of a drug and alcohol overdose," he said, his expression tightening with disgust. "Did she seem high to you when you were talking to her?"

"What? No," I said, and shook my head. "She didn't seem high or spacy. Her eyes were clear and except for the headache she seemed as normal as you and I."

"She had a headache?"

"Yes," I said. "She got a sharp pain and closed her eyes, pressing her temples. She told me it was a flash headache and she got them sometimes."

"So that's what you talked about at your sister's wedding reception?" he asked.

I sat back and put my hands in my lap. "She made these great cocktails. I had never tried them before. Bobby was a beer guy. Anyway, I was interested in the cocktails because I thought I might do a 1950s theme at one of my proposals. So I talked to her about them. She told me she served them at a couple of weddings."

"So she was a regular at the country club," he assumed.

"No, weirdly, she told me this was her first country club gig and I believed her. She didn't really look the country club server type. But then this strange thing happened."

"What strange thing?" he asked.

"These two kids came up. They looked about eighteen or nineteen and the guy demanded that she make him a cocktail."

"Did she?"

"No, she refused and the guy got upset and started to

tell Ashley he was going to have her fired for insubordination, but the girl, Samantha Lyn, tells him to cool it. She orders them both sodas—Cokes, I think she said. Anyway, Ashley gave the kids a glass of soda each. The guy, Clark Fulcrum, made some threat—like he was going to tell his Mom that Ashley wouldn't serve him and she would never work another country club wedding."

"That seems a bit extreme," Detective Murphy said.

"Yes, I thought so, but then Samantha Lyn apologized and she and Ashley talked for a while. It seems that Ashley had a run-in with Clark and Samantha Lyn at another event. Both times, I guess, the guy was all talk and no action. You know sullen, spoiled stuff." I shrugged. "The weird part is these kids are so young and yet their parents are pushing for them to get married. Mrs. Fulcrum called me today to set up a meeting to plan their engagement."

"What?"

"I know, right? As soon as Clark's mom—Sugar Fulcrum learned I planned Warren's proposal, she searched me out at the wedding and asked for my card. She and Samantha Lyn's mom are meeting me tomorrow at the Pavilion to plan 'The proposal of the century,'" I said, and used air quotes.

"What parent would want their kid to get married under the age of twenty-one?"

"Apparently these two do. The kids should at least be of drinking age before they get married. Don't you think?"

"Yeah, I think," he said. "Apparently Ashley thought so, too?"

"I don't know. Ashley didn't speak to me about them,"

"I see," he said. "When was the last time you spoke to Ashley?"

"Toward the end of the party," I said. "She showed me how to make a couple more cocktails. Then her head still hurt so I suggested she drink some coffee and she poured herself a cup. I offered to meet with her another afternoon to talk about bartending for me. She agreed and I went to the ladies' room. When I came out, she had collapsed."

"I see." He wrote down *coffee* on his notepad and sucked on his teeth. "Are you going back to the country club soon for anything like a luncheon or party?"

"There's nothing planned, but that doesn't mean I won't be back at the club," I said, and shrugged. "Warren's family is big into that scene."

"If you do go back, keep your ears open for me, will you?"

That got my curiosity up. "Why?"

Detective Murphy paused as if weighing how much to tell me. I bit my bottom lip. One thing I had learned was that if I kept quiet, he'd eventually tell me something. I was right.

"Ashley has a bit of a history," he said.

"How so?"

"She attended Morduray College for two years."

"Morduray College?"

"Yes, it's a small, private school in Michigan. The country club has a high population of alumni from Morduray."

"So are you suggesting that Ashley knew people from the country club?"

"Maybe, but she may not remember," he said. "Ashley and another girl were attacked and sustained gunshot wounds on homecoming night of her junior year there."

"That's right," I said. "She told me about the attack. She said she thought it was what caused her headaches. She also mentioned she couldn't remember anything but waking up in the hospital. What happened?"

"The friend, Kiera, was killed instantly. Ashley was left for dead," he said, his expression fierce. "Although she survived, Ashley was shot in the head and shoulder and spent weeks in a coma. The head shot looked bad but she was lucky. She survived it relatively intact. When she woke up from the coma, she had no memory of the incident. She didn't know who'd shot them. She couldn't even remember who they'd been with that night."

"You know, she showed me the scar. Does that kind of memory loss happen a lot with gunshot wounds to the head?"

"It's pretty common for an injury of that magnitude," he said. "She'd suffered extensive brain damage from the gunshot wound. Her parents told me that the doctors feared she'd never remember completely. They were warned that a wound that bad could change her personality. Sadly, the prognosis proved to be true.

"Ashley eventually returned to Morduray after rehabilitation, but couldn't concentrate anymore, couldn't study. Her mom said she was frustrated and quit college. Without an eyewitness, there wasn't any progress on finding the killer," Detective Murphy said. "Ashley floated from job to job and racked up a small-time police record. She had a couple of disorderly conducts, an arrest for unlawfully discharging a weapon, plus a citation for the gun being unlicensed."

"Oh, no, that doesn't sound like the girl I met," I said, and tapped my chin thoughtfully. "That said, if I had been shot and left for dead, I'd probably carry a gun, too—especially if I had no idea who did it. You never know when a killer will come back and attempt to finish the job."

He nodded. "The judge took that into consideration. Ashley was fined and did community service for those crimes. But then she dies of an unintentional drug overdose?" He looked at me. "It just doesn't add up. You say she didn't appear high when you interacted with her."

"No, she didn't."

He shook his head. "I don't like it. I can't put my finger on it, but something isn't right. Anyway," he said as a way of dismissing me, "the autopsy isn't complete yet. I'll keep digging. If you hear anything . . ."

"I'll let you know," I said.

"The thing is," Murphy said, "she never had any drug convictions. Not even any drug arrests. Maybe she was lucky, but not likely, given her behavior issues. I believe she was clean."

"I agree," I said, and stood. "Like I said, I'll keep an ear open. I can plan a country club proposal with the Fulcrums. Maybe I can learn a bit more."

"Make sure you don't get in over your head," he said

with a shake of his head. "Leave the heavy lifting to the professionals. All right?"

"Okay, well," I paused, "you call before you pop over to my house and I'll keep you abreast of anything I find out. Does that sound like a deal?"

"Deal," he said. "Now get out of here."

"I will," I said, and turned on my heel. I left him to his musing. Ashley had been through a lot. No wonder she looked so much older than me. Maybe meeting with Clark and Samantha would help me get to the bottom of Ashley's death. It seemed like the least I could do to help a woman who wanted to be a fast friend.

Chapter 8

"So, Pepper, what kinds of things do you suggest for a proposal?" Laura asked me. It was five o'clock and I had gone from the police station straight to Rosa's where I'd promised Laura I'd meet her. She was waiting when I got there. We hugged and settled down in a comfortable booth, ordering coffee from an attentive waitress.

Laura had her dark brunette hair pulled back into a low ponytail. She wore a pale pink button-down shirt with a navy cardigan sweater and a pair of high-quality jeans. She rested the ankle of her long right leg on the knee of her left. Her manicured fingers were wrapped around her coffee cup. Her makeup was minimal and yet highlighted her almond-shaped eyes and bow-shaped mouth.

"The first thing I do is ask you a lot of personal questions," I said, and dug out my notebook from the tote at my feet. I clicked on my pen and wrote *Laura's Proposal* at the top of the page. "Are you up for the questions?"

"Sure," Laura said, and shrugged.

I could tell she was a bit uncertain so I sent her an encouraging smile. "Don't worry. No one sees the notes but me. Privacy is very important. Wedding proposals are very personal and I want to get it right."

"Oh, good," Laura said, and relaxed her shoulders.

"I know you told me, but please explain again how you and Monica met?"

"It's kind of a cute story," Laura said with a soft smile. "My brother was visiting from New York and I wanted to impress him with this dish I saw online and thought I could make. You see, I'm not much of a cook. My brother always teased me that any time he visited all we did was get take-out. I wanted to prove that I was cool and hip now that I lived in Chicago."

"I get that," I said, and leaned in toward her. "I gave up on being cool or hip a few years ago. My ex-boyfriend didn't care what I cooked as long as I had cold beer in the fridge."

"Oh, wow."

"It's okay," I said, and waved my hand. "We're history and this is not about me. It's about you and Monica. You were making a dish to impress your brother."

"Yes, I was in the middle of making Kung Pao chicken when the recipe called for sugar."

"Sugar?"

"I know, right? I mean, who knew you put sugar in a spicy Asian dish. Well, I didn't and so I didn't have any sugar on hand. I dug around and thought maybe I had some honey, but no. Then I contemplated using maple pancake syrup."

I winced.

"I know, the last thing I wanted was to screw up my first homemade dinner. So I got desperate and started knocking on my neighbors' doors. Monica was three doors down and the only one to answer. She opened the door and there was this gorgeous woman with soft caramel-colored hair and big green eyes, and my heart went to my feet."

"What happened?" I asked when she slipped into a quiet memory.

"I forgot what I knocked for," she said with a small laugh and sipped her coffee. "That's what I said after a moment of just staring." Her cheeks turned a gorgeous pink. "It was horrifyingly embarrassing. I mean, it's hard sometimes. An instant crush can go sideways really fast. She could have had a big burly guy in the next room, you know?"

"It's the same no matter who you are," I said with a quiet smile. "When you fall fast for someone it can get awkward if they have a girlfriend or whatever."

"So you know what I mean?"

"Yes, I know." My thoughts turned to Gage. I had to drag them back to Laura. "What happened when you told her that you forgot why you knocked?"

"She was so sweet. She merely laughed. Then she said that she heard me knocking on other doors and figured I must need something sort of urgent. That brought me out of my attraction coma. I laughed and said, yes. I explained about the Kung Pao. She had sugar and went so far as to ask me for the recipe."

"Nice."

"It was," she said with a soft smile. "I invited her to dinner with my brother, but she said no, of course."

"Oh," I said, my heart breaking a bit even though I knew it all worked out.

"No, no, she said the most amazing thing. She said, if I didn't mind, she'd really like to have me to herself."

"Ohhh."

"So we made plans for lunch the next day."

"And the Kung Pao?"

"Was awful," she admitted with a laugh. "But Monica can cook. So she made this fabulous steak salad for lunch. We ate out on her tiny fire escape, which she had dressed up with a bistro table and chairs and filled with flower boxes full of blooming plants. She told me her story and I told her mine."

"Story?"

"Of how we discovered we were gay and how difficult it was to tell our families. My family was very accepting," Laura went on to say. "Her family, not so much."

I frowned. "I plan an engagement party immediately following the proposal. Many times the family and friends want to be there to see it and so we combine both. It sounds like that might not be a good fit for you and Monica."

"No," Laura said. "No, we have friends and my family would like to celebrate. But if we could, I'd like keep it simple and beautiful and private."

"I can do that," I said. "This is all about what you want."

Laura relaxed a bit. "Okay, good. Some people are good with the splashy, in-your-face wedding thing. I applaud them, but it's not for me."

"Okay," I said. "What do you and Monica like to do when you're together?"

"Besides cooking? We like to Rollerblade in the park. We like to bike with our pups, Harry and Sally."

"Oh, you have puppies? What kind?"

"Harry is a corgi and Sally is a pomapoo."

"So small dogs," I said, and drew my eyebrows together. "How do you bike ride with them?" I tried to imagine their tiny legs keeping up with two women on bicycles.

"Oh," Laura said, and chuckled. "We have picnic baskets on the front of our bikes and we pop the dogs inside. They love to ride with the wind in their hair."

"Now that's cute," I said, and wrote down *dogs in picnic baskets*.

"You like outdoor things," I stated. "Too bad it's the middle of winter. I could do a sweet picnic proposal."

"Oh, yes," Laura said with a smile. "In Grant Park. How fun would that be?"

"We could still do it," I said, my mind working through the idea. "It would certainly be a surprise."

"A picnic in Grant Park in winter? She'd be surprised and frozen."

"Right, maybe there is something else food related we could do." I pursed my lips thoughtfully. "Listen, I know this chef who gives cooking lessons in her home. We could set it up to look like you are doing a cooking class date. We'll re-create your Kung Pao dinner . . ."

"Hopefully better tasting," she teased.

"Most certainly better tasting," I said with a smile. "We can decorate with Monica's favorite flowers."

"She likes daisies."

"Great," I said, and wrote it down. "Her favorite color?"

"Yellow and green," Laura said. "Not exactly winter colors."

"Still, okay," I said. "I'll bring in other couples who Monica has never met to make it look like a real cooking class. We'll set up a small party with your friends and family in the second of the two dining rooms the chef has available. That way you can do the proposal in the first dining room and then we'll open the second and all your friends and family will be there for an engagement party. It will be a big surprise and a lot of fun. Are you up for it?"

"I do like the idea," she said.

"Great, now, I'd like to meet Monica. I like to get a feel for both people in the couple. That way I'm sure it will be a fantastic event."

Laura winced. "Do you mind if you don't meet Monica? I really want to surprise her and I don't want her to wonder why I'm introducing her to a proposal planner."

"You could introduce me as a friend. After all, you know my aunts."

Laura blushed. "I'd really like to keep it low key."

"Oh, sure, no problem," I said. "Is it okay if I secretly film the event? Even though it's low-key, I've found people like to have professional video of the event. We can tell her the chef is filming a documentary. Is that okay?"

"Okay, I guess," Laura said. "It would be nice to have it on film."

"Great. I've already gone through as much of her Facebook page as I can without friending her. I don't want to give it away by friending her. Does she have another website or blog so that I can sort of stalk her a bit and get a good feel for other things she may like?"

"Sure," Laura said, and pulled out a business card. She wrote down a Web address. "You can find her here. Also, she's a librarian."

"Seriously?"

"Seriously," Laura said with a laugh. "She works at the Schaumburg Library and collects cookbooks as a side hobby. It's why I never have to worry about cooking."

"Sounds like she'll like the cooking class idea."

Laura laughed. "Learning how to make Kung Pao chicken would be really funny."

"I'm certain it will bring back warm memories of when you first met," I said, and stood. I held out my hand and shook hers. "Let me do a little more research on Monica and put together a quote for you."

"Great," Laura said, her eyes sparkling. "I'm looking forward to it."

The next day I got to the Pavilion fifteen minutes ahead of time. The hostess took me to a large table in the glass corner that looked out at the Chicago skyline from two sides. It was indeed the nicest table in the tearoom. At thirty stories up the views were spectacular. I had just enough time to look over my notes of things I thought might work for a high society proposal before the ladies arrived. Sugar Fulcrum was fashionably thin with brunette, shoulder length hair that was expertly cut and styled. Today she wore a silk blouse in cream, a Navy blue skirt, and black suede booties. She handed the hostess her coat and gloves. Behind her was Mrs. Thomson, who was also thin. Her blonde hair was styled in a conservative chin length blunt cut. She was dressed as impeccably as Mrs. Fulcrum. Behind them slumped Clark. He wore a leather bomber jacket, graphic T-shirt, and jeans and walked with his hands in his pockets looking bored.

I stood when the hostess brought them over. We said our hellos and the ladies gave me air kisses on both cheeks. I found the gesture affected, but did the same to make them comfortable. Clark simply flopped down in a chair and greeted me with a shrugged shoulder.

The waitstaff brought over teas and cakes.

"I hope you don't mind that I ordered for the table," Mrs. Fulcrum said as she took a seat. "Now let's talk proposals."

"We want something so spectacular it will make the tabloids as well as the society pages," Mrs. Thomson said. "We want this to be seen as elegant as JFK Junior's wedding event."

I looked at Clark. "What about you Clark? What do you want for Samantha Lyn?"

"I want her to say yes," he said and called the waitress over to order a Pepsi.

"I usually get a description of what the potential bride wants, her likes, her dreams, what she and her friends think is wonderful."

"Samantha Lyn wants over the top, glitter. Think diamonds are a girl's best friend," Mrs. Thomson said.

"Clark, are there any special moments when you were dating that you might want to recreate?" I ignored Mrs. Thomson and looked at the slouching boy.

"Whatever they want," he said and thumbed through his phone. "Look, this has been real, but I have to go."

"Don't you want more input in the proposal?" I asked.

"I'm good with what Mom wants," he said, stood and gave his mother a kiss on the cheek. "Bye."

"Whatever Mom wants," Mrs. Thomson said with admiration in her tone. "You raised that boy right."

"Thank you, dear," Mrs. Fulcrum said. "Well, Pepper what are your suggestions?"

"I make it a policy not to make suggestions on the first meeting," I lied. "I use the time to get to know the bride and groom and figure out what makes them special and create an event to suit them."

"You've met the kids," Mrs. Thomson said. "They make a gorgeous couple, don't they?"

"Yes," I said. "But I like to make it truly personal."

"Samantha loves diamonds and all things that glitter," Mrs. Thomson said. "Make it something romantic and dreamy like the season. Something that will look great on camera, I want this to hit all the morning shows."

"I have a great cameraman," Mrs. Fulcrum said and pulled out a card. "Call him. He knows what I like."

"Here's a band for you." Mrs. Thomson gave me a card. "They have a following with the kids."

"We want you to give us three venues and themes and we'll let you know if you're close," Mrs. Fulcrum said and sipped her cup of tea. No one touched the platter of tea cakes and cookies. No wonder the ladies were so thin. They didn't seem to eat. I didn't touch anything simply because I was at a business meeting. I used the time to write notes for the event based on my thoughts and feelings and so far, my notes were filled with question marks and half-formed ideas.

"And your budget?" I asked.

"Mr. Fulcrum doesn't care what you spend as long as I'm happy," Mrs. Fulcrum said.

Mrs. Thomson chuckled. "You have him properly trained as well."

"Thank you, ladies," I said and stood, reaching out my hand. "I'll have something for you soon."

"We expect a spectacle," Mrs. Thomson said as both ladies ignored my hand.

"I'll be sure to bring you the best," I said and lowered my hand. "I'll be in touch."

* * *

An hour later I met Brad at McGee's Pub and Grill. I approached the booth to find that Jennifer sat next to him.

"Hi," I said, and looked from one to the other. Brad told me Jen wanted to be here, but I had hoped he was kidding.

"Hi, Pepper," Jennifer said with a wide smile.

"Hi, Jennifer," I said, and slid into the booth across from them. "I thought you wanted this to be a surprise. How can we do that if you're part of the planning?"

The waitress stopped by. "What can I get you?"

"I'll take—"

"She'll take an iced tea and I'll take a hot green tea and Brad will have a black coffee, strong, right, dear?"

"Right," he said, and smiled softly at Jennifer.

The waitress took the order and walked off. It was pretty clear that Jennifer wanted to control the situation. "What if I didn't want iced tea?" I asked.

"Oh." Jen laughed. "Sorry, you look like an iced tea kind of person. Should I call her back?"

"No," I said with a small sigh. "Iced tea will be fine. Why don't you tell me why you're here despite wanting to be surprised."

"I want everything to be perfect for the big event," she said, and grabbed Brad's hand, pulling it toward her. "There isn't any other way to get it perfect than for me to be involved in the planning, right? You can figure out the surprise part later."

I bit the inside of my cheek. This was going to be a very difficult event. Maybe I shouldn't have said I would try.

"Don't worry," she said, as if reading my thoughts. "I promise we'll pay you top dollar. Whatever you want to charge, right, Brad?"

"Yes, dear," he said. It was pretty clear he was enamored with her.

"I need a ten-thousand-dollar retainer," I said. "Fifty percent is nonrefundable. You understand, of course."

"Of course," she said. "I understand Mrs. Fulcrum hired you to do Clark's proposal to Samantha Lyn. Is that true?"

"Mrs. Fulcrum and Mrs. Thomson and I are in talks, yes."

"Good, I thought so." She sent Brad a knowing look. "Mrs. Fulcrum only hires the best where Clark is concerned."

"How do you know so much about Mrs. Fulcrum?" I had to ask. She and Jen were at least twenty years apart in age. I highly doubted they ran in the same circles.

"Mrs. Fulcrum was my sponsor for my college sorority," Jen said with a great deal of pride. "Our families are very close. I trust her judgment. If she is hiring you, then I want to hire you."

"I'm not exactly sure—"

"If you can pull off the perfect proposal, we'll give you a two-thousand-dollar bonus. Won't we, dear?" She glanced at Brad.

"Of course," Brad said with an indulgent smile.

"All you have to do is make it perfect and surprise me," Jennifer said. "That's not so hard, now is it?"

"Okay," I said, feeling as if I were lying again.

"So how do we start?"

"I usually ask the person setting up the proposal a series of questions, to start," I said. "But it sounds like you already have an idea in mind."

NANCY J. PARRA

"Oh, no, let's start like you usually do," she said, and let the waitress put down the drinks. "I want the full experience. So, ask away."

"Okay," I said. The whole setup was more than a little weird, but if I was going to do this, then I was going to do it right. If I could pull it off, it would be a huge boon for my business. "How old are you?"

"Oh, I'm twenty-five and Brad is twenty-six," Jennifer said, and squeezed his hand.

"Okay," I said, and wrote that down. I had expected as much. "What are some of your hobbies?"

"I like salsa dancing," Jen said. "Brad likes to watch the Cubs and the Bears and hockey . . . any kind of hockey."

"Okay," I said, and made a note. "It sounds like you don't have any hobbies in common. Is there anything you like to do together?"

"Like movies?"

"Sure," I said, and nodded my encouragement. "Movies are good. I just did a movie engagement. It was great with old black and white films."

"Movies are okay," Brad said, and sat back. He tugged his hand from Jen and put his arm up along the cushion at the back of the booth. "We usually watch them at home on the couch. I think Jen wants something bigger, more romantic."

"Brad falls asleep halfway through every movie," Jen said, and sipped her drink. "I don't think that would work for an engagement."

"Okay," I said, and doodled on my pad. "What about

104

food? Do you have favorite restaurants? Any annual traditions? What about your first date? What did you do on your first date?"

"I took her to Pete's Roadhouse," Brad said with a smile. "She hated it."

"I did not," Jen protested.

"Yes, you did," he argued, then sent me a direct look. "After that I wasn't sure she would go out with me again."

"What changed your mind?" I asked Jen, suddenly finding a topic of interest.

"I fell for his cute smile and quick wit," she said, and patted his cheek. "I thought, if this is going to go anywhere, then I need to be honest with him."

"So you told him you hated it?"

"She did," Brad said. "She also made me promise never to take her back there ever."

Jen nodded. "That's right, and you know what? He hasn't."

"It's easier for me to tell you what she doesn't like than what she likes," Brad said. "Would that help?"

"Anything helps at this point," I said, and doodled the word *contrary* on the paper out of eyesight of Jen.

Brad chuckled. "I'll e-mail you a list."

"Okay," I said, and sat back. This entire proposal felt completely out of my control and I didn't like that. My mind reeled. There had to be something I could talk to these two about. They were both at Felicity's reception. "You mentioned Jennifer likes the movie *Serendipity*. Jen, what was it you liked about it?"

"I loved how they got together in the end. You know,

on the ice rink. It was so romantic. I mean, how did he know to go there? Why did she show up there? It was all so . . . serendipitous. Plus, it was pretty with all the twinkling lights and the snow. I like twinkle lights."

"She also likes glitter and diamonds and anything sparkly," Brad said.

I made a few notes. There was no way I could do an iceskating proposal. Jennifer would figure it out the moment they went to the rink. "Let me think about that some more." I sipped my tea and leaned toward them. "So, how do you know Warren?"

"Oh, his mother and my mom play tennis together," Brad said. "My family got a wedding invitation from Mrs. Evans and Mom wanted to go, so we went."

"Do you play tennis?" I was struggling to get any ideas, no matter how random.

"Oh, yes," Jen said. "Brad is killer in doubles. I don't play, of course."

"Of course," I muttered. I sighed and thought about the wedding reception. "Wasn't it terrible . . . you know, that poor bartender dying the other night. I mean, you were still there when it happened, weren't you?"

"Yes," Jen said with a nod of her head. "It was awful. Poor thing. I read in the papers that it was a suspected overdose. She looked so thin. I bet it didn't take much to put her over the edge. You were brave though, to jump in and try CPR like that." She took a sip of her drink. "I wouldn't have been so brave."

"I took CPR last year," Brad said. "It was one of the courses I needed to coach intermural tennis. It looked like you did a bang-up job."

"It didn't work," I said, with a shake of my head. "They never did revive her."

"You can't save some people," Jen said, patting my hand. "No matter how hard you try."

She was right, of course. We continued to chat, but I had a feeling this couple was a lost cause. Maybe the list of things Jen didn't like would give me an idea of how to make a big, bold surprise statement with her proposal.

I walked out of McGee's nearly two hours later completely disappointed. Looking at my doodled notes, there wasn't a whole lot to go on for a proposal. I was just about to my car when my cell phone rang. I pulled it out of my purse and saw that it was Toby.

Poor lovelorn Toby was super wealthy but a bit of a schlump. After he helped me in a couple of proposals, he sort of unofficially made me his guide in all matters of the heart.

Gage wondered why Toby kept hanging out with me when he should be pursuing his own girls. I didn't mind. Toby and I were friends, but it was hard for Gage to understand. I tried to explain it by reminding him that he and I had been friends for years. That didn't help. Gage pointed out that our friendship had turned into romance. I swore there wasn't anything romantic between me and Toby. Why would there be? I had Gage.

"Hi, Toby, how are you?" I answered my phone.

"I'm not bad, Pepper," Toby said. "Could be better, could be worse."

I laughed. "That sounds typical," I said. "What can I do for you?"

"So you know I'm not all that ready for the big leagues in love just yet, right?"

"Right," I said, nodding my head even though he couldn't see me. "Are you in the minor leagues?" The last I knew he wasn't seeing anyone at all.

"Yeah, so, can we meet?" he asked. "I have this girl I think might work."

"Have you met her in person?" I asked. The last girl he had brought to me was merely a picture of a woman he'd seen on the street.

"Not yet," he answered honestly. That was the best thing about Toby. He was always brutally honest. It was an annoying but admirable trait. "I want to meet with you first and get your opinion on her. You know, whether we're a good fit or not. Plus, you know how to take the next step, and stuff like that."

I had warm feelings for Toby. He was so clueless. I found it charming. "Okay. How about tonight?"

"Sure, meet me at the coffee shop at eight."

"I can do that," I said, and put the appointment in my mobile calendar. "See you then." The bookstore is where I first met Toby. He'd heard about my services and had asked to meet me at Centre City Books. I had gone expecting a cup of coffee and a serious chat about what he and his soon-to-be fiancée did on their dates, et cetera. When I arrived, I found a rumpled man with a George Clooney air. He didn't even bother to look me in the eye. Instead, he'd wandered the store filling a shopping cart and off-handedly answering my questions. It didn't take long for me to discover that he'd never been on a date with the woman. Toby was brilliant in business, but completely clueless in relationships.

Gage suspected he had a bit of a crush on me. I hoped not and was glad Toby had another target . . . er, woman in mind. It meant that I could officially tell Gage he had nothing to worry about.

Chapter 9

It was early afternoon and I sat next to the coffee shop window and watched the cars go by. I noticed a powder blue BMW Mini roar into the parking lot. Samantha Lyn parked badly, and without a second look, hit the lock as she stepped toward the coffee shop.

Today she looked all of nineteen years old in her skinny jeans, pink polo, and blue peacoat. Her pretty blond hair was pulled back into a messy bun. Her black thigh-high boots rang out on the walk as she hurried to the shop. I waved when she stopped just inside the door looking for me.

"Hi, Pepper," Samantha said, and leaned over to give me a quick peck on the cheek. "Thanks for meeting me. I didn't know who I could talk to about this."

"Any time," I said, and handed her a triple raspberry

mocha I had ordered for her. "I thought you might enjoy this flavor combination. It's my favorite!"

"It smells wonderful," she said, breathing in the steam rising from her cup, then sat down across from me. "Thank you. And thanks for, like, you know, meeting me here."

"No problem," I said. She took off her coat and draped it on the chair back behind her and then wrapped her fingers around the cup I gave her. I noted that her manicure was a soft pink ombre that moved from light to darker tips.

"I'm so upset," she admitted. Her blue gaze held a watery look as if she fought back tears. "Ashley was so kind to me. I never knew anyone like her and now she's gone. Just like that." Samantha snapped her fingers. "I don't know what to do. I don't know how to handle myself. My mom won't listen. All she can talk about is the upcoming proposal with Clark."

"Wait, you know about the proposal? I thought it was a surprise."

Samantha Lyn sighed and shook her head. "Our moms have been talking about it for months. Mom tells anyone who is willing to listen. She told me they hired you. So, I know it's coming, but just not when."

"And you're okay with that?"

"I haven't had a chance to think too much about it. I'm too upset over Ashley's death. Like I said, it's awful and heartbreaking and I'm having trouble dealing."

"I know," I said and patted her hand.

"You liked Ashley, too, didn't you? I saw you two talking off and on that night."

"Yes, we sort of had a connection," I agreed, and tilted

my head. "I felt out of place and so did she. She was helping me come up with cocktail ideas because I plan events and thought it would be nice to know. Then she told me a bit about her history and how she knew you." Samantha Lyn seemed really upset and it didn't make any sense. From what I understood, the teen had hardly known Ashley. Why was she having such a hard time dealing with this? "You mentioned on the phone that you knew Ashley from another wedding. I remember talking to Ashley about this the night she died."

"Yeah," Samantha said, and clung to her coffee cup. "She probably didn't tell you the whole story, though. She wouldn't because she was so nice."

"What happened?" I asked. Tears welled up in Samantha's eyes and she dashed them away. "You don't have to tell me if you don't want to," I said, and patted her hand.

"Stupid mascara." Samantha Lyn got a tissue out of her Michael Kors bag and dabbed at her eyes. "No, no, I don't mind telling. I'm sure you'll understand. You see, when I first met Ashley it was at the wedding you're referring to. Clark was being a complete jerk."

"Oh," I said encouragingly. I wasn't surprised. From what I saw the other night, Clark was not a naturally nice person.

"He said something really mean to me. Usually I can blow it off, but not that time. I'd had enough and ran out of the reception." Tears filled her eyes and she used the tissue to dab them away. I reached into my bag and pulled out a new tissue and handed it to her.

Samantha Lyn took the second tissue and dabbed at her eyes then twisted the two tissues in her hands. "He said I was a fat cow."

"No!"

"I know, right?" Samantha said. "He said it because I caught him flirting with this other girl there, at the wedding. Hanna Anderson. We go to school with her. When I called him on it, he got mean."

"I'm so sorry," I said, and patted her hand. "Is that when you met Ashley?"

"Yes," she said. "I ran out of the building and Ashley was taking a cigarette break. When she saw me crying, she came over and said, 'Whoever he is, he isn't worth it.'"

"She was right," I said.

"I know." Samantha Lyn shrugged her shoulders. "It's complicated. But Ashley just sat down with me and listened as I went on and on. I know she was supposed to be working. I even asked her to go since I knew she was missing out on tips and such. She said no. She said I needed to talk and she was not going until I was okay."

"That sounds like the girl I met," I said, my mind going back to my conversation with Ashley the night of my sister's wedding.

"Anyway, she listened for a long time and then told me that I should break up with Clark." Samantha's big blue gaze looked up at me. "She said I should trust my gut because guts don't lie."

I nodded. "She was a very smart woman."

"Yes, she was," Ashley agreed, and tears welled up in

her eyes again. "I told her something I hadn't told anyone else."

I waited but Samantha simply dabbed at her eyes with a tissue. "I'm sure whatever you told her was kept in the highest of confidence."

"I think so, too," Samantha Lyn said. She paused and looked at me, then leaned in. "I told her that I wanted to break up with Clark, but with my parents involved it was tough."

I waited a heartbeat. "What did she tell you?"

"She did the most amazing thing," Samantha said, and leaned away from me. "She said for me to wait right there. Then she went inside and when she came out a few minutes later she had her purse and car keys. She put her arm through mine and told me that she apologized to the other bartenders and explained to them that an emergency had come up and she needed to leave. Just like that, she left her job and all those tips for me. Then she drove me home so I wouldn't have to go back in and face Clark."

"That was a really nice thing to do."

"I agree," Samantha Lyn said with a nod. "In the car, Ashley encouraged me to go out and see the world. She said I should learn more about who I was and give myself a chance to grow before tying myself down forever."

"That sounds like very good advice."

"But I let her down." She leaned back as tears welled in her eyes. "I didn't break up with Clark. I tried, but my parents talked me into giving him another chance."

"I still don't understand the pressure to get married," I said. "What about college?"

Samantha shrugged. "I wanted to study engineering, but my parents think that's not an appropriate major for me. They think it's silly to get an education when all I need to do is marry well and give them grandchildren. They sent me off to college to join a sorority and make good connections. They expect me to get my Mrs. degree and drop out. Not actually graduate with a college degree. You see, my parents have never let me have a job. They pay for everything and then they threaten to cut me off if I disobey their wishes."

"They said that?" I frowned. "In this day and age, people actually still think that way?"

"No, no, you misunderstand," Samantha Lyn said. "They mean well, they really do. They want what's best for me. I'm the one who is wishy-washy." She blinked. "It's because I'm young."

"You're almost twenty years old," I said. "You are an adult. You don't have to listen to them."

"It's not that easy." Samantha Lyn shook her head. "Until I can afford to live on my own, I *do* have to listen to them. But I can't afford to live on my own because I can't get a good job without an education, which I don't have because they want me to spend my time at society events instead of in class. It's all a vicious circle."

I patted her hand again. "There are lots of things you can do to put yourself through college. Kids do it all the time. It takes longer than if your parents are supporting you financially, but it can be done. This is your life, Samantha. You have to stand up and fight for it."

She frowned at me. "I tried. But my mom was so disappointed. I just." She paused and her shoulders slumped. "I caved."

I muttered something appropriately soothing like "I understand" even though I didn't. I had learned there was a point where people refuse to listen to good advice and it sounded like I hit that point with Samantha. What I wanted was more information. Maybe she knew something about Ashley that would help me figure out what happened to her. "Can I ask you something? Do you know if Ashley was doing drugs? I mean, she didn't seem to be the druggie type when I met her. But you met with her before and I thought maybe you might have a better feel for who she was."

Samantha looked appalled. "Absolutely not. It's weird how much she and I talked that one night. But I can tell you that she was completely against that sort of thing."

"Seems like you knew her pretty well in that short time," I said.

"You know how sometimes you get to know a person really fast and you want to stay friends forever?" Samantha shrugged. "I felt that way about Ashley." Samantha paused and sighed. "The worst part is that she died so very young."

"I agree, it's a terrible loss." I wrapped my hands around my coffee cup.

"I think she'd be disappointed if I married Clark,"

Samantha said in a near whisper. Then she looked at me so sadly.

"If you don't want to, then don't," I stressed.

"I wish it was that easy."

I bit my tongue. We talked a bit more, but mostly about what happened when someone died. How to dress and act at a wake. What to do for a funeral. It was all things that I had learned through my parents and my big family. By the time Samantha and I left the coffee shop she had settled down. I felt confident that she could drive safely and I gave her a hug and waved as she drove off. Samantha Lyn was a lovely person. I really hated the fact that she felt pressured into being with Clark. I would do my best to discourage the proposal. I had to be careful, though. Clark's mother was well connected in the community. If I went against her wishes, she was completely capable of seeing that I didn't get any more work. Perfect Proposals was too new. I couldn't afford to make enemies—especially influential enemies like Sugar Fulcrum. I would have to be very, very careful.

* * *

My cell phone rang as I got into my car. "Perfect Proposals, this is Pepper, how can I help you?"

"Pepper? It's Murphy."

"Hi, Detective Murphy. What can I do for you?"

"I wanted to let you know that the official autopsy report came through."

"Oh, that was fast. Do they know what happened?"

"The report confirms that Ashley was killed by a deadly mixture of drugs and alcohol," he said, his tone flat.

"I just don't think she was on drugs," I protested. "She didn't seem high to me at all."

"It was an overdose of Xanax combined with alcohol," he said. "It's a killer combination."

I remembered Ashley finishing my martini and I felt pangs of guilt in the pit of my stomach. "Lots of people take Xanax," I said. "I'm sure some people drink alcohol, too. How come we don't hear about people dropping dead all over the place?"

"Mixing any drugs with alcohol is a bad idea," Murphy said sternly.

"Yes, I know," I said. "I would never do that, but people do and they don't die."

"Pepper, the amount in Ashley's system was off the charts."

"I don't understand," I said. "Did she have a prescription for Xanax? I mean, if she had a script then she should have known she shouldn't mix it with alcohol."

"She didn't have a script, Pepper. We checked."

I didn't like his tone. "What are you implying?"

"If she didn't have a script, then she could have bought the drug off the street," he said. "She probably didn't realize you can't mix Xanax and alcohol."

"I just don't think she was a drug addict," I said. "I was with her for a few hours. I could be wrong, but she didn't seem strung out to me."

"I'm sorry, Pepper, I know this is bad news. But someone with her track record probably knows how to get illegal drugs."

"I don't understand," I said, and frowned. "Just yesterday you thought that something was wonky about this whole thing. Now you get the autopsy results and suddenly Ashley is a drug addict who overdosed?"

"Look, the chief says the results were definitive."

"What does that mean?"

"It means the case is closed, Pepper," he said. "It has been labeled an accidental overdose. There's nothing more to do. Anyway, I thought you should know. I know you took a shine to this girl."

"Thanks, I guess," I said, and hung up. I stared out my windshield. I couldn't wrap my head around the fact that Ashely would be the victim of an accidental overdose. She seemed too aware, too nice.

I decided then and there to dig a little into Ashley's story, if for no other reason than to help Samantha Lyn understand the loss of a person she thought could be a real friend.

Chapter 10

I stopped home and hopped on my computer. A quick Google search brought up Ashely's Facebook page. Like most kids she left it public. Ashley's family and friends were writing on her Facebook page about their memories of the happy girl she had once been. The stories from friends and family told the tale of a middle-class sorority girl with good grades. There were several pictures of her and her best friend, Kiera.

"Such a terrible loss," a woman named Blake wrote on Ashley's page. "It is hard to imagine the Ashley I knew ever doing drugs and drinking. When we were in college she was so health conscious. But then when Kiera was murdered, it seems Ashley fell apart and never recovered."

"I know, sad," a girl named Clarissa added in a comment. "Kiera's death and the horrible incident really scarred Ashley. It is so tragic to have to bury both of these beautiful, caring women."

"I agree," Blake went on to say. "Hard to connect the story of Ashley's death with the hard-working, straight-A girl we all knew."

"Remember the pranks she and Kiera used to pull?" a girl named Deirdre wrote on the page. "When they took Dean Ordant's moped and ran it up the flag pole? That was so funny."

"I remember that," Clarissa commented. "Kiera painted it to resemble the American flag and then they pulled it up the flag pole with ropes. The look on Dean Ordant's face was priceless."

"I miss them both," a girl named Angela wrote. "It's a terrible loss."

"I agree," I muttered and glanced at the time on my computer. I had to shut down right now or I would be late meeting Toby.

"Hey, Pepper," Toby said as I hurried toward his table at the local coffee shop. "Thanks for coming."

"No problem," I said, and kissed his cheek in a welcome. I put down my tote and unzipped my coat. "The weather is good."

"Thirty-five degrees and clear is a decent day for Chicagoland in December," Toby agreed. "I bought you a coffee just the way you like it." He pushed the cup toward me.

"Thanks," I said, and took off my coat, hanging it on the back of my chair. "So you have a new girl?"

"Yes," he said, matter-of-factly. "I found her on an online dating site. I have the profile right here." He pulled out his cell phone and brought up the website. "Her name is Greta. She has a PhD in physics and works for a tech company." He gave me his phone.

I didn't know exactly how old Toby was but he looked to be in his mid to late forties. A man of average build and height, he had a full head of dark, wavy hair, and an ever-present five-o'clock shadow. I wasn't sure if he merely forgot to shave most days or if he was intentionally clipping his beard at that level. In the last few months Toby had become a dear friend. When I first met him I thought he could be good-looking in an older George Clooney kind of way. Unfortunately, despite his vast wealth, he was always as rumpled as that funny old television detective Colombo. Today he wore a stained T-shirt, droopy jeans with completely frayed hems, and his favorite ripped white skateboarder shoes.

I took his phone and looked at the site he'd brought up. The picture was of a girl who looked like she was a natural for a model, not a PhD in physics. But I wasn't going to judge. Not when Toby seemed so happy. "She's pretty," I said.

"And smart," he said. "She says she is looking for intelligent geeky guys. That would be me."

"Yes," I agreed as I handed him the phone. "That would be you. Still . . ."

"What?" he asked as he took the phone back and perused her profile.

"Nothing," I said, and chewed on my bottom lip.

"It's not nothing," he said, his eyes narrowing. "You are the expert in matters of the heart. I appreciate your opinion."

"I'm not sure," I dodged. "But she could be phishing."

"What do you mean?"

"This profile seems too good to be true," I pointed out.

"Are you saying a girl can't be pretty and smart? Because I disagree. You are living proof that they can."

I felt the heat of a blush rush up my neck and into my cheeks. "Thanks, Toby. But the problem with websites like this is that you don't really know who this person is. I mean, she could be a guy looking for a nerd with a fat wallet."

"A guy?" Toby looked at his phone. "She does not look like any guy I've ever met."

"That's just it," I said. "The picture could be of any random model. People do that. They put pictures up on the Internet trying to snare an unsuspecting guy. They get close to you via e-mail and such and then get you to rescue them by sending money. Or worse, they come to your house, plant some scene, and then blackmail you."

"So, you're saying she could be looking for marks. You know, people to scam."

"Yes," I said with a nod. "It could be a guy looking for marks."

"Hmmm," Toby said, and put the phone down. "I could vet them through my sources."

"Yes," I agreed. "You could vet them. But it's always better to meet someone through your friends. I mean, friends tend to set people up with people they know. A girl who has already been vetted by your friends is a wiser choice."

"I don't have that many friends, Pepper," Toby said bluntly. "You and one guy are it, and Harold isn't exactly a social butterfly."

"I see," I said, and sipped my coffee. He was right. He had ordered me the exact flavor I preferred with just the right amount of creamer.

"That leaves me with very few options, unless you are willing to vet women for me," Toby said. He looked away as if he really didn't want me to find him a girl. Was Gage right? Did Toby have a crush on me? Would he say no to every woman I mentioned just to keep me in his life?

"I'm not a professional matchmaker," I said. "I'm more of an after-the-relationship-works kind of girl."

"Yeah," he said, and sipped his coffee. "I know. How's the business going?"

"Pretty good," I said. "I've got four projects going right now."

"Anything I can help with?" His tone was hopeful.

"Maybe," I said. "I have this one woman who demands that I surprise her."

"Okay, well, you surprise all your clients."

"The catch is that she feels like she needs to be involved in every stage of the planning," I said. "She wants her experience to be perfect, and the only way to do that, according to her, is that she plan the entire thing."

"I see," he said, and put his coffee cup down. "There is one small issue with that."

"The surprise," I said. "I know. I don't know what I'm going to do. I thought maybe I could plan a pseudo-event and then have you help with the real event. That way she wouldn't see it coming."

"That sounds like a lot of work," he said. "Why don't you just do what you did with me? Tell her she's going to observe a few events and then have one of those events be her proposal."

"You are brilliant!" I stood up and hugged him. "That is much easier. Of course, I'll have to ask the other clients if Brad and Jen can tag along, but I don't think they will mind."

"You can use me as the guy who you are planning the proposal for," he said. "I'm sure you know someone you can use as the 'girlfriend.'" He said the term with air quotes. "That way I'm helping but you don't have to do everything twice."

I sat back down and ignored the slight panic in my gut at the idea that I might be planning another proposal event for Toby and a woman who didn't love him. I would have to walk a very careful line with this.

"What else has been going on?" he asked.

"There's this bartender who died at Felicity's reception."

"What?" He leaned forward. "Another death? If I were your sister I'd begin to wonder what kind of death karma was following me around."

"She doesn't know," I said. "We did our best to shield her from it until she and Warren get back from their honeymoon."

"How can you not know someone died at your own

wedding reception?" he asked. "That's kind of a big thing. I'm sure the police were called as well as an ambulance. You can't miss that."

"They were," I said. "But Ashley—the girl who died—didn't pass out until the end of the reception. Felicity and Warren were long gone." I shook my head at the memory of Ashley lying there hopeless on the ground. "I tried to perform CPR, but I wasn't able to revive her. In fact, the paramedics took over and pretty much called her time of death right then and there."

"What happened?" He leaned forward, his gaze filled with concern. "Are you okay?"

"Yes, no, I don't know," I answered honestly. "She was a nice girl. We sort of bonded about being misfits at the country club." I shrugged. "I spent some time talking with her about 1950s cocktails and life in general. She seemed like one of those people you meet and know right away you are meant to be friends. The last thing I talked to her about was getting together some afternoon. Then she was gone."

"That is a testament to what a nice person you are," Toby said, and patted my hand. "You took me under your wing pretty quickly, too. So, what happened? Did she slip and fall? Get accidentally electrocuted?"

"What?" I pulled my hand away from him. "No, no."

"Gunshot? Stabbing?"

"No." I shook my head at the absurdity of his suggestions. "No, she passed out and never came to," I said. "She had complained of a headache when I was with her.

Detective Murphy told me the autopsy suggests she over-dosed on Xanax and alcohol."

"Terrible," he said with a shake of his head. "How could the country club hire a drug user to work the bar? I will lodge a complaint."

"You're a country club member?" I asked. "Oh, wait, don't answer that." I put my hand up in a stop-sign palm toward him. "Let me guess, you joined the club after you earned your first million dollars."

"Yes," he said, and nodded. "It's—"

"What you do," I finished the sentence for him. Then I leaned in. "So, Toby, the country club is a perfect place to meet the appropriate woman for you."

He frowned. "Do you really think so?"

"It can't hurt," I said, and sat back. "It would seem to me that people of the appropriate income level would be members of the club, right?"

"Yes," he said. "I do suppose that's true."

"The club membership board would rule out anyone inappropriate, therefore there would be no chance of phishing."

"There may be some gold digging," he said, and glanced at me. "That is a possibility."

"Yes, I suppose that's true," I said with a shrug. "But for the most part you'll be in a place ripe with women of the proper socioeconomic status. You should get to know the other members of the club. Then you can eventually vet your potential dates through them."

"It's an idea," he said. "I could go tomorrow afternoon. They serve a nice two-martini lunch there."

I chewed my bottom lip and tried not to wince at the idea of Toby showing up for lunch at the country club dressed like a forty-year-old skater boy. "Yes, yes, you most certainly can, but before you go, perhaps you should step up on the grooming. You know, so that people get the right impression of you."

"What do you mean, my grooming?" he asked and looked down at his T-shirt and jeans. "I wear this to the club all the time. They don't judge me there. They like my money."

"Yes, I'm sure they do, but if you are looking for a suitable wife there, you should wear a nice dress shirt. Perhaps put a clean white T-shirt under it to give it a nice finish. Then I'd replace the shoes with something more appropriate."

"Good god, do I need to wear a tie and jacket?"

"I don't think they are necessary for making an impression at lunch," I said, and pursed my lips as I contemplated him. "But you could comb your hair a bit."

"Fine." His tone clued me in to the fact that he wasn't at all fine with my thoughts on his grooming.

"Think of it as setting the stage," I said, and patted his hand. "If you want a beautiful, intelligent woman, you have to give them what they want—a smart, well-groomed man."

He blew out a long breath. "I suppose that's true."

"If you want, I'll go with you," I offered. "I don't have a membership to the club so I'll have to go as your guest."

"You know, that's not a bad idea," Toby said. "I'll be more approachable with you there. I've discovered that a single man alone is a bit intimidating to women."

I smiled at the idea that anyone would be intimidated by Toby. "If it's okay with you, there may be some people who were at the country club the night Ashley died. I would really like to talk to them and see if they thought she was on drugs."

"You want to validate your hypothesis," he said with a nod. "I can understand that. Let's go, then. I can help you with your new investigation and you can help me sort through eligible women."

"Sounds great," I said. "You are the best." I stood and gave Toby a hug. "I've got to go. It was nice catching up. I'm really looking forward to talking at lunch tomorrow."

"Meet me there at noon," he said. "You can ensure I'm impeccably groomed and I can have lunch with a beautiful woman. We both win."

"See you, Toby," I said, and walked out to my car. The frozen wind had died down a bit. The sky was dark early. Frankly, I hated the time of year when it was dark early. The only good thing about winter was the fact that the cold made the sky very clear. Which meant you could see a few stars peeking through the city lamp light. It was a beautiful evening.

I got into my car and pointed it toward home. It had been a busy day. Tomorrow would be even busier, now that I'd added investigating Ashley's death to my to-do list. I felt as if I owed it to her to look into the mysterious circumstances behind her death. After all, she had been kind to me and I was a perfect stranger. Someone like that didn't deserve the label of addict who overdosed. Especially if that's not what really happened.

* * *

"Why all the phone calls?" Gage asked from his perch on my living room couch. He had come over to cook me dinner and spend time with me. I had enjoyed his famous beef stew, but then had excused myself to do a little work.

"The usual," I said and flopped down on the couch beside him. "Leaving messages for venues and flowers and caterers."

"I wouldn't have guessed that the evenings were a good time to get ahold of businesses."

"Actually, it's a good time to leave messages. Sometimes I get ahold of the real person because they are working late trying to catch up and the daytime staff has left."

"So there are no gatekeepers telling you the person you want is in a meeting."

"Exactly," I said and rested my head on his broad shoulder. "Detective Murphy called me today. He said that the autopsy results proved that Ashley died of an overdose of Xanax and alcohol."

"That's terrible," Gage said.

"I agree," I said, and rested my head on his wide shoulder. "She didn't seem the type. Detective Murphy confirmed that she didn't have a prescription for Xanax, so she had to have gotten the pills illegally." I sat up and turned my body toward Gage. "But I'm telling you that I had a few conversations with her that night. She was not stoned. She looked very sober."

"Was she drinking?" Gage asked. "Maybe she was an alcoholic. Sometimes you get high-functioning ones who appear to be sober the entire time they are swallowing two six-packs of beer."

I winced. "She did take a few sips of the cocktails she was creating for me to taste."

"I know you want to think the best of this person," Gage said and patted my knee. "But she might just be what the report says. You can't tell anything about people by simply talking to them a few times. Think of all the people who get scammed every day."

I slumped back down and grabbed a couch pillow and hugged it. "I'm a good judge of people."

"You are," he said. "But this situation may be more of a reflection on how you see the world than how the world really is. That's what I like about you, Pepper. You believe the best in people."

"Yes, until proven otherwise, I do," I said. "I feel strongly about this, Gage. I'm going to do some digging. I talked Toby into taking me to the country club for lunch tomorrow. I thought we'd work on his social skills and perhaps how to meet the perfect girl for him."

"He isn't going to meet anyone with you there," Gage said, and raised his hand to stop me before I could speak.

"Not because you can't coach him, but because that man is half in love with you. You will be the only woman he sees there. I know. I have the same problem."

"Oooh," I said, and planted a tender kiss on Gage's mouth. "That is so sweet."

"But you're going, aren't you?"

"Of course, I'm going," I said, and snuggled in beside Gage. "Toby needs my help. You should have seen the prospect he brought me to check out for him. It was an Internet scammer. There's no way I'm going to leave Toby to his own devices. I'm going to lunch at the country club."

Gage put his arm around me and gathered me to his chest. "It doesn't hurt that you may run into some of the people from the reception, does it?"

I shrugged and didn't bother to hide the rising blush. "If I run into someone from the reception and the topic comes up, I won't shy away from asking them their opinion on the matter."

He squeezed me closer and planted a soft kiss on my lips. "You wouldn't be my Pepper if you didn't."

Chapter 11

♂

The next morning I called Jen to suggest the idea of tagging along to see how the other proposal events go. "Hi, Jen. So, I had an idea last night."

"What's your idea?" Her voice was strong over my cell phone. I sat in my living room and looked out the window at the mailman delivering the mail. He wore a long, heavy coat, a warm postman hat with ear flaps, and gloves. It was another cold, clear day, but there were predictions of snow in the future.

"How do you feel about accompanying me to a couple of proposal events? You can view firsthand what I do and I can get a better idea of what you like and don't like."

"Huh," she said. "Can I do that?"

"Sure."

"What about the person paying you? Will they be okay with that?"

"I'll tell them you are my assistant. They'll let you in."

"Okay, I'm in," she said, her voice brightening. "It will be fun to see up close if you surprise them or not."

"Great," I said, and tried to remain cheerful and not feel insulted by her skepticism. "I have a proposal planned for Saturday morning. It's at the F.A.O. Schwarz, but I think you'll see that it doesn't have to have a lot of flash to be classy, sweet, and perfect for the couple. I'll e-mail you the details."

"Fine, Saturday it is," she said.

I made notes on my laptop. "One more thing," I said. "It's about Ashley."

"The bartender?"

"You remember talking to her at all?"

"I remember she was good at making mojitos," she said. "I had my fair share of those that night. Weddings make me a little crazy."

"I remember," I said. "Did you talk to her?"

"No, Brad got most of our drinks. No, wait, I did pick up one or two rounds, I think," she said. "It's kind of a blur. Your sister was beautiful. I remember that part, and also how much she and Warren glowed with love."

"Yeah, they really had that in-love glow, didn't they?" I asked. "So when you did order from Ashley, did you think she was high when she served you?"

"Let me think," Jen said, and paused for a second. "Honestly, I can't remember. But if she was, I think I would have noticed."

"Do you know if anyone saw her taking drugs?"

"What? No, no, I didn't hear that rumor. I'm usually tuned in to the gossip after these events, and that would have been something people talked about," Jen said.

"Do you know if anyone had a grievance against her?"

"What, for her bad haircut?" Jen said, and snickered into the phone. "No, like I said, we barely knew the girl. I think this was her first time bartending at the club. So are we good? You'll send me the details for Saturday morning?"

"We're good," I said. "I've sent you the e-mail just now. See you then, if not before."

"Super." Jen hung up.

I called Brad to let him know that I asked Jen to tag along. "You can come as well, if you'd like to see how I work."

"I suppose I'll come, but frankly, I'm not that interested," Brad said with a low chuckle. "What I'm interested in seeing is how you pull this off."

"If anyone can do it, it's me," I said with more bravado than I felt. "Quick question, though. Do you remember that bartender, Ashley?"

"The girl who died?"

"Jen says she made you mojitos at the wedding. Do you remember if she seemed to be acting strangely at all?

"No, I don't remember her acting strangely. In fact, I don't really remember anything about her at all. Why do you ask?"

"The police think she died of an overdose by mixing Xanax and alcohol," I said. "It's sad."

"Yes, very sad," Brad said. "I understand you have to be really careful when you're taking those kinds of drugs."

"Yes, I guess you do," I said. "She didn't seem like she was drunk or drugged to you?"

"Like I said, I don't remember. I doubt I would have even noticed unless the drinks tasted odd or she was moving slow or something. She seemed okay with the service," he said. "I went back to her because she put the right amount of alcohol in the drinks. You know? Some bartenders put in too little. The drinks always looked nice. Like she cared."

"Do you know of anyone who might have wanted to hurt her?"

"No," he said. "Why? Do the cops think she was murdered?"

"No," I said. "They have closed the case as an accidental overdose. I was simply wondering who stood to gain from her death."

"I doubt it was anyone at the wedding," Brad said. "She didn't look like a person that ran in our circles. I remember thinking she could be a looker if she took better care of herself. Seems to me the cops have it right on this one. "

"Thanks," I said. We hung up with my promising to take pictures of Jen working at the event on Saturday. Brad seemed to think he and Jen tagging along would be more work than it was worth. I didn't tell him yet that I would plan his surprise to be one of my events. Now all I had to do was figure out which one.

I called Sherry to ask her permission for Jen to attend her proposal. "She doesn't believe that people can really be surprised," I said. "I'd like her to see firsthand how wonderful the perfect proposal can be, but not at the expense of your event."

"Oh, yes, of course," Sherry said. "The more the merrier!"

"Wonderful! I'm glad it's okay with you," I said. "I was able to get the Macy's tearoom and I'm planning to cater a gorgeous brunch. I've sent you pictures of decorations and two cakes for you to choose from. I think this is going to be a great proposal."

"I'm getting so excited."

"Oh, one more thing . . . The Rockettes are in Chicago for their traveling show this week. I know a guy who's got connections in the Chicago theater scene. I may be able to get them to come and do a routine to 'Dance of the Toy Soldiers' right before you propose. What do you think?"

"Oh, my gosh!" Sherry sounded excited. "That would be awesome."

"It could be pretty pricey, but it is a once-in-a-lifetime opportunity," I said.

"My dad will pay," she said. "Whatever it costs. That would be so cool."

"Great," I said. "I'll let you know if it's a go. See you Saturday. Don't forget the ring."

"Oh, I won't," she said. "William is going to be so surprised. His mom and dad are helping me. We have a plan on getting him there."

"Wonderful," I said. "Also, I need you to send me the list of people you want at the brunch. I'll send out supersecret Evites today."

She squealed. "I'm so excited."

I laughed. "Sounds like it. I'll talk with you soon."

I hung up and made a few notes. I called Gage.

"Hey, sweetheart," he said. "What's up?"

"Hi, I have a client who wants to have a toy-store-proposal event. I see the Rockettes are in town this week for their Christmas show. Do you think I could hire them to come in and do a dance number?"

"Hmmm, I know the stage manager. I'll get you his number," Gage said. "It's going to be expensive."

"Money's no object," I said.

"Timing might be an issue if they have a matinee," he said.

"Oh, right, I'll remember to factor that in."

"You might be able to get a couple of the understudies," he said thoughtfully. "Would that work?"

"Yes," I said, excited by my idea. "Thank you, Gage! You're the best."

"I know," he said with a chuckle. "That's why you love me."

I took the stage manager's name and number and gave him a call. It took an hour but he got back to me. They could do it. I would only get six dancers, but they would come in costume and perform one number. I excitedly approved the price with Sherry and faxed some paperwork over to the stage manager.

One small dance number at F.A.O. Schwarz at ten A.M. on Saturday. Done. I was on a roll. Next up, I needed to call Laura and see if she was okay with Brad and Jen attending her proposal.

"Hi, Laura," I said when she answered the phone. "This is Pepper Pomeroy. Listen, I have a client who needs to see a couple of proposals before she'll commit to one of her own. Can I include her and her boyfriend in your event? They can be stand-ins."

There was a long moment of silence. "I'm not sure. You know I want things to be low-key."

"I'm putting together a cooking class idea, remember? They could be one of the other couples at the class. There has to be a full class or it won't feel authentic. Trust me, Monica won't know the others are in on it. The other couples have been told to treat it like any cooking class date night." I paused for a heartbeat. "It will help her to be more comfortable for her proposal."

"Oh . . . okay, then," Laura agreed reluctantly. "If somehow my event can help her event, then I'm okay with it."

"Thanks for letting me bring Jen and her boyfriend to your proposal. I promise it will all go off as planned."

"I'm counting on you, Pepper. I'm really nervous. You only get one chance at proposing to the woman you love, you know? I don't want anything to ruin it."

"It won't. My business is named Perfect Proposals for a reason. I guarantee it."

* * *

I met Toby at the country club at noon. The parking lot was full. The valet took Old Blue and hurried away with it. I tried not to think of the incongruity of my big ancient

Buick at a ritzy country club. Toby waited for me near the entrance. He cleaned up well when he put effort into it. It was pretty clear he'd taken my advice. His hair was neatly trimmed and I swear there was product in it. His face was clean-shaven. His suit was clearly Armani, but the expensive dress shirt underneath held a hint of the wrinkles that Toby usually dressed with. I was glad to see he hadn't cleaned up too much.

"Hi," I said, and brushed a kiss on his cheek. "You look nice."

"I had my assistant make me a salon appointment and pick out the clothes," he said, and ran his finger around his collar. "I thought when you earned enough money you didn't have to wear a tie anymore. Unless you were negotiating venture capital."

I smiled and patted his cheek as he opened the door for me. "Think of this as a venture opportunity that might establish the foundation for your future family."

He nodded. "As I've indicated in the past, the only reason to marry is to leverage fortunes for your children and their children to come."

"So romantic," I muttered as the hostess asked for the name.

"Toby Mallard. I have a reservation for two," Toby said.

"Ah, yes, Mr. Mallard, so nice to see you again. We have your table ready for you. This way, please." The hostess was a tall woman of Eastern European descent. She was thin with high cheekbones and slanted eyes. Her blond hair was piled effortlessly on her head and she wore a designer white shirt and black wool skirt. Her shoes flashed red on the soles. I wondered who made enough money as a hostess to wear Christian Louboutin shoes. "As per your standing order, this is our finest lunch table," she said, and waited for Toby and me to sit. I paused for a moment to see if Toby would pull out my chair. He didn't even notice and sat down immediately, grabbed his napkin off the table and stuffed it in his shirt collar like a bib.

I sat and tried not to look the hostess in the eye. She didn't seem to blink as she handed us our menus.

"Alexander will be your waiter today," she said. "Bon appétit."

"The last time I was here, the service was fine but the meal was a bit goopy," Toby said from behind his menu.

"I assure you sir, the cook would not serve you anything goopy," the waiter said as he reached our table in time for Toby's comments.

"Yes, well, we'll see about that, won't we?" Toby said, and lowered the menu long enough to look the waiter in the eye.

"I'm sorry, Mr. Mallard, I didn't realize you were our guest today. Welcome back. Can I get you something to drink?" the waiter asked, appearing contrite once he realized who he was serving. "We have sparkling water, iced tea, and, of course, several wines and cocktails."

"We'll take a bottle of sparkling water," Toby said. "Then I want iced tea. Pepper?"

"I'll take an iced tea as well," I said. The waiter turned on his heel and left. "Toby, did you ever take a business etiquette class?"

"Yes," he said, his gaze on the menu. "Of course, I do business with many foreign investors. I didn't want to offend. So I read several books on proper etiquette."

"Of course you did," I muttered.

"The waiter should know better than to contradict a patron. Especially a patron he should know will leave a big tip."

The waiter arrived with a bottle of sparkling water and poured both glasses. Then he explained the lunch specials. I ordered a simple steak salad and Toby ordered prime rib. When the waiter left, I smiled at Toby. "It might not hurt to take a refresher course," I said gently. "A woman of the stature you are looking for has certain expectations when it comes to the man she dates."

"That may be true," Toby said, and picked up his water glass. "But if marriage is the intended outcome, then it is only fair to be myself during the courtship. If I put on airs for the courtship, she will be sadly disappointed once we marry. Don't you think? Divorce can be so expensive."

"You think she'd divorce you over bad manners?"

"I've heard of divorces for something as simple as sneezing wrong," Toby said absently. "Of course, I will ask for a prenup before we wed."

"Yes," I said, and tried not to shake my head. "That is really romantic."

"Romance is overrated when looking for a bride," he said.

"Really, Toby? After attending my proposal events you still think that romance isn't important?"

"I didn't say romance wasn't important," Toby said.

He wasn't all that good at direct eye contact, so I couldn't see what he was thinking. "I said it was overrated."

"People take dancing lessons so they can dance at their wedding," I informed him. "Manners are a lifelong skill that need to be practiced whether you are courting someone or not."

He blew out a long breath that was almost a sigh. "I'll have my assistant Francine schedule me for the proper class."

"Wonderful."

"And dance classes as well. I didn't realize there would be dance expectations at a wedding."

I tilted my head and studied him. "Haven't you ever gone to a wedding, Toby?"

"No," he said.

"No one you know has ever invited you to a wedding?" My tone went up at the end of the sentence. I couldn't imagine having never been to a wedding.

"A few of my colleagues invite me to their children's affairs, but I'm certain they have no expectations that I would actually show up. Usually the invitation is merely a bid for a gift. I have my assistant send along something appropriate and that takes care of the matter."

"Oh, boy," I said, and took a sip of my water. The man had a lot to learn.

After our meal, I excused myself to go to the ladies' room. On my way I saw Mrs. Fulcrum and Mrs. Thomson. It seemed Samantha Lyn and Clark's moms were more in love with each other than their kids.

"Hello, ladies," I said as I stopped by their table. Neither one had eaten, which was obvious by the picked-at plates of food that had been pushed aside for coffee and gossip. "How are you?"

"Pepper," Mrs. Fulcrum said. "How nice to see you here. Are you a club member?"

"No," I said with a shake of my head. "I'm here with a friend who needs mingling advice." I waved toward Toby, who had removed his napkin and was currently thumbing through his cell phone.

"Oh, you know Mr. Mallard?" Mrs. Thomson asked. "I heard he was a member of the country club, but I'd never seen him here." Her expression was full of curiosity.

"I suggested that he come," I said. "It's good for him to get out more and meet people."

"Indeed," Mrs. Fulcrum said, her gaze thoughtful. "I understand he's single."

"Yes," I said. "Toby's a great guy."

"Maybe we should go say hello," Mrs. Thomson suggested.

"I can introduce you, if you'd like," I said. "But first I'm off to the ladies' room."

"Of course, dear, yes, do stop by on your way back. We would love to meet your host."

"One more thing," I said as I straightened. "I was wondering if you knew anything more about the bartender who died at my sister's reception."

"Terrible," Mrs. Thomson said. "The hiring manager

should have never hired her. I've had a word with the board about that."

"I'm sorry?" I wasn't sure why she felt that way. "Why?"

"The club has standards, dear," Mrs. Fulcrum said. "Drug-addicted employees are below those standards completely."

"Indeed," Mrs. Thomson said with a nod. "I didn't like her from the start. She had the look of a drug addict. I understand she died of an overdose."

"I don't mean to speak ill of the dead," Mrs. Fulcrum said. "But it's her own fault. She should never have mixed drugs and alcohol."

"Typical addict," Mrs. Thomson agreed. "Those people get what they deserve."

"Oh," I said, unable to digest how horrible these two women were. "Addiction is a disease."

"Well, it's a disease we don't want at the club," Mrs. Fulcrum stated. "Seriously, I've made it my mission to see that whoever hired her gets fired. They should have more sense than that."

"I understand she went to college with some of the members her age," I said. "Morduray College is quite picky about who gets in, isn't it? I understand Ashley was a good student."

"Oh, dear, Morduray is my alma mater. They must have lowered their standards. I will have to have a talk with the Dean of Admissions," Mrs. Thomson said with a rude frown. "Hiring that woman caused the club all kinds of grief. Not to mention ruining Warren Evans' wedding reception. When Samantha Lyn and Clark get married, I'm going to go over the staff myself and ensure that no one looks out of place."

"A good drug screening the morning of the wedding will take care of that," Mrs. Fulcrum said. "I implement it at all my Xi Omicron Mu functions. It helps keep the riffraff out. We'll write that into the contract."

"Excuse me, ladies," I said, and bowed out. I walked to the restroom, my thoughts saddened by the animosity of those two busybodies. As far as I could tell, Ashley hadn't done anything to either of them. At the most she had chided Clark for attempting to indulge in underage drinking. Instead of cursing Ashley, they should be thanking her. It was also clear that Mrs. Thomson thought college, even at a small private institution, was merely a place to find a rich husband. I sighed. What decade did she drop out of?

* * *

Later that afternoon, I had a meeting with Laura about her cooking class proposal. I picked a nice class that took place in an old Victorian home setting. It was time to take Laura through the venue and give her an idea of how the proposal would work and why it was okay to have Jen and Brad and a few other couples participate in the class.

"Wow, this place is great," Laura said as she entered the parlor of the house.

"I thought you would like it," I said, and gave her a quick hug. "Here, let me take your coat." I waited for her to take off her puffy down coat. The weather was darn cold today. The gray sky and bare black branches of the nearby trees were the perfect backdrop for the blue and white twinkle lights the homeowner had strung from the trees and along the wraparound porch.

I hung up Laura's coat with mine on a wrought iron coat rack near the door. I showed her through the parlor to the twin dining rooms that flanked the center foyer of the house. The place was tastefully decorated to show off the original dark wood trim.

"Wow," Laura said. "This place could host a huge party."

"That's the idea," I said. "The kitchen is through here." I opened the door to showcase the large open kitchen. It was clearly an add-on to the back of the house. The room could hold up to ten people cooking at the same time. The kitchen was set up with two sides that mirrored each other. Both sides had a professional Viking stove with a shining stainless-steel hood. Then there were twin stainless-steel ovens in the wall. A giant Sub-Zero built-in fridge flanked a pot sink. The décor was turn of the twentieth century with black and white subway tiles for a backsplash. White painted cabinets reached up to the ten-foot ceilings. Twin islands faced each other. They had butcher-block countertops with an inset vegetable sink and a portion of marble for rolling out pastry dough. The entire room spoke of a love for cooking.

Angela, the chef and homeowner, waited for us in the kitchen. "Laura, this is Angela Hart. Angela, this is Laura, our prospective proposer."

"Hi, Laura," Angela said. I met Angela when I did an event for my old employer. The employer who let me go due to budget cuts. I had no regrets about my old job. The best thing I got out of that job was my connection to great people like Angela, who ran her own small business. She was a middle-aged woman about five feet tall and nearly as big around. Today she wore a chef's jacket and black pants. Her gray hair was pulled back into a no-nonsense bun and she wore little makeup. She didn't need to, as her skin was porcelain and her cornflower blue eyes twinkled.

"This place is fantastic," Laura said.

"Thank you," Angela said.

"I thought we'd keep it intimate," I explained. "Angela worked up a nice menu in honor of your Kung Pao chicken."

Laura laughed. "I hope you're prepared for mistakes."

Angela smiled. "I'm always prepared."

"Angela suggested that we have four other couples for the class to fill the kitchen and make it feel like a real event. As I mentioned, I picked out four couples that will be in on the event, including my clients Brad and Jennifer. Everyone will be in on the proposal and will have strict instructions on how to act. I promise no one will give away your surprise. Now, the dining room on the left will be decorated to match your apartment where you first started dating."

"Oh, my gosh, mismatched blue plates and white cups?"

"Exactly," I said. "I have a friend who works for a prop house. I forwarded him the pictures you sent me. We'll be able to re-create the setting down to the decorations on the fireplace."

"Wow," Laura said. "That's awesome."

"I've got a copy of the playlist of your favorite songs. We'll have music on in the background. Once dinner is made, we'll all gravitate to the dining area. When Monica's favorite song comes on, you'll propose. Meanwhile, your friends and family will be waiting in the other dining room." I pointed toward the second dining room across the foyer. "When Monica says yes, we'll open the doors and your family and friends will be there."

"I've got a matching dinner menu for the engagement party," Angela said. "We'll cater it completely. So there's no need to fear that you are cooking for it."

"Sounds perfect," Laura said, with tears in her eyes. "I'm starting to get excited."

"So am I," I said.

We went over a few of the details and Angela had a tiny tasting menu prepared so that Laura could decide on the dishes and desserts for the family. Laura and I sat at a small table in the parlor with a cup of peppermint tea to finish off the tasting. "So, are you happy with the plans?" I asked.

Laura's face lit up. "I think it's going to be perfect. Just as I asked, intimate and yet reminiscent of our first meeting."

"Good, I'm glad. So we're all set. Are you ready for your big day?"

"I'm ready," Laura said with a happy smile. "Everything is going to be perfect."

"I couldn't agree more."

Chapter 12

My cell phone rang as I left the Victorian house and headed toward where my car was parked on the street. It was Clark's mother. "Hello?"

"Hello, Pepper, this is Mrs. Fulcrum."

"Hello again, Mrs. Fulcrum. What can I do for you?"

"Mrs. Thomson and I want to get the ball rolling on the engagement. It seems so silly that the kids should have to wait. We were thinking it could be done tomorrow."

"I'm sorry?" I said as I unlocked Old Blue and climbed inside. "Tomorrow? That's rushing things, isn't it? I mean, it takes time to plan out a big fancy proposal. I need to have a venue and props and such. I haven't had time to really talk to Clark and Samantha Lyn about their relationship."

"Please," Mrs. Fulcrum said. "What's there to talk

about? They are two young people completely in love. I'm sure you do these romantic things all the time."

"Yes, but you asked for sparkle and glitz and video recordings. That is not something I can just do in twenty-four hours."

"I'm sure you can if we pay you enough." Mrs. Fulcrum's tone was no-nonsense. "I've already got a wedding planner hired and she tells me she can pull off the wedding of the century in thirty days. If she can do that, you can pull off a proposal in twenty-four hours."

"The kids are so young, why the rush? We should let them savor this time in their lives," I said. "What is the name of the wedding planner? Because I'm not sure you got a good one if she thinks she can do all that in one month."

"Oh, please, we all know money talks, now. I'm giving you free rein. In fact, money is no object. I expect you can pull something off quickly."

I scratched my head. "It's just that Samantha Lyn seems kind of upset over the death of Ashley. Can you give me a couple of days? To make it special?"

"Oh, please! Samantha Lyn barely knew the girl."

"Did you know her, Mrs. Fulcrum? Because it sounds to me like you did."

"It sounds to me like you are obsessed with a drug addict. Listen, Clark is going to marry Samantha Lyn in thirty days. Either you can do the proposal or I'll find someone else to do it. You have until the end of next week." She hung up the phone.

I stared at my phone, not sure at all what the right thing

to do was. If I went through and planned this thing, then Perfect Proposals stood to earn a lot of money. If I held my moral ground and refused, Mrs. Fulcrum would just find someone else to take her money. I sighed long and hard.

Maybe I could convince Samantha Lyn to say no. I dialed the girl's cell.

"Hey, Pepper, what's up?" Samantha answered her phone. It was clear she had marked my number in her contacts.

"Hi, Samantha," I said. "Mrs. Fulcrum just called and she wants me to move forward with the proposal planning. Before I do that, I need to check that you are okay with this. I mean, you mentioned that you told Ashley you wanted to break up with Clark. I can't in good conscience plan a proposal event if you don't want to marry the boy."

She paused for two heartbeats. "It's okay, Pepper," she said. "I want to marry Clark."

"Really?" I tried not to wince. "Are you sure?"

"Yeah, sure, I'm sure," she said. "I talked to the moms and it really is for the best. They aren't going to stop until we're married." I could hear the defeat in her voice. "Whatever our moms want. It will be the next great adventure."

"Listen," I said. "Do you know anyone who takes Xanax?"

"Sure," Samantha Lyn said. "Clark takes it. Both our moms take it. Heck, half the people I know from college take it. It helps with all the stress they're under to get good grades and get good jobs."

"Huh," I said. "Then you know you shouldn't mix the drug with alcohol."

"Yeah, I tell Clark that all the time. He just rolls his eyes at me."

"You are a good and caring person, Samantha Lyn."

"Thanks," she said. "It's nice to hear that someone thinks so. Listen, I have to go. I'm sure whatever you come up with for our proposal will be wonderful. If I were you, I'd spend whatever money my mother and Clark's mother are offering. I'd rather you get it than some lame event planner I don't even know."

"Thanks, Samantha," I said. "I'll try to make it beautiful."

"You're the best. Bye, Pepper."

She hung up and I tossed my phone onto the passenger seat. I would have to come up with a proposal event that would please the mothers and perhaps remind them of just how young Samantha and Clark really were.

*　*　*

Next up was a meeting with Brad. He asked that I stop by his office to discuss how the plans were going for his proposal. I took the Metra train downtown and walked the short distance to his office building. Brad worked near the lakeshore just off Michigan Avenue. It was a swanky forty-floor building. I entered and pulled off my hat, letting the fresh snow that covered me shake off onto the floor.

"Can I help you?" the security guard said from behind the big desk.

"Hi, yes, I'm Pepper Pomeroy. I'm here to see Brad Hurst."

The security guard was older with a bald head that he shaved to disguise his halo. His neck was as thick as his head on wide shoulders. I had a feeling he'd been a Marine in his early life. He filled out his white security shirt and dark blue pants in a very muscular way. He looked over his list. "Yes, I have you here." He reached up and pushed a clipboard to me. "Sign in."

I signed my name and the time.

"Wear this badge," he said, and pushed a yellow visitor badge toward me. "Take the elevators on the right. It's the thirty-second floor, office 3210."

"Thanks," I said, and picked up the badge. I dutifully pinned it on the lapel of my navy wool coat. I always dressed business casual when I was working, even if I did most of my work from home. It helped me to feel professional. Today I wore black wool slacks and a cream pullover sweater. The cream looked nice against my pale skin. I had my red hair pulled back into a sleek low ponytail. I got into the elevator with two other people, both of whom had employee badges on. As I waited for my floor, I took the time to remove my black leather gloves and stuffed them into my hat. I was the first off. The thirty-second floor had a cool carpeted hallway filled with tall cherry wood doors. A quick look at the room numbers and I found Brad's door.

I walked in and there was a receptionist at the desk that separated the small entryway from the wall of windows behind her. "Hi," I said. "Pepper Pomeroy to see Brad Hurst."

"Sure, I'll let him know you're here," the receptionist

said. She was a beautiful brunette in a bodycon bandage dress that flattered her figure. I resisted the urge to compare myself to her. I was very thankful that Gage didn't have a woman as beautiful as her working in his office.

"Thanks," I said, and sent her a small smile. There was a giant canvas of modern art across from her desk. It had bold stripes of red and blue with splatters of orange, not something I would want to have to stare at day in and day out.

"Pepper!" Brad said as he came around from behind the receptionist. "Thanks for coming all this way. Jeanette, Pepper is the event planner who is going to ensure that Jen is surprised when I propose to her."

"Good luck!" the receptionist said breezily.

"I see she's met Jen," I said as Brad gently guided me toward his office.

"I'm dying to know how you're going to surprise Jen," Brad said as he ushered me into his office. "Have a seat. Can I get you something to drink?"

"No, I'm good," I said as I unbuttoned my coat and sat down. "Nice view."

The wall behind Brad's desk was floor-to-ceiling glass and looked out over the marina and Lake Michigan. You could see the gray clouds swirling and the snow falling like heavy rain.

"Yes," he agreed. "The funny thing is, you get used to it and barely see it some days." He sat down. "So tell me, how's the planning going?"

"Good," I said. "You didn't tell Jen we were meeting, did you?"

He flushed bright red. "Yeah, I did. She hates secrets."

"Oh, right," I said. It was a good thing then that I had decided not to share with Brad the details of my plan to surprise Jen. I had the sneaking suspicion he'd run and tell her right away. "Remember how I decided to have Jen and you join me on a few of my proposals to critique them and give me a feel for what she likes and doesn't like?"

"I remember."

"And I mentioned that the first one is Saturday morning at F.A.O. Schwarz in Macy's?"

"Yes, I have that on my calendar."

"Good. The next one is Sunday night. It's a low-key proposal and I'm setting it up at a cooking class because the couple met when Laura knocked on Monica's door to borrow a cup of sugar."

"Oh, nice . . ." He paused. "Two women?"

"Yes," I said. "I thought you and Jen could come and be part of the cooking class. It will help the surprise to have strangers in the class. Are you okay with that?"

"Sure, why not?" He shrugged in his light blue shirt, shifting. Brad's hair was in a perfect preppy cut. His light blue shirt contrasted perfectly with his maroon and blue striped tie. I noted he had a suitcoat that matched his slacks hanging from the back of his office chair.

"Great, this way I can populate the class with people who are in on the proposal but still strangers to Laura and Monica. It will help Monica be surprised. We will be making vegetable egg rolls, Kung Pao chicken, and chocolate mochi for desert. Once everything is cooked and plated, we'll adjourn to the dining area to eat. That's when background music will start to play Laura and Monica's song. Laura will pull out the ring and get down on one knee and propose."

"In a room full of strangers?" he asked.

"It's not any different than a flash mob proposal. You know, where a group of people suddenly show up on the street and all dance to the same song?"

"I know what a flash mob is," he said, and nodded. "I tried that, by the way. Jen shook her head, laughed and said she saw it coming a mile away. I mean, how often did we walk through Grant Park with a bunch of strangers flocking toward us."

"Using a flash mob has been overdone," I agreed. "I'll think of something else."

"Jen wanted to be here today, but she had an appointment," he said. "I think she'll agree with you, though, that flash mobs have been overdone."

"How does she expect to be surprised if she is in on every meeting we have?" I asked him, and tried not to sigh.

He grinned. "I know she seems controlling."

"Do you think?" I asked, and we both laughed.

"If you think she's controlling, you should meet her parents," he said, and shook his head. "Don't get me wrong, they're great, but they are super protective. It took me years to get them to understand that I wasn't going anywhere. I had to really prove my commitment."

It dawned on me then. "That's why you keep trying to propose."

"Yes," he said, and smiled. "I haven't given up trying yet and Jen tells her parents everything. They have to know I'm committed to her."

"Do you have the ring?" I asked.

"Yes, I brought it like you asked." He reached into his desk drawer and pulled out a teal blue Tiffany box. "It's one of a kind." Brad opened the box and drew out a smaller ring box and handed it to me.

I opened it to see a blue sapphire in a princess cut flanked by one-carat diamonds in baguette style set in platinum. "It's gorgeous."

"Thanks, I saved for six months to buy it."

"I didn't expect the sapphire," I said.

"Blue is Jen's favorite color. She already told you she likes lots of bling."

"You tried a flash mob in Grant Park?"

"And ice skating near the bean sculpture. She loves snow and I thought it would be like that movie *Serendipity*. I suspect that she has a thing for the actor John Cusack."

I smiled. "Are you going to walk around with the ring in your pocket until I give you the go sign to propose?"

He laughed. "That would be dangerous," he said. "It's a $100,000 ring."

"Oh." I think my face blanched a bit and my hand shook. My reaction caused him to laugh harder.

"It's insured," he said. "So, how about you keep it and surprise me. When you give it to me, I'll know it's time to propose."

"You trust me with this ring?"

"You're bonded and insured, right?"

"Yes, of course," I said. With a ring this big I figured I'd better call my insurance guy and add more coverage. I wasn't going to tell Brad that.

"Then you keep the ring. When the moment is right for me to propose, hand it to me. I'll drop down on my knee and pop the question."

"Okay," I said with a nod, and closed the box and put it back into the Tiffany box. "This works." I looked him in the eye. "You're okay with being surprised, too?"

"Oh, yeah," he said, and waved his hand to dismiss the notion. "I'm easy to surprise. It's Jen you have to worry about. Here, I'll make a deal. Since Jen will tell me the moment she figures out what's up, let's have a signal. If I tug on my ear, then the jig is up and you have to try again. Sound fair?"

"Sounds fair," I said. "I'm still working out how I'm going to get your friends and family there to witness and have an engagement party if every one of you can't keep a secret."

He laughed and tilted his head. "You can do it. I have faith."

"I'm glad someone does," I muttered, and put the ring carefully into my purse. "You said Jen comes by her control freak nature naturally. Why?"

"Her parents are worse than she is, if you can believe it." He ran a hand through his hair. "I think they had some serious family tragedy and they're afraid Jennifer will get hurt."

"What happened?" I asked, and drew my eyebrows together.

"No idea," he said. "She won't talk about it. But it had to be something that really scared her because her parents didn't want her staying in Chicago. It took a lot of convincing before they understood that Jennifer and I were serious and that I'd watch out for her."

"I'm surprised there was any discussion at all once Jen made her mind up. She is such a force of nature."

"You haven't met them yet. They insist we relocate to California to live near them after we get married."

"Will you?"

He shrugs. "I'm okay with it."

"But you'll lose all of this," I said, and gestured to encompass his corner office and the full-wall view.

"If it means having Jen for the rest of my life, I'll do it."

"You are a good guy," I told Brad. "It's clear you really love Jen. She's lucky to have you."

"We'll be there Saturday. I can't wait to see firsthand what one of these parties is like."

"You should be pleasantly surprised." I smiled and stood. "Remember to act natural. We don't want to give away the surprise."

Brad chuckled and led me out. "I'm not the best actor, but I think I can shop in a toy store and pretend to be disinterested."

"I don't know," I said with a grin. "I've got the Rockettes booked to do a number."

"Really?"

"Don't worry, you can watch. The proposal will still be a surprise. Unlike Jen, this prospective fiancé isn't part of the plan."

Brad chuckled. "Just be careful with how many of these you have us attend," he warned. "Jen's cunning. She'll start to see a pattern and then she'll figure you out."

"I promise, no patterns in my work," I said.

"Let's hope not," he said. "I really want to marry my girl. A girl that pretty and smart doesn't come along every day, you know."

"Oh, I know," I said. "Too bad she's so controlling."

"It's a safety mechanism," he said as he walked me out. "She grew up in an unstable household. Controlling as many outcomes as possible was a coping mechanism. Once you realize she's just trying to be safe, it's a lot easier to handle. Trust me, showing her your proposals might be a good thing. It will get her to see that surprises can be fun and not scary. That's my hope, anyway."

"I'll make it fun," I said. "You can count on me."

* * *

Driving home from the Metra station was a bit of a night-mare as the snow had come down just enough to be slushy. The first few snows of the season always had people driving crazy. I passed two cars in ditches. It was a relief to pull into my driveway and park in front of my garage. When I got out I realized for the first time that I was living in a house now, not an apartment. That meant when it snowed there wasn't anyone coming to shovel but me. I sighed and stepped into four inches of slush.

There was nothing to do but trudge inside and change my clothes. I quickly put on jeans, proper socks, and warm boots. Back outside, I opened the garage and turned on the light. There were all kinds of tools in the garage. It was pretty clear that Detective Murphy's family had everything it took to be a homeowner in the Chicago area. Even two snow shovels. I grabbed one and looked at its straight handle.

"Too bad they don't have a snow blower," I muttered. I turned on the outside lights and kept the garage door open. It was dark out. That meant that shoveling had to be done in the dark. Not such a fun thing to do. "I'm going to the store and to get some Christmas lights. They'll look great against the dark sky and the white snow."

"Oh, honey, everyone smart put their lights up at the end of October before the snow," my nosy new neighbor, Mrs. Crivitz, said.

Startled, I glanced over to find her standing on the corner of her porch watching my every move. "Hello, Mrs. Crivitz, I didn't see you there." Although I should have suspected she was watching. Ever since I moved in I'd noticed that if anything moved at my house, she knew about it. In fact, she was one of the original neighborhood watch people.

"I thought you were talking to me," she said, and frowned. "If you didn't see me, who were you talking to?"

"I talk to myself sometimes," I said, and shrugged. "It's

a habit I got from living alone." I put the shovel down and pushed it toward her house. The neighborhood was old and the driveway spanned the difference between her house and mine. I had to shovel toward the neighbor's house across the drive and then push that lengthwise toward the garage or there wouldn't be enough room to get Old Blue down the driveway. The last thing I wanted was to have to park my Buick on the street. The snowplows would plow it in and I'd never get it dug out.

"I saw Detective Murphy here the other day," she said. "Is everything alright?"

I glanced at her. She wore her gray hair up in curlers. A thick scarf wound around her head so that the curlers and her face were the only parts sticking out. She wore a big overcoat and what looked like thick stockings and bunny slippers. "Aren't you going to get cold out here?" I asked.

"Oh, no, I have a nice hot cup of cocoa," she said, and lifted her hands to show me the steaming white mug. "What did Detective Murphy say about you bringing a man over to his mother's house?"

I paused in my shoveling. "It's really none of his business," I said. "He was here to ask me about a woman I tried to save with CPR."

"Oh, that girl at the country club?"

"Yes, how did you know?"

"It's all over the news, dear," she said, and sipped. "When I heard it was at the country club the night of your sister's wedding reception, I put two and two together. It wasn't hard, dear. I'm a smart cookie."

"I'm sure you are," I said, and pushed the snow toward the garage.

"Let's get back to Detective Murphy, shall we?" she asked. "Do you know if he's dating anyone? My Mary Ellen just broke up with her boyfriend. I always thought they would be the perfect couple."

"Who? Mary Ellen and her old boyfriend?" I asked. I knew who she meant but I wanted to be perverse.

"No, Detective Murphy, silly. He and Mary Ellen grew up together. I always thought they would marry. You know? The romantic boy falls for the girl next door story."

I'd seen Mary Ellen. She was a plain woman with thinning hair and a couple of missing teeth. "I think he's still in love with his ex," I said.

"Well, if he ever says anything about dating, put a bug in his ear. Okay? He and Mary Ellen have so much in common. I would hate for him to miss a chance to love the girl next door."

"I'll let him know you were asking about him the next time I see him," I said, and continued to push the snow away.

"You do that, dear," Mrs. Crivitz said, but didn't leave. I tried to ignore her as much as was polite. But it was difficult when she leaned against the porch rail and watched me like a hawk.

After I managed to push enough snow out of the driveway, I got into my car and pulled it into the tiny garage that was situated between the house and the alley. The yard was fenced in the back so that whoever traveled the alley couldn't get into the yard without scaling a six-foot fence. Detective Murphy had installed motion-sensor lights on the back of the garage so that they flickered on whenever anything taller than two feet walked by. It was unnerving at first, but after a while I didn't even see them turn on and off.

I squeezed out of Old Blue and went back to shoveling. It was some relief to see that Mrs. Crivitz had gone inside. The dining room curtains moved so I knew that she still watched me, but at least I didn't have that odd feeling that I should be making conversation. Another twenty minutes and I was finally down to the mailbox.

I spotted the neighbor across the street from me as he shuffled out his door to the mailbox. "Hey, Mr. Mead, how's everything with you?"

"Terrible," he said, and pulled his mailbox open and took out a handful of mail.

"I'm sorry to hear that."

"Why should you be sorry?" he asked. "You didn't do anything."

"Right," I muttered. Mr. Mead was dressed in a thick overcoat that covered a pair of blue and white striped boxers and a dingy T-shirt. His legs were bare and he wore snow boots that came up to his mid-calf and were untied. I'd spoken to him perhaps six times since I had moved into the house, and each time he was doing "terrible." At least he was consistent.

He muttered something dark under his breath as he bent to dig his newspaper out from under the bushes. "That paper boy ought to be shot," he said. "I pay all that money for daily service and I get an incompetent idiot who can't hit the broad side of a barn. I mean seriously, how difficult is it to hit my porch?" He waved toward his bungalow. The brick building had a thick sturdy front porch with a double-wide opening and four steps up. "Do you have this problem?"

"I don't get the paper," I said.

"Of course you don't," he grumbled. "Young people today are so darn illiterate."

"I read it online," I said, as if that would convince him that I was smart.

"Nothing better than real words on good old-fashioned paper," he said with a shake of his head. "Online . . . sheesh." He looked up and gave me the stink eye. "Don't you be pulling any noisy parties," he warned. "I'll call the police."

"I don't have parties, Mr. Mead."

"Don't think you can play your music at all hours of the night, either," he said, and shook his fist at me. "I have a hotline straight to the precinct."

"I don't have a stereo," I said. "So you have nothing to fear."

"Yeah, well, keep it that way." He walked back through his unshoveled drive up to the porch.

I shook my head and smiled. Crazy old neighbors came along with cheap rent and a lovely neighborhood bungalow. I accepted it as part of the charm of the place. Pulling my mail out, I noted I had two catalogs and a water bill. Well worth the twenty minutes it took to shovel my way to the mailbox . . . not.

I turned and made it halfway to the house when a snow plow came through and blew three feet of snow across the bottom third of the drive. I resisted the urge to flip him off. Mr. Mead didn't have my self-restraint as I noted the inelegant gesture he made with his arms.

Finally inside and away from the neighbors, I turned on the lights, deposited my keys in the dish on the edge of the kitchen counter, took off my boots and left them on the mat by the door to dry. My coat went on a hanger in the small coat closet just inside the summer porch at the back of the house. I closed and locked my doors.

The bungalow went back to front, summer porch, closet, stairs to the basement, kitchen, short hall to the right that ended in the only bathroom. There was a bedroom to the left and the right of the bathroom. I used the left back bedroom and the right bedroom was set up as my office. Straight in front of the kitchen was the dining room that had side windows which mirrored Mrs. C's and in fact looked right into her house. Mrs. Murphy had hung lace curtains to let in the light. I hung a second set of light-blocking curtains to keep the nosy neighbors guessing.

The dining room flowed into a living room complete with a gas fireplace. There were windows on the front and side walls. Again during the day the lace curtains let in the light, but at night I closed off the light-blocking curtains. This kept the cold out and helped muffle any road noises. To the left of the living room was a third bedroom. That was a complete luxury for a single girl. I used it as a guest bedroom and had had a good time at Ikea buying simple furniture to decorate it. I went for cute and cozy. I thought the peach and cream colors and soft curtains were welcoming.

Mrs. Murphy had decorated the place so nicely that I pretty much moved in without a thought. The front bedroom was the only place I'd taken the time to make my own.

I hadn't had any guests over yet, but I was working on getting my college friend Alice to come to Chicago for a visit. She lived in St. Louis and complained of the Chicago winters. I suppose she had a point, but when you lived in Chicago your whole life, the winters didn't feel any less than normal.

I stepped into the kitchen to start heating a kettle of water on the stove for a nice cup of tea. Then I turned on my computer, which sat on a built-in desk, brought up my Internet browser, and sorted e-mails as I waited.

The teakettle started to squeal. I got up, turned off the burner, and poured the hot water into my favorite mug and dipped in a peppermint tea bag. I sat back down and did some digging on the Internet to see what I could learn about Ashley and the others that were working at the country club the night she died. After only an hour, I had come to the end of everything I could learn about Ashley online. I sighed. Maybe Detective Murphy was right. Maybe there wasn't anything here. Maybe I'd simply gotten used to thinking murder when someone died.

I shook my head at myself and decided to forget about Ashley's death for a moment and go back over what I had to do for my current clients. Maybe it was a full moon or bad biorhythms, or maybe it was because my sister was off on her honeymoon and my life was changing at a rapid pace, but everything seemed a bit off these days. I mean, Sherry was proposing and announcing her pregnancy. That was a little odd; sweet, but odd. Laura wouldn't let me meet Monica before the proposal event. That was against my own business rules, but I had done some research online with Facebook and Twitter and Instagram. Laura had so many pictures of her and Monica that their romance was undeniable.

Then there was the Fulcrum/Thomson engagement. I hated getting mixed up in what I considered a train wreck. Those two kids were far too young to get married. Still the Fulcrum name and money was good for my business and the moms were going see that it happened whether I did it or someone else did. At least if I were in charge, I could see Samantha took the time to make a real choice.

Finally, Jen acting so strange, wanting to be in complete control and yet demanding to be surprised. Then Brad said her parents were worse and that her household while growing up was unstable. It didn't help that each of these couples was somehow connected to the wedding reception. Maybe it was just me, but Ashley's death seemed to put a gloomy cloud over every one of these events.

The good news was I had asked for a huge retainer from Brad and Jen. Brad had given me a check for the full amount and my bank said it cleared. So at least there was that. I pulled the engagement ring out of my purse and put the box on the desk next to me.

I had a small safe. Mrs. Murphy had shown it to me when I moved in. It was in the floor under the master bedroom dresser. I was glad I had it now. The last thing I needed was to get robbed and lose this ring. Sure, I was insured—a call to my agent had informed me that I was indeed covered for a ring of this price point—but my business was new and taking a claim that big would really hurt. I opened the box and looked at the ring. It was lovely. A little showy for my taste, but it looked like just the sort of thing Jen would love.

I put the ring back into the box and went into my bedroom. Careful that the curtains were closed, I moved the dresser aside and pulled out the fake floorboard, dialed the safe combo, and put the ring inside, then closed everything up. By the time I was back at my computer the tea was drinkable.

I typed my zip code into a website and brought up all the crimes in the area over the last six months. There was one speeding ticket. No robberies or break-ins, so my worries over the ring were relieved. The chances of a random break-in were low. It helped that the neighborhood was known to be a place where firefighters and policemen lived.

There was a knock at the back door. I got up and glanced out to see Gage standing on the steps to the summer porch. He waved when he saw me. I opened the kitchen door and then the porch door. "Hi," I said, and kissed his cheek.

"Hi." He grinned back and grabbed me, pulled me into his arms, and gave me a proper kiss. The cold from his jacket dissipated between us. "Nice welcome," he whispered against my lips. He touched his forehead to mine. "I brought dinner." He raised his left hand to display the bag from a chicken take-out place.

"Come in," I said. I took the bag of chicken while he took off his coat, shook the snow off of it, hung it in the closet, then took off his shoes and put them on the mat next to mine. I put the bag on the tiny kitchen table and pulled plates and silverware out of the cupboard.

"I'll wash up," he said, and made his way to the bathroom. By the time he came out I had the table set and dinner all ready.

"Thanks for dinner," I said as he kissed me on the cheek and pulled out the chair across from me.

"It's the least I could do," he said. "I see you shoveled your drive."

I glanced out the window. The snow was still coming down and covered his car with a new inch. "How could you tell?" It looked as if I hadn't done anything.

"The end of the driveway is about four inches deep from the snow plow," he said with a chuckle and bit into his chicken. "I'll shovel it again for you before I leave."

"Oh, you are a doll," I said, and enjoyed watching him blush.

"What was your day like?" he asked, changing the subject.

I gave him the lowdown on my day. "I wasn't able to

find out anything more about Ashley. I still don't feel right about her death. I don't think it was accidental."

"You have to trust Detective Murphy to do his job, Pepper," he said.

"I know," I said, and shrugged. "I do, but it's got me feeling as if everything is a little off.

"What do you mean by *off*?" he asked, and tilted his head.

"There's nothing I can point to exactly, but I have this weird feeling I can't shake. I just don't want it to be because one of my engagements isn't going to work out."

"That's one of the things I really like about you," he said. "You throw yourself into these people's stories. You really do care. I know you investigate your couples fully in order to give them the best proposal ever, don't you?"

I felt the heat of a blush rush over me. "I want every couple to be successful, not just in the proposal but in their life together."

"You can't predict what will happen five, ten, or twenty years down the road, Pepper," Gage said, and reached out to squeeze my hand. "People are people. All you can do is take care of them in the now."

I sighed. "I wish I could have taken care of Ashley."

"I know her death hit you really hard."

"I don't think it's right that they closed the case," I said with a shake of my head. "My gut says that someone killed her."

"Any idea who?"

"No, not really."

"But you suspect someone."

I chewed on my bottom lip then leaned toward him. "I think maybe Clark and Samantha Lyn's moms had something to do with Ashley's death."

"What makes you think that?"

"They are so unreasonably certain she deserved to die," I said. When I got upset I had a tendency to gesture with my hands. I couldn't help it. Sometimes words weren't enough to emphasize my meaning. I gestured wildly now. "They keep saying she should have never been hired. That she deserved to die for mixing pills and alcohol. Well, let me tell you, Samantha Lyn told me that both her mother and Clark's mother are taking Xanax and yet both of them were drinking that night. That tells me one thing . . ."

"What's that?" Gage had a smile on his face as he took in my active hands.

"It takes a lot of Xanax to cause the small amount of alcohol I saw Ashley drink kill her like an overdose."

Gage rested his elbow on the table and his chin in his left hand and studied me. "You may be right. Then again, if I remember correctly, you said that Ashley was a very thin girl."

"She was thin, too thin if you ask me." I tapped my chin. "I don't think she intentionally took the Xanax. I think the moms could have slipped her the drug. You know? They might have meant to make her sick but then accidentally killed her."

"I love you, Pepper," Gage said, and grasped my hand. "But I think you're reaching. Why would they want to kill

Ashley? And if they were only trying to make her sick, wouldn't they be horrified that she died? I mean, playing a mean-spirited prank and then realizing you accidentally murdered someone are two very different things. One or both of them should have been horrified. Did they appear horrified that night?"

I thought about the two moms at the reception. Neither looked horrified. They both looked annoyed at the delay in getting home. I frowned. "No, neither of them appeared horrified."

He patted my hand and went back to eating his chicken dinner. "Don't worry, Pepper. If there is a case to solve, you'll solve it. But right now why don't we enjoy dinner. I'll be heading out soon to shovel. I'd like to spend time with my girlfriend without any dead bodies between us."

"You're right," I agreed. "I'm sorry."

"Don't be sorry," he said. "I love that you care so much. Now, do you want to know what plays are coming into town next year? I happen to have a sneak preview of the new season."

Chapter 13

Saturday morning I was up at five A.M. to shovel my drive. We had another two inches of snow. The air was ice cold and barely breathable. I wore a full face mask cap so only my eyes and mouth peeked out. I'm sure I gave Mrs. Crivitz a little scare when she glanced out the window. I waved.

By six thirty I was showered, dressed, and ready. The plan was to get to the store by eight thirty A.M., ensure that everything was ready for the Rockettes and the proposal in the toy area, and then double check with the caterer and florist for the engagement party in the tearoom above.

By the time the store opened, everything was ready. Sherry and William's family and friends were up in the tearoom sipping mimosas and Bloody Marys and snacking on brunch appetizers. My video guy, Cesar, was set up in the toy soldier area where the store had cleared part of the floor and set up a stage for the Rockettes, who were in the back in toy soldier costumes and ready for their cue. A video feed was run up to the tearoom on a jumbo-sized screen.

Brad and Jen entered the store just then.

"Is this going to work?" Jen asked as she craned her neck to see around a pile of stuffed toys.

"I certainly hope so," I said. "I've got fifty guests upstairs in the tearoom and a table full of engagement gifts. I told them all to bring baby gifts as a gag."

"Wait, so the family doesn't know she's pregnant?" Jen said, and gestured with her hands.

"No, she wanted William to find out first," I said. I got a text on my phone. "Okay, they are at the front door. Places everyone."

We watched as Sherry came in with William. Sherry was dressed in a blue wool skater coat that just covered a sweet cobalt blue dress. She had on knee-high black boots and black leather gloves. She wore a blue beret perched jauntily on her head. William was stoic in a black wool dress coat, dark wash jeans, and what looked like a hand-made knit scarf around his neck.

Sherry chatted away as she guided him toward the toy soldier section.

"Okay, go," I said to Jen and Brad. "Remember, you're shopping for a gift for your nephew for Christmas."

Brad nodded and he and Jen went out into the room that

housed the green army soldiers and tin army action heroes to make it look and feel less empty.

When Sherry got William into the toy soldier area, I cued Cesar to come out with the camera on his shoulder. He appeared to ignore the couple as music began to blare on the speakers and the Rockettes came out and filed onto the stage.

"Look, look," Sherry said as Cesar got them on camera. The Rockettes did their dance of the toy soldier routine. Sherry and William watched. The routine ended with one of the girls coming down and taking William by the hand. Drawn to the area by the music and camera, customers gathered in clumps around the stage. Another Rockette came down and took Sherry's hand and led her to the stage. There Sherry went down on one knee and William's eyes widened in surprise. A big grin spread on his face as Sherry presented him with a ring.

"William Herald, I love you now and always. Will you marry me?"

I held my breath as William looked at her and took a moment, as if considering saying no. Then he grinned. "Yes!" He grabbed her and swung her around. "Yes, yes, you silly girl. But I wanted to be the one to propose."

The Rockettes and the crowd burst out in applause. More music started as Sherry put the ring on William's finger and the color guard from William's squad came out and made an arch out of their guns. "There's more," Sherry said, and took his hand. "Come with me."

I smiled and nodded as she led him off the stage and

through the arched guns to the baby toys section of the toy store where Santa sat holding a tiny T-shirt that said "I love my daddy."

William stopped. He had his arms around Sherry and his eyebrows drawn together in happy confusion. "What does this mean?"

Sherry smiled and bumped him with her hip. "It means I'm glad you said yes to marrying me because—"

"Oh, my God!" William shouted, and picked Sherry up and spun her. "You're pregnant!"

Sherry had her hands on his broad shoulders and blushed. "Yes."

William let out a loud shout. The guys from his squad all gathered around and pounded him on the back. I could hear the cheers from the tearoom in my earpiece. I made my way through the crowd and tapped Sherry on the shoulder. William had not let go of her hand.

"Come on, you guys, there are some people here who would like to say congratulations," I said, and hustled them into the elevator. William barely noticed me. As soon as the door closed, he embraced Sherry in a passionate kiss.

When we hit the tearoom floor, I cleared my throat, held the door open, and tapped William on the shoulder. "Come on, guys, you have family waiting."

"Let them wait," William said in a growly tone.

Sherry laughed and pushed him away. "Come on, this is all part of the engagement plan." She took his hand and followed me to the tearoom. I opened the door, and Gage handed me a microphone.

"Ladies and gentlemen," I said into the mic, getting everyone's attention. "I'd like to introduce the newly engaged couple, Sherry Burlingham and William Herald." I waved the couple into the room. They were surrounded by friends and family. Cesar had come up the stairs and shot footage of the couple's welcome.

My heart soared. It was a great event and a good start to the day.

An hour later, Jen and Brad came over to congratulate me.

"This was nice," Jen said. "He really was surprised."

"For both announcements," Brad said. He had his hand on Jen's back. They had dressed in dark wash jeans. Brad wore a pale pink button-down with a wool coat. Jen had worn a brown silk shirt and a wool trench coat. They were both stylish and yet looked the part of shoppers.

"Thanks for letting us see up close what you do," Jen said. "Of course, I don't want the toy store. It's too pedestrian."

"But it works for a guy," I said.

"Especially the green army men display in the action-hero section," Brad said.

"I've got a couple of others planned," I said. "I'll see you two at the cooking class proposal tomorrow night?"

"Yes," Jen said.

"What's the third proposal?" Brad asked.

"The Fulcrum/Thomson event. The families want me to put together the proposal event of the century for the kids," I said. "By seeing this fun event, the next quiet event, and then the Fulcrum's glitzy event, I hope you can help me narrow down exactly what you think is perfect for your event."

"Sounds good," Jen said. "Does this mean our event will be happening in the next couple of weeks?"

I shook my head with a smile. "I'm thinking after Christmas. I mean, if it happened now, you'd expect it, right?"

"Ah," Jen said with a knowing smile. "A New Year's Eve proposal."

"Perhaps," I said with a shrug, then walked them both out. "Thanks for helping. See you tomorrow night."

"Bye, Pepper," Jen said. "Good show."

I blew out a long breath. One down. Two to go.

Chapter 14

"Thank you for meeting with me," I said as Mrs. Fulcrum and Mrs. Thomson took their seats at Tea and Crumpets, a posh tea shop in the Chicago Gold Coast neighborhood. It was our second meeting and I was fully prepared to pitch them.

"It's not a problem," Mrs. Fulcrum said as she unbuttoned her coat. "I understand you have the plans ready for Clark and Samantha Lyn's proposal."

"Yes," I said, and handed each of the women a glossy full-color presentation binder with the outline of the event details and costs. "Before you look at it, I need to ask a favor of you both."

"Really?" Mrs. Thomson said as she draped her coat

on the back of her chair and took a seat. She wore a red pencil skirt, a cream bow blouse, and gold hoop earrings. "Isn't your fee enough?"

"This isn't about my fee," I said. "This about Jen McCutchen and Brad Hurst."

"What about Jennifer?" Mrs. Fulcrum asked, turning her laser gaze on me.

"She and Brad have hired me to do their proposal, but Jen wants to know all the details and yet be surprised."

"Sounds like Jennifer," Mrs. Thomson said. "That girl has always been a handful."

The waitress stopped by and we ordered tea and a sampler plate of cookies.

"What is your favor, dear?" Mrs. Fulcrum asked.

"I would like to do a double engagement," I said. "I would tell Jen that the event is for Samantha Lyn and Clark and I would tell Samantha Lyn that it was for Jen. Mrs. Fulcrum, I understand you sponsored Jen into her sorority."

"It's a coed fraternity, dear," Mrs. Fulcrum said. "And yes, I sponsored her. Jen and her family have been family friends for years."

"And I know Jen knows Samantha Lyn through Clark, right?"

"Yes," Mrs. Thomson said. "We attend many of the same functions."

"So, since they know each other and they both know me, they shouldn't suspect anything."

"Interesting," Mrs. Fulcrum said as the waitress brought

our tea and cookies. "Is this included in the proposal you've worked up for us?"

"Yes," I said with a nod. "I'm proposing an ice event filled with glitter, silver, gold, and sparkles everywhere. I will set up publicity as a fund-raiser for autism."

"That is a nice touch," Mrs. Fulcrum said. "Autism is one of our foundation causes."

"Yes," I said with a smile and a nod. "No one will suspect anything when they find out your involvement." I looked toward Mrs. Thomson. "I will create a costume ball. In the middle of the event, Brad will surprise Jen with his proposal."

"And Samantha Lyn and Clark?"

"They will go second, sealing the evening with romance. Everyone will walk away thinking that Clark was carried away by the moment. It will feel special and a double proposal at a charity event will not only make the social pages, it should make the evening news."

"Hmm," Mrs. Fulcrum said, and sipped her tea.

"You did want to make the evening news, right?" I asked.

"Yes," Mrs. Thomson said. "We did."

"By doing it this way it will also highlight your cause," I said. "Mr. Fulcrum could deduct a portion from his taxes."

"You know the way to my husband's heart," Mrs. Fulcrum said with a laugh. "Will Samantha Lyn be disappointed?" she asked Mrs. Thomson.

"Samantha Lyn is a good girl. She will be happy however we do this," Mrs. Thomson said, and bit into a frosted sugar cookie.

"Then we'll do it," Mrs. Fulcrum said. "Now let's dive into the details of your proposal, shall we?"

"As you'll see, I have covered all the details in this presentation," I said. "From the venue at the Ice Pit, to the costumes from Trinity Prop House, to male and female stylists to ensure everyone looks their best in the video."

We opened the presentation booklets in front of us and spent the next hour going over all the details. I was relieved that they would agree to the double engagement. I had arranged it with a fund-raiser in case Samantha Lyn decided to say no. The event could still benefit the Fulcrums. In a way it would be win-win no matter the outcome as long as these two ladies could keep the matter from Jen's all-knowing gaze.

* * *

The next night Jen and Brad showed up first for the cooking class. I introduced them to the chef and let Jen talk to her about the classes she taught and her business model. Meanwhile I pulled Brad aside.

"Are you sure you want me to keep the ring?" I had to ask.

He smiled and shrugged. "How else will I know to have it on the night of the surprise?"

I bit my bottom lip. "I know, it sort of makes sense, but it's a big responsibility."

"If you can pull off surprise proposals and engagement parties, then I think you can take good care of one little engagement ring."

"I want you to know that I went out this morning and

put it in my safe-deposit box at the bank. The only one who has access to that box is my dad, and only in case I die."

"Well, let's hope that doesn't happen any time soon," he teased.

"Brad, she teaches at Le Cordon Blue." Jen came over to us all excited. "It's a three-month class. We could take it together. It might be fun."

"Whatever you want to do, dear," Brad said. "Just remember that your parents are expecting us to move to California."

"Then we'd better sign up for classes tonight," Jen said. "I'm sure Pepper will be able to surprise me in the next three months and, after I say yes, we'll be spending a lot of time on the wedding. It only makes sense to have the wedding here with all our family and friends. California can wait now." Jen threaded her arm through Brad's and pulled him toward the chef.

The door opened and Cesar came in with his tripod on his shoulder. "Hi, Cesar," I said. "You can set up in the kitchen and then in the dining room area."

"You're taping this?" Toby asked as he entered the house. "Isn't that going to give it away?"

"No," I said with a shake of my head. "Mrs. Hart sent out an e-mail today telling everyone in the class that her marketing group was taking a video for her website. She promised that she would keep the cameras small so they wouldn't intrude. Everyone agreed that was fine."

"Brilliant," Toby said, and took off his coat, hanging it on the coat rack near the door. "Do I have a date?"

"Yes," I said with a smile. "My friend Amelia Galesberry is coming. She doesn't know about the proposal. She thinks it's a double date."

"Double date?" Toby asked.

"Yes, Gage is going to be here. We're going to be the fourth couple," I explained. Toby looked a little down.

"Gage will be here?"

"Yes," I said, and patted Toby's shoulder. "He wants to watch me attempt a cooking class."

"Okay, that's you and me and Gage and your friend, the couple who wants you to surprise them, and the couple who is proposing," Toby counted out on his fingers. "The class is for five couples. Who's the last couple?"

"Martha and Bob Dixon," I said. "They are friends of my mother. Martha always wanted to try a cooking class, and since I'm paying, Bob agreed."

"I see," Toby said.

Gage came in next, followed by the Dixons. Then Amelia arrived. Amelia was petite with a cute brunette bob and big eyes. Her nose was pert and her face heart-shaped. She wore a blue scoop-neck T-shirt and dressy jeans. Her feet were firmly ensconced in skater-style athletic shoes. "Amelia, this is Toby," I said as I took Amelia's coat. "Toby, Amelia."

They said their awkward hellos. I could tell from Amelia's expression that she found Toby attractive. Like I said, he was cute for a slouchy kind of guy. Toby stared at Amelia awkwardly.

The last to arrive was Laura and the woman I assumed

was Monica. Angela handled the couple by showing them where the coats were to be hung and then offered everyone a glass of wine.

"Come in, folks," Angela said as she gathered everyone. "Let's get you started with simple introductions. Part of the fun is getting to know the other people in class."

I sent Gage a look. He smiled at me. Laura introduced herself to me and I shook her hand. "Hi, Laura, nice to meet you."

"This is my partner, Monica," Laura said.

"Hi, Monica, nice to meet you." I shook Monica's hand. While Laura seemed introverted and slightly awkward, Monica was warm and easygoing.

"Hi," Monica said. "Have you done one of these cooking classes before?" She sipped her chardonnay. Monica was a tall woman, thin with a sweet smile and kind eyes. I could see why Laura fell instantly in love.

"This is our first," Gage said. "Hi, I'm Gage, Pepper's boyfriend." He shook Monica's and Laura's hands. "Nice to meet you."

"Gage thought it would be entertaining to watch me try to cook," I said, and sent Gage a soft smile.

"You don't cook?" Laura asked.

"No," I said with a shake of my head. "My mom's the cook."

"I think she's better than she lets on," Gage said.

"Well, of course," I replied. "If I claimed I was a good cook then I'd be the one doing all the cooking." I winked at Monica. "It's better to keep them guessing, don't you think?"

"Not me," Monica said. "I love to cook. In fact, that's sort of how we met."

"It is?" I raised my right eyebrow.

"Yes," Laura said with a soft smile. "I was trying to impress my brother and ran out of sugar. So I knocked on her door and asked if I could borrow some. It turns out Monica is a great cook."

"Very nice way to meet," Gage said.

"Okay, everyone," Angela said. "Let's move into the kitchen. You'll find a station for each couple. There are aprons for you to wear and ingredients set out. So, let's wash our hands, suit up, and enjoy the class."

I grabbed Toby's arm and Amelia's arm and walked with them into the kitchen. "Hi, guys, are we having fun yet?"

"The wine's good," Amelia said, her brown eyes sparkling.

"Amelia tells me she works for Myers and Higgs," Toby said, his expression one of interest. "George Myers and I have done business together for a few years. He's a good lawyer."

"So is Amelia," I pointed out, and put them at the station next to Gage and me. "It's great that you have things in common to talk about." I pushed them together and went to Gage, filled with pride at my matchmaking.

"Toby doesn't look bored," Gage said as he handed me my apron. "Good job."

"Amelia's a Harvard Law grad and her family has money," I said, and watched the two interact. "I don't know if it's a match, but they certainly seem interested in each other."

"I still say Toby's half in love with you," Gage teased me.

"Well, he's going to have to get over that. I have a boyfriend." I reached up and gave Gage a quick kiss.

"Laura and Monica seem like a great couple," Gage said. "I don't think you have anything to worry about here."

"I agree." I wiggled my eyebrows at him.

Chef Angela took over. She walked us through the menu step by step. Twenty minutes in, I excused myself and slipped out the side door. Gage and I were in the far back of the kitchen so that I could come and go without being noticed or missed.

I checked on Angela's assistant, Sandra. She was stationed at the side door and her job was to usher in Laura and Monica's family and friends. They were to remain hidden in the other dining area until after the proposal. Then both rooms would be opened and everyone would enjoy the catered engagement party.

I slipped back into the kitchen as Chef was walking everyone through how to make mochi. The Japanese ice cream dessert was time consuming. In advance of our class, Angela had frozen little ice cream balls in a variety of flavors. The only thing we had to make was the mochi covering. The wine flowed and we laughed while we rolled out the sticky sweet dough, made wide circles, and put them back in the refrigerator to cool for fifteen minutes.

"Your circles are perfect," Amelia said as she put her stack of mochi next to ours in the fridge.

"Gage is very precise," I said.

"So is Toby," Amelia said. "Thanks for inviting me, this is fun."

"Thank you for coming," I said. "Looks like everyone is having a good time."

We both noted that Laura and Monica appeared to be in their element and very much in love. Meanwhile, Brad watched Jen as she earnestly tried to roll the perfect mochi.

"They are cute," Amelia agreed. "Especially the two ladies. They seem to be so in love." Amelia sighed. "I hope to be that in love one day."

"I'm sure you will be," I said.

We went on to deep-fry vegetable egg rolls in woks and place them on appetizer plates. Next was more wine and Kung Pao chicken time. That went well, as we all learned not to breathe over the pot while the chilies roasted and popped. The air around them became so spicy it burned your eyes.

Finally it was mochi-filling time. I laughed at how particular Gage was at plopping the ice cream into the mochi wrapper and closing it back up into perfect balls.

"Aren't you going to try?" he asked.

I sipped my wine and smiled. "I think you're doing just fine all on your own."

Next we made the main course and finally we plated our meals and took them out to the empty dining room. I winced when I heard laughter come from the other dining room and hurried to turn up the music on our side.

"What's going on over there?" Monica asked, and looked toward the closed door.

"Angela's assistant is hosting a cocktail party," I said.

"Huh," Monica said.

I glanced at Jen, who gave me a narrow-eyed look. I refused to sweat. This was a surprise and it was going to work. The music changed to Laura and Monica's song.

"Oh," Monica said, and turned to Laura. "It's our song."

At the mention of their song, Laura pulled the ring box out of her apron pocket and got down on one knee. "I know," Laura said. "Monica, you are the love of my life. Without you, I'm incomplete."

The room was quiet as Monica covered her mouth with her hand in surprise.

"Monica," Laura said. "Will you do me the honor of being my wife?"

"Yes," Monica said with tears in her eyes. "Oh, yes!"

I reached over and took the wineglass out of her hand. Laura placed the ring on Monica's finger and they embraced. Tears filled my eyes as they kissed. Tears of joy ran down both their cheeks. I waved for Sandra to open the doors. She did and Laura and Monica's friends and family streamed over to congratulate them.

The house was filled with laughter and congratulations. Both dining rooms were opened and the staff quickly filled tables in the foyer with buffet foods that included our plated selections. Lines were formed and everyone grabbed a plate.

"Wow," Amelia said as she sidled up to me. "I did not see that coming. Was this one of your events?"

"Yes," I said. "I think it went well."

"Oh, it was very romantic," Amelia said, her brown gaze sparkling. "Thanks for letting me be a part of their special day."

"Amelia," Toby called. "I think your vegetable rolls turned out very good."

Amelia glanced at me. "Thanks for introducing me to Toby. He's cute." She went over to spend time with her date. I watched them for a moment and then turned to my date.

"Your mochi is wonderful," I told Gage as I bit into the ice cream delight.

"I happen to be a good cook," Gage said, and raised his right eyebrow as if waiting for me to dispute that. I didn't.

"You're going to make some girl very happy someday," I said, teasing.

"Let's hope someday soon," Gage said, and the look he gave me made my heartbeat speed up.

"Well, this was a lot of fun," Jen said as she and Brad moved toward us. "She certainly looked surprised."

"Yes, she did," Gage agreed.

"It was a very nice, low-key moment," Brad said.

Just then, Laura and Monica caught the crowd's attention by clinking a spoon to their wineglasses. "Everyone's attention, please," Laura said. "I wanted to take a moment and thank Pepper Pomeroy of Perfect Proposals for putting together this memorable evening. Here's to Pepper and many more perfect proposals." She raised her glass and everyone said, "Hear, hear."

I blushed and lifted my wineglass to the toast and took a sip.

"They do look happy," Jen said. "You did a great job. But next time I hope there's more bling. I do like loud, splashy sparkle. Not exactly what you did here."

"Bling was not what was best for this couple," I said. "You need to come to a few more of my proposals and you'll see how I tailor each event to the particular couple's needs."

"It's a date," Brad said with a smile as he collected their coats. "Flashy or not, I had a great time learning how to make Asian food. Thanks, Pepper." He leaned over and gave me a kiss on the cheek. "It was great meeting your friends."

"See you next time," I said. "In the meantime, Jen, think about what you liked and didn't like about tonight. E-mail me suggestions. Okay?"

"Okay," Jen said. She put on her coat and gave me a hug. She held out her hand to Gage. "Bye, Gage. It was nice to meet you."

"Have a good night," Gage said as the couple went out the door. They were soon followed by the Dixons, who told me they had a great time watching me in action.

"I let Chef Angela know we'll be back for more classes," Bob Dixon said. "Even if I have to pay."

"Don't forget to tell your friends about the proposal," I said. "You never know when someone's kids might want to plan a perfect proposal." I pressed my card into their hands.

They left with smiles on their faces. Next Toby and Amelia stepped up. They were both wearing their coats.

"Thanks for inviting me," Amelia said.

"Are you two leaving?" I asked, looking from one to the other. "Amelia, do you need a ride?"

"I'll see she gets home," Toby said. He gave me a nod. "I'll call you tomorrow."

"Night, folks," Gage said. We watched them walk out the door. "Well, looks like you might have made a successful match."

"That would be nice," I said. "I wasn't sure. Toby's a bit . . . unusual."

"Amelia didn't seem to have a problem with it. Did you notice they were both wearing skateboarder athletic shoes?"

"I did," I said, and wiggled my eyebrows. "If I say so myself, this date was a stroke of sheer genius. When I ran into Amelia a couple of days ago I noticed she wore skater shoes. I took the chance and told her about Toby and asked if she wanted a blind date. I promised we'd be here to double and she said, 'Why not?'" I laughed. "Let's hope it works or I might be in hot water with both friends."

"Matchmaking is not for the faint of heart," Gage said with a laugh. He looked at Laura and Monica. The two women glowed brighter than the diamond that sparkled on Monica's finger. "Looks like this is going to be a very happy marriage."

"I couldn't agree more."

Chapter 15

That night I had a dream that Ashley stood at the bottom of my bed looking at me. I swear there was an expression on her face that said she was counting on me to figure out who killed her. I sat up straight with a gasp. A quick look at the clock told me it was five A.M. I turned on the bedroom light to dispel the unease I still felt from my dream. I put my head back down on my pillow but couldn't sleep, so I got up. After making coffee, I turned on my computer and brought up the file I had on my persons of interest in Ashley's case. It was a list of people at the reception who were also country club members. I was certain none of my relatives had a reason to see Ashley gone.

I opened my search engine and entered Mrs. Fulcrum's name. There were a couple of local news articles on the woman. She came from Chicago high society, which meant big money. Her father was in advertising and made a killing in the fifties and sixties. Her grandfather was an architect and real estate magnate. Her great-grandfather started the family fortunes with a department store that went nationwide. Mrs. Fulcrum herself married into money as well, doubling the size of her son Clark's fortune before he was even born.

That said, she wasn't simply a lady who shopped and went to lunch with her friends. She was an active alumnus of Morduray College. There was also an article about her volunteer activities in her church and another article about her holding the honor of being named person of the year by the Chicago Ladies Auxiliary Club. Twice. There was an article about her influence in Chicago social circles and another one on her tireless work with homeless children. According to the papers, Mrs. Fulcrum was a saint. I sighed and looked at the information I wrote in her file. Maybe Gage was right. Maybe I was barking up the wrong tree with my suspicions.

I forged on and did a search of Mrs. Thomson, Samantha Lyn's mom. She wasn't quite as pedigreed as Mrs. Fulcrum. Mrs. Thomson was a local girl whose parents were university professors. She met and married Rick Thomson in 1984. Rick's family ran a successful brokerage firm, elevating Josie to the ranks of Chicago society. The couple had two boys and a girl, Samantha Lyn. Josie was a member of a handful of exclusive clubs and had earned her reputation as a person of note by serving on committees and boards in the clubs. Her eldest son, Richard Junior, had married well, bringing money and prestige to the family. Her middle boy, Theodore, was currently at Berkeley Law and a member of the prestigious fraternity Delta Epsilon. It was pretty clear that Josie Thomson was salivating over a match with the Fulcrum fortune.

I could understand Mrs. Thomson's hurry for the kids to marry, but why would Mrs. Fulcrum want Clark to marry Samantha Lyn? The best I could tell, Clark was a bit of a ne'er-do-well. Mrs. Fulcrum had to be looking for a girl who could attract Clark's attention and yet had a head on her shoulders. After all, it was Clark's wife who would ensure there was a fortune left for Mrs. Fulcrum's grandchildren. Samantha Lyn had graduated at the top of her class at a private girl's academy. She was in her first year of college when she met Clark. After her freshman year, she hadn't returned to school. I could only guess that it was because her east coast school was too far from Clark, who had dropped out halfway through his freshman year and was currently working in his father's office in Chicago. It was pretty clear that the two older women were set on making this match, regardless of what was right for Clark and Samantha Lyn. There was little I could do to convince them otherwise. After all, as Samantha Lyn had said, "It was a complicated situation."

But was it complicated enough for murder? As far as I could tell, while they both had means, neither lady had a good motive to kill Ashley. Not even by accident. Except for the fact that Clark had complained that Ashley had done her job and refused to serve alcohol to a minor. I sighed and studied the computer. There wasn't a whole lot left for me to dig up. I shut it down and got dressed. There had to be another angle I was missing.

Maybe Detective Murphy knew something that would help in my search. I pulled on navy blue wool dress pants and a pressed, long-sleeved pale blue blouse. I did my makeup in my usual minimalistic yet businesslike way. Then I ran a comb through my wayward red hair, slapped on some lipstick, and headed off to the police station.

If there was one thing I had learned about Detective Murphy, it was that he rarely gave up any secrets on the phone. If I was going to find out anything further, I would have to face the lion in his den.

The snow had stopped shortly before Gage had finished shoveling my driveway after dinner the other night, so the drive remained clear. I pulled Old Blue out of the garage and noticed Mrs. Crivitz peering out her dining room window. I waved her a good morning as I closed and locked the garage then headed back into Old Blue. The big Buick warmed up fast and had heated seats—something that was needed in cold Chicagoland.

My cell phone rang as I pulled into a coffee shop parking lot. I parked the car and dug through my purse. I managed to answer the phone before it went to voice mail.

"Perfect Proposals, this is Pepper. How can I help you?"

"Pepper, it's Toby," he said. "I told you I would call."

"Right," I said, and glanced at my watch. "Thanks for being part of the proposal last night. Did you have fun with Amelia?"

"Yes," he said. "She is very pretty."

"I thought you two might have something in common . . . well, besides me," I said with a laugh. "Do you?"

"We do," he said. "She reminds me of you in many ways."

"Thanks," I said, and tried not to overthink that comment. "Good. Listen, I was wondering if you would help me with another proposal?"

"Sure," he said. "What do you need me to do?"

"You remember Brad and Jen from last night?"

"The couple that had never cooked before?"

"What?"

"They had never cooked before," Toby said. "I believe I'm wealthier and I still learned to cook. So I found it strange that neither had cooked before."

"I think they were pretending for the class," I said.

"No, they really didn't know a wok from a saucepan," he said. "Thankfully Amelia at least knew that much."

"Amelia is a good cook. You should have her make you dinner sometime," I suggested.

"She said the same thing," he said. "So what are you planning?"

"Brad and Jen are the couple you suggested I involve in a few of my proposal events."

"Ah," Toby said. "The ones I suggested you plan a

proposal for me as a dummy for theirs? You really shouldn't have introduced me to them if you wanted me to pretend to be a client."

"What I would like is for you to call Brad and set up a meeting for the night of the next proposal event. That way, Jen won't think I'm preparing her event because Brad can't come."

"Alright," he said. "I think that makes sense."

"Thank you," I said, and quickly rattled off the when and where of the event.

"And what about Amelia?" he asked. "Will she be at this next proposal?"

I stopped short at the unexpected question. "I can ask her if you want me to," I said. "But really this would be a great reason to call her. Tell her what you are doing and have her help you with Brad. Maybe she could be an associate at the meeting. I'm sure you could think of something."

"Right," he said. "It would be better if you invite her to the proposal event and I meet her there, don't you think?"

"No, I don't think," I said.

"Fine, I'll have my secretary call her and set up the meeting with Brad and Amelia," he said.

"No," I said as gently as I could. "If you are interested in Amelia as a date, you need to call her yourself."

"Fine," he said. "I'll call Amelia and have my secretary set up a meeting with this Brad person at the time and place you requested."

"Thanks, Toby, I knew I could count on you," I said.

"You might want to send my secretary an e-mail to remind me of this commitment," he said. "And send her Amelia's contact information."

"Toby," I warned.

"I'll call her," he said. "I need you to send Francine the information so she can put it in my digital database."

"Okay," I said. "I've got to go. Thanks for doing this."

"Any time, Pepper," he said. "Your business is fun in a cloak and dagger sort of way."

I tapped into my cell phone as we talked. "I've texted Francine the details and Amelia's contact information. See you soon, Toby."

"Always a pleasure, Pepper."

I hung up the phone and stepped out into the frigid air to pick up coffee for Detective Murphy. It was always a sure bet that I would get in to see him if I brought coffee. I added a few lattes and a box of scones to my order for the rest of the guys at the station to fight over.

"Well, good morning," Detective Murphy said as I handed him his coffee.

"Peppermint mocha, triple shot with extra whip," I said, and then handed him a smaller bag. "Plus two cinnamon scones."

"You are my best friend ever," he said with a grin and sipped the coffee, then dove into the bag of scones.

I sat in the small plastic chair across from his desk and watched him attack his snack. "Are you on a diet or something?"

"My doctor insists. I told her it was foolish, what with the holidays approaching," he said between bites of scone. "She set me up to see a nutritionist. They want me to eat egg whites scrambled with no salt and dry whole wheat toast in the morning. I think they're secretly trying to kill me."

"I won't tell," I said. "But my dad had the same thing happen last year."

Detective Murphy made a face. "They called my daughter and now she's on my case about the diet."

"Then definitely don't tell her that I brought you a snack," I said. "I don't want her to give me the evil eye."

"Don't worry," he said with a grin as he dug out the second scone. "Your secret is safe with me."

"Good," I said, and smiled. "How are you? Mrs. Crivitz was asking after you."

"What? Why?" He stopped eating and looked a little pale.

I grinned. "She thinks you and her Mary Ellen would make a lovely couple. So romantic," I mimicked her. "The handsome detective marrying the girl next door."

"Ugh." He dropped the scone. "The last thing I need is to be set up with Mary Ellen. Have you seen her?"

I giggled. "But she's perfect for you."

"Right."

"Speaking of perfect," I segued not too subtly. "How's Emily?"

"She's good. I talked to her last night," he said, and wiped the sugar off his hands with a napkin. "I got to thinking about what you said."

"What did I say?" I asked, and sipped my coffee.

"That I had to let her live her life. I think you're right. I can get a little too . . . involved."

"You're her father. That's what you do," I said, and let him off the hook.

"Yeah, well, I called Emily and I promised that if she moved back I'd give her space . . . no strings attached. I'll be there for her when she wants and keep my distance when she needs me to." He leaned back and sipped his coffee.

"Good for you," I said.

"I even went so far as to tell her she could bring her loser boyfriend if she wanted to."

"Please tell me you didn't."

"No, I didn't use the word *loser*," he said and blew out a long breath. "I said boyfriend. And I told her I'd welcome any friend of hers with open arms. Anyway, Emily was happy." He looked at me, his dark eyes shining. "I haven't heard her sound so happy in a long time. In fact she actually cried and thanked me." He cleared his throat. "It got me a bit choked up."

"I see that. Good for you both."

"No word on whether she'll come or not, but I put it out there and she appreciated the effort."

"I'm glad," I said.

"You didn't come here to talk about Emily," he surmised.

"No, I wanted to continue the conversation about Ashley's death," I admitted, and leaned forward. "It feels all wrong. I have to know. Despite what the autopsy reports indicate, do you truly believe it was an accidental overdose? Do you really think the case should be closed like the chief says?"

I noticed him wince slightly.

"You don't, do you?" I said, certain I'd read his expression correctly.

"You know I can't work on a case that is officially closed, Pepper," he said, and looked down at his desk. "I've got plenty of work to do on cases that are active."

"But we both know this case isn't closed," I pressed. "Someone killed Ashley, and I'm not going to let a convenient story keep that person from justice. I know that I only had a few conversations with her that night, but she was so easy to like. She was caring and she was fun and she was kind to Samantha Lyn, and let me tell you, that little girl needs someone caring in her life."

"The fact of the matter is that Ashley died from taking too much Xanax and then drinking alcohol." Detective Murphy's voice was gruff. He picked up a pencil and tapped it on the desk pad he had on top of his desk.

"According to my sources, half the people at the country club take Xanax," I pointed out. "Any one of them could have slipped the drug into Ashley's drink. I mean, maybe they didn't intend to kill her. Maybe they meant to make her sick."

"Why would anyone do that?" Detective Murphy asked.

"I don't know, maybe they were mad at Ashley. Take

Clark Fulcrum, for instance. He was upset that Ashley wouldn't serve him alcohol. I distinctly heard him say that he was going to tell his mom that Ashley was being insubordinate and that his mom would do something about it."

"It sounds like a childish threat," Detective Murphy said.

"That's what I thought at the time," I said. "But I've learned that Ashley had a history with Clark and his girlfriend Samantha Lyn."

"Besides meeting them at another event where Ashley bartended?"

"Well, no, at that event. You see, that was the only time Samantha Lyn admitted to anyone that Clark was not a good guy."

Detective Murphy straightened. "What did she mean by that? Has Clark abused Samantha in any way?"

"No." I shook my head. "Not that she's said, anyway. But Samantha Lyn told me she doesn't really love Clark, but her mom and his mom are dead set on the union. Samantha is young and wants to please her parents. She told me that Clark was being horrible to her that day and she confessed it all to Ashley. Ashley left the event early, missing out on tips and wages she clearly needed just to take Samantha Lyn home and see that the girl was okay." I paused for a moment to let that information sink in. "I think the mothers found out and were out to get Ashley."

"Why?" Detective Murphy asked. "Why would they see a protective bartender as a threat?"

"Because Ashley made friends with Samantha Lyn. Everyone knows that peers are hugely influential when you are Samantha Lyn's age. The moms must have seen Ashley as a threat to their plans. They could have wanted her out of the picture. You know, a little Xanax slipped into a drink and Ashley would have gone home, leaving the kids alone. Both Mrs. Fulcrum and Mrs. Thomson have a prescription for the drug. With Clark complaining about Ashley yet again, it wouldn't have been hard to slip her something to get her out of there."

"Do you know how crazy that sounds?" Detective Murphy said. "Like I've said, Pepper, you get too emotionally involved in your couples. You are there to facilitate the proposal. You aren't their life coach or their counselor."

"I know that," I said, and sighed. "But I can't rest thinking that Ashley killed herself accidentally. From what you've told me, she's been through a lot. If she were going to hurt herself—accidentally or not—she would have done it years ago. Right?"

"Maybe," Detective Murphy hedged. "Sometimes these things lie dormant for a while. We don't know. Something could have triggered her that night."

"If it did, then I have to know what it was," I said. "Tell me what you know. Please. I can bring in more scones."

He gave me a long look. "You are not going to leave this alone, are you?"

"No."

"Fine," he said, and took a folder out of a pile on his desk and opened it. "I've been looking into Ashley's apartment. She lived alone, renting a room from a Polish woman near Lincoln Park. Her landlady told me that Ashley insisted on staying in the attic bedroom. There's a full-size one-bedroom apartment in the basement, but Ashley was—and I quote—too scared of sleeping on the first floor."

"That's something," I said, and studied the papers in the folder. I was pretty good at reading upside down. "Wait. Is that Ashley's mom's name and address?" I asked, pointing to the left-hand paper that listed a Mrs. Pamela Klein.

"Yes," Detective Murphy said.

"It's a Chicago address," I pointed out. I knew because I once went to a friend's bridal shower in that area. "I thought you said Ashley's family lived in Michigan."

"No," he said. "She went to college in Michigan, and that's where she was almost killed, but she was born and raised here in the city." He closed the file and frowned at me. "You aren't supposed to see confidential stuff."

"I want to talk to Ashley's mom," I said. "You know, pay my condolences and such."

"I don't think that's such a good idea, Pepper. That woman has been through enough."

"Really?" I asked. "What if something happened to Emily? Hmm? Wouldn't you want to talk to one of the last people she spoke to? Wouldn't you want to know about the efforts to save Emily's life?"

"She isn't me," Detective Murphy said softly.

"No, she's a grieving mother," I agreed. "Look, I won't

tell her where I got her address. I promise. I'll take her a casserole. I know that would mean something to my mother."

"Fine," he said. "But I don't want to know about it."

"Cool," I said, energized. "Thanks, Detective Murphy." I bussed a kiss on his cheek. "You're the best."

He scowled at me. "Don't do anything stupid."

I winked. "I'm taking a casserole to a grieving mom. How is that stupid?"

Chapter 16

"The days spent waiting for Ashley to wake up were a nightmare," Mrs. Klein said. "I thought those were the worst days of my life. I was wrong."

I patted her hand. We were sitting in the small living room of the two-story flat that Mrs. Klein owned. Inside it was decorated like a 1990s Pottery Barn advertisement. The couch was blue and white toile with spots of yellow in the pillows and accessories. Mrs. Klein looked like a less thin, older version of Ashley with long blond hair and beautiful expressive eyes. There were wrinkles bracketing her thin lips and worry lines around her eyes. She wore a black, long-sleeved sweater and a pair of yoga pants. Her feet were bare and her toenails were painted in neon blue. She had told me it was a tribute to Ashley. It seemed that

Ashley had loved to paint her toenails in crazy outrageous colors.

"I'm so sorry," I said, and passed a tissue box to her. "Ashley was a good person. She didn't deserve to die like that."

"I agree," Mrs. Klein said, and dabbed at her eyes and blew her nose. "She had lived this wonderful charmed life until she went away to college. Did you know her in high school?"

I had wormed my way in by saying that Ashley and I were fast friends and that I was missing her. Which wasn't exactly a lie. Plus the lasagna, loaf of garlic bread, and bottle of wine had helped ease my way into the Kleins' home. "No, I went to Fenwick."

"Oh, well, your high school plays hers in sports. She was the head cheerleader. You might have seen her at basketball games," Mrs. Klein said. "I have her scrapbook right here." She reached over and pulled out the book.

I just smiled and nodded. I was a band geek. If I was at a basketball game at all in high school it was because I was assigned to play for band. But I wasn't going to burst her bubble.

"Here she is her sophomore year," Mrs. Klein showed me a picture of a gorgeous, fit Ashley smiling while flying in the air and doing perfect splits. "She made the varsity team that year. She was so talented."

"Wow," I said, and listened to her talk about Ashley's high school years.

"She was prom queen her senior year," Mrs. Klein said,

and showed me the picture of Ashley wearing a gorgeous Tiffany blue gown and a crystal tiara. "She was so smart. Did you know she got a full scholarship to Morduray? She was going to teach kids with learning disabilities. She always wanted to give back."

"Ashley never told me she had a full scholarship," I said honestly. "She was so different than the Ashley you are showing me. But I really liked her. She was so personable and kind and she had this quality about her that made me want to be her friend."

"Everything changed that night," Mrs. Klein said, and turned the pages of the scrapbook. "When they found her just barely holding on to life, I prayed and prayed. She was in a coma while we buried Kiera. The police interviewed several witnesses who saw the girls at the parade and then the bonfire after. It seems the girls left the bonfire early. No one saw them go, but they were shot in a nearby park sometime during the bonfire event. The police never solved the crime. I think that was the worst part of it for Ashley. She was here and alive but unable to help the police understand what happened. She couldn't remember the parade, the bonfire, or even why they left. In fact, she had no idea she was even in that park where she was shot. She lived with a lot of survivor's guilt over Kiera's death. She felt as if she should have died that day, too, but she couldn't tell anyone why." Mrs. Klein paused. "Whatever happened, Ashley suffered terribly."

"She told me about the headaches," I said. "They were awful. She refused to take anything for them."

"I know," Mrs. Klein said. "Ashley hated to take any kind of drug. She always did. She wasn't a rule breaker. It's why her arrests were so horribly out of character. I couldn't get through to her. No one could."

"She told me that she sometimes had flashes about that night," I said carefully, watching Mrs. Klein's reaction. "Maybe there were triggers of some sort."

She shook her head. "If there were triggers we couldn't figure out what they were. It was all so maddening for us and for her . . . my poor, poor baby." Mrs. Klein put the book away and pulled out another, smaller one. "This one is strictly college pictures. I put it together thinking that if she felt comfortable seeing her friends and surroundings like this—and if they were familiar—then maybe it would ease her memory back to her." She sighed. "But it never worked."

"Here's Kiera," she said, and pointed to a couple of the photos. "They were assigned as roommates Ashley's freshman year and they became inseparable." She turned the page and showed me two photos. "This one and this one seemed to trigger a reaction from her every time she looked at them. But then she'd forget again, until she'd open the book and get startled. I can guess why one might be important, but not the other."

I looked at the pictures she was pointing at. The first photo was a crowd scene with about a hundred people in it, all cheering or dancing or waving their hands in the air. Behind them was a banner announcing the Morduray homecoming. There was a large group of students around a bonfire in the foreground and in the far background, a couple of parade floats. "That's a picture from the night Ashley was shot," Mrs. Klein said. "I included it hoping it would jog her memory."

Most of the faces in the photo were either blurred or were of people looking away. "Is Ashley in this picture or did she take it?" I asked.

"There," her mother said. "That's her."

I followed where she pointed and recognized Ashley. "Of course," I said. "She was younger then, carrying a little more weight. It looked good on her, though," I muttered. Her hair wasn't lifeless, her face not quite so worn-looking. "She was beautiful."

"She was once," her mother agreed. "The incident took its toll on her."

"And this picture? "I asked, and pointed at the second one. "Was that taken the same night?"

"That's a picture of the homecoming parade," she said. "Ashley helped decorate her sorority's float. She took this picture."

I looked at it carefully but didn't see anything that would remind her of a shooting. The photo was of three sorority floats in a row. You could make out the back of the first float, all of Ashley's sorority's float, and the front of the next float.

"She was so proud to have helped design her house's float."

The last item in the scrapbook was a large fabric sign, so big that it needed to be kept folded. "May I?" I asked and, when Mrs. Klein nodded her agreement, I unfolded the fabric. The sign was blue and white with three Greek symbols. "Was this from her sorority?"

"No," Mrs. Klein said. "Ashley belonged to a different one. I don't even know why she had this. Her father and I cleaned out her dorm and brought everything here after the . . . incident. We didn't want to throw anything away. I didn't know what its significance was, but the moment she came across it, she froze and nearly passed out. I decided it must be important." She patted it. "So it went in here."

Xi Omicron Mu. "That sounds familiar, but I can't quite place it." I folded the fabric back up and made a mental note of the letters and colors. I had no idea what any of the things Mrs. Klein told me meant, but they were small clues that might lead to something bigger. "Thank you so much for sharing your memories of Ashley with me," I said, and stood. "I wanted you to know that she might not have been the head cheerleader anymore, but she still made a difference in my life and in the life of a young girl she befriended at a wedding."

Mrs. Klein stood with me and gave me a hug. "I'm so glad you stopped by. I needed to hear about Ashley's last hours. Thank you again for trying CPR. I'm grateful that you were there to try to save my baby."

Tears welled up in my eyes. "But I didn't save her," I said.

She patted my back. "It's enough to know that you tried," she said. "Thank you."

I wanted to tell her that I wouldn't rest until whoever did this to Ashley would be found and prosecuted, but one look in her eyes and I bit my tongue. At this point I only had suspicions. Giving Mrs. Klein false hope wasn't helping anyone.

* * *

I went straight home and turned on my computer and browsed the Morduray College website to see if I could get any of those homecoming pictures from two years ago. After speaking to Ashely's mom, I was certain that somehow the shooting that night had to be connected to Ashley's death. If the person who shot Ashley at homecoming was the same person who killed her at the country club, there had to be a connection between Morduray College and someone at my sister's wedding.

I knew that my sister and I didn't go to Morduray. In fact, no one from my family had gone there, which meant it had to be someone from the groom's side or another one of the servers. Maybe more pictures would give me a different angle or help to clarify the story of what happened to Ashley and Kiera. I had a feeling that if I solved the shooting, I'd know who killed Ashley. I clicked on a link to a photographer. It looked like they had this year's photos up for people to order. I dug up their phone number and made a quick call.

"Morgan Photography, the official Morduray College photographer. This is Kathi, how can I help you?"

"Hi, Kathi," I said. "My name is Pepper Pomeroy. I'm working on a collage for a friend's mom and I was wondering if you still have pictures from the Morduray College homecoming from two years ago. My friend was part of the bonfire and in the homecoming parade. She died recently and I thought it might be nice to do something for her mom."

"Oh, my condolences," Kathi said. "Yes, we do have all those pictures available. We keep pictures for ten years."

"Do you have some sort of proof page where I can go and pick out the ones I want?"

"Yes," she said. "Are you on our website?"

"Yes," I said.

"Go to the top left and click on 'Buy Pictures.' When the page comes up, go to the search box and type in 'Morduray College homecoming' and the year. All the pictures we have will pop up. They are all watermarked so you can't download them, but you can click on the ones you want and order them. Once they are in your shopping cart, you can pay online. We will print them out to the size you request and will ship them to you as soon as possible. Where do you live?"

"I'm in the Chicago area," I said. "Will it take long to get the pictures? I'm hoping to have this collage for a memorial service two days from now."

"We can get those pictures rushed to you and you can have them within forty-eight hours."

"Sounds perfect," I said. "Thanks." I clicked through the steps and up popped one hundred proof pictures of that night. The bonfire, the parade, the game, and the homecoming queen were all there. I chose shots that appeared to be close to the picture that Mrs. Klein had in Ashley's scrapbook. In the end I ordered fifteen digital copies to be e-mailed to me. Once they took off the proof lettering I could better see what was underneath. The cost set me back a hundred dollars, but it seemed like a small price to pay if they helped me identify Ashley's killer.

Next on my to-do list was to look into Xi Omicron Mu. It turned out it was a coed fraternity. They posted pictures of their members from the last five years. I printed them out, but the pictures were group shots and I didn't have access to facial recognition software, so I stacked up the pictures into a pile to be reviewed with a magnifying glass later tonight.

Finally, I contacted the fraternity.

"Xi Omicron Mu, this is Hanna, how can I help you?"

"Hi, Hanna," I said. "My name is Pepper Pomeroy. I'm putting together a memorial collage for a friend of mine who died recently. She went to Morduray and I wondered if I could get some copies of your homecoming pictures from two years ago."

"Was she a member?"

"No," I said. "Her mother said she wasn't, but she did have a piece of fabric with your Greek letters on it and your colors. So I thought maybe she was at some of your functions? She might even have had a friend or two in the fraternity."

"I'm sorry, I can't help you," Hanna said. "Our pictures and activities are restricted to members only. Do you know a member? If so, they could sponsor you and get you access to the shots you are looking for."

"No," I said. "I don't know a member." I frowned. Why did it sound familiar? Did I know a member? Clearly it wasn't Ashley.

"I'm sorry, then," she said. "Access to party pictures is restricted. With social media and people able to Photoshop people into pictures, we've made it a policy to restrict access to our party pictures. I'm sure you understand."

"Certainly," I said.

"Thank you for calling Xi Omicron Mu. Have a nice day." She hung up on me and I frowned. Xi Omicron Mu was a dead end.

Or was it? I put the name into my search engine and a whole lot of pictures popped up. In fact, there were 1,245 pictures. That was too general so I typed in homecoming and the date two years earlier. This time a hundred pictures popped up. People don't understand that their Twitter, Tumblr, and Instagram accounts can be easily searched.

I started to go through the pictures, but it was a long, slow slog and I still had to finish the details for an important party. The nagging thought that I knew someone who went to Xi Omicron Mu stayed with me. I sighed, finally, and put the sleuthing work away. It was time to concentrate on the Brad and Jen extravaganza and how it tied in to Samantha Lyn and Clark's proposal.

Everyone, including Samantha Lyn, knew I was against Clark proposing to her, but Mrs. Fulcrum and Mrs. Thomson were adamant that they would have a proposal. I liked Samantha Lyn, and even if I couldn't prevent her from marrying Clark, at least I could give her a party.

The event was going to be couched as a fund-raiser for autism. I put in multiple hours' worth of work designing posters that explained the fund-raiser. The title was going to be 'Cool Cats on Ice'—a jazz-age event with cocktails and dancing. I ran off a half dozen posters. I planned to place the posters around the country club and other areas where Brad and Jen and the Fulcrums and Thomsons hung out. It would give authenticity to the event. The families and members of the country club would buy tickets to the event. Brad and Jen would think the night was staged for Samantha Lyn and Clark and they were coming to watch. Samantha Lyn would think it was a fund-raiser and get her surprise engagement as special as I could make it. If it worked the way I hoped, I would walk away with two satisfied customers and maybe raise some funds for a good cause.

* * *

That night, Gage was over at my house. I was elbow deep in the double-proposal event. "So, I've got the Ice Pit rented," I said. "There is seating for one hundred and fifty and all the tables and chairs and everything inside is made of ice—even the glasses. So it all glitters and, see, it's lit from underneath with Jennifer's favorite colors." I pulled up pictures that the venue had sent me.

"It looks cold, but cool," Gage said with a grin. He sat across from me on the couch with his laptop on his lap.

"They supply these great faux fur coats for everyone who enters." I showed him a picture of the coats. "But I really want to jazz it up a bit."

"That's where I come in," Gage said. "I'm delivering jazz-age costumes for all the guests to dress in prior to entering the space. I've got racks of flapper gowns in all sizes and shapes. There are bins of pearls and sparkling cubic zirconium necklaces, chandelier earrings, and tiaras. The guys have a full range of zoot suits to wear under their faux fur."

"Yes, I'm hiding the proposal by announcing that it's a fund-raiser for my autism charity. Everyone must come in costume. I made these posters this afternoon and put them up at the country club. Tomorrow I'm doing an e-mail campaign. It's sort of last minute, but the Fulcrums and Thomsons didn't give me enough time to make it look like a real deal. You know, an event that people plan for a year in advance."

"It doesn't matter that it's rushed," Gage said. "What matters is that it appears like the real thing. I'm certain it will, with my help, of course."

"Of course," I said. "Now, there will be three tents outside the Ice Pit set up as dressing rooms. One tent will be specifically for Jen and Brad and for Samantha Lyn and Clark's guests. Then the other two will hold Jen and Brad's friends and family—one for the guys and one for the dolls. You have the tents ready, right?"

"I do," he said, his blue eyes twinkling. "Are you going to have fake guests this time? You know, to mingle with the families?"

"Well, with the posters and tiny bit of publicity, I'm hoping for a few people coming who expect the fund-raiser.

I sent a note to the local autism charity board and they will be promoting it as well. Then I've asked Samantha Lyn, Clark, and their parents to participate. Samantha Lyn at least was excited to help. She has a friend who has an autistic brother. The moms are in on the event, of course."

"Of course," Gage said.

"Finally, I told Jen the proposal event is for Samantha Lyn and asked her to kind of handle the mothers since they all know each other from the country club. Jen agreed."

"What about Brad?"

"Well, I couldn't have him be a part of this proposal, as that would seem too obvious," I said. "So I got Toby to meet with Brad under the pretext of doing some work for his firm. Toby agreed and he has already made plans to meet with Brad at the coffee shop around the corner from the event. It's close but not suspiciously close to the Ice Pit."

"Wait, Brad met Toby at your last proposal event, won't he suspect Toby of helping you?" Gage asked.

"You know, Toby," I said. "He isn't exactly the most social."

"That's true."

I smiled. "Toby's business reputation turns heads. Brad said he's looking for a job in California. Toby has some venture capital in start-ups out there. I'm sure the last thing Brad is thinking about is my proposal business."

"Right," Gage said with a nod.

"Toby will explain after they arrive at the coffeehouse that he has to attend this fund-raiser. Brad will say, 'Hey, Jen is there.' Toby will take Brad with him and when they arrive, Toby and I will hide Brad. I'll give him the ring, and the moment the band starts to play their song, I'll get Brad behind the screen so that he is backlit. He'll get down on one knee and I'll light up the screen with the words 'Jen, will you marry me?' Brad will say the words into a microphone. Then, when Jen has her mouth covered and tears in her eyes, the screen will go up and Brad will step out with the ring, get back on his knee, and she will say yes."

"Wow," Gage said. "I'm always amazed by how you do this. You really have this all worked out."

"I have help from my friends," I said, and put my laptop aside. I moved over next to Gage. "I couldn't pull off these fun events if I didn't have you."

"Is that right?" He put his tablet aside and pulled me into his arms.

"Yes," I said, and wrapped my arms around his neck. "I'm a very lucky girl."

He smiled and kissed me. "I'm a lucky man to have such a lucky girl in my arms and in my life."

That was the end of proposal planning for the night. After all, there's more to life than working and amateur sleuthing.

Chapter 17

I met my mom for lunch at Samboni's Pasta House. "Hi, Mom." I kissed her on the cheek and unbuttoned my coat. "How are things?"

"Not too bad," she said, and watched me take off my coat and hang it on the back of my chair before I sat down. "You look good."

I glanced down at the black turtleneck sweater and jeans I wore. "Thanks, Mom."

"How are things with you and Gage?"

I couldn't stop the grin that spread across my face at the mention of Gage's name. "Good."

Mom tilted her head and studied me. "Good. It's nice to see that look in your eye."

"What look?" I picked up my menu and pretended that her close attention wasn't bothering me. I mean, who wants their mom to know they had a great date the night before?

"The one your sister had when she started dating Warren," Mom said. "When's the wedding?"

"What!" I put down my menu. "We have only been dating for a few months."

It was Mom's turn to grin as she perused the menu. "When it's right, it's right."

I gave her the stink eye but she ignored me.

"What's up with your proposals?" she asked. "How did the foodie one go?"

"It went great. Laura and Monica are so cute together and their friends and family were so happy for them."

"Good," Mom said. The waitress came over and took our orders for drinks, soup, and pasta. Mom handed her the menus and then leaned on her elbows. "So, how's the investigation coming along?"

"Investigation?" I tried to act casual but there's no ignoring my mom. She somehow always knows all.

"The one for that dear girl who died at Felicity's reception."

"You haven't told Felicity about that, have you?" I asked, and sipped my water. "I don't want her to feel like her entire marriage is cursed."

"Of course I haven't told her. She's still on her honeymoon." Mom leaned back. "The kids won't be home for another three days."

"Have you heard from her?" I asked. The waitress brought us soup and breadsticks.

"She's on her honeymoon," Mom said, and picked up her soup spoon. "She's not going to contact her mother."

"I thought maybe she'd send pictures of the trip," I said, and shrugged. My soup was made with potatoes, leeks, and Italian sausage. It was warm and wonderful on a cold, dreary winter day.

"I'm sure they'll share pictures when they get back," Mom said. "Not everyone feels the need to post constant selfies."

I paused. "How do you know what a selfie is?"

"It's all over the Internet," Mom said with a shrug and dipped her spoon into her chicken tortilla soup. "Everyone's into taking pictures of themselves or their food." Mom sighed. "All the knowledge in the world at their fingertips and all anyone wants to do is take a snapshot of their smiling face."

"Well, not me," I said, and went back to my soup.

"Yeah, I noticed," Mom said. "I thought maybe you'd post one or two of you and Gage. Are you two keeping it on the down low?"

"What?" I asked. "Mom, where are you getting these terms?"

"What, I can't be modern and up to date?" Mom asked back. She looked disappointed.

"It's fine, Mom," I said, giving in to her pout. "No, we're not hiding our dating status."

"But you still have 'single' listed on your Facebook

page," Mom pointed out. "I figured after a couple of months you would switch that to 'in a relationship.'"

"Gage and I haven't talked about our status," I said. "I won't post anything until we do."

"What are you waiting for?"

I squirmed, uncomfortable with the conversation. "Stop pressuring me. I'm sure when the time is right, Gage will broach the subject."

"Maybe he's waiting for you to broach it," Mom said, and gestured with her spoon. "Men do that, you know. Did you tell him you were still uncertain about you and him and Bobby?"

"Yes, but that was two months ago," I said.

"Time is nothing to a man," Mom pointed out. "Look at how long he followed you around before he got the nerve to ask you out. What was it eleven or twelve years?"

"I was dating Bobby."

"Don't let him wait another eleven or twelve years before he takes the next step," Mom said. "Nobody wants to have kids when they are old."

"Mom." I really tried not to roll my eyes.

"What? Twelve years from now you'll be forty. That's old for having kids. I'm just saying."

I pushed my empty soup bowl away. "Why did you ask me to lunch? Was it to badger me about my relationship?"

"No," Mom said. "Tell me about your investigation into that girl's death."

"Ashley," I said. "Her name was Ashley Klein. She was from here. I went to see her mother the other day."

"Did you bring her a casserole?"

"Yes," I said with a nod. "Lasagna and bread and wine. All ready to freeze and eat whenever. That way if she was inundated with casseroles she could freeze it, or if she wanted to—"

"She could eat it that night," Mom finished. "That's my girl. How was her mother? Poor thing, nobody wants to outlive their children."

"She seemed okay . . . at peace with it. Ashley really suffered the last few years. She and her best friend were gunned down. Ashley survived, but her friend Kiera died on the scene. When Ashley came out of her coma she didn't remember anything . . . for a while."

"Was she remembering things? Do you think that's why she was killed?"

"You know, she told me she was having headaches and strange flashes, but couldn't put things together."

"So she wasn't killed for remembering," Mom said as the waitress placed plates of pasta in front of us.

"I'm not sure," I said. "Her mother has this scrapbook that shows Ashley growing up. She was head cheerleader and prom queen. She had a full scholarship until that day she was shot and left for dead. After she woke up she couldn't get over her grief and her guilt to continue with school. She acted up and dropped out of school. When I met her I thought she was ten years older than me. She was skinny and clearly unhappy. She had that rough look, you know?"

"Yes, dear, I remember her," Mom said, and expertly

twirled her pasta with a spoon and fork. "I thought she didn't look like the usual bartender type for a high-society event."

"I know, right? But here's the thing, she'd done a few other high-society weddings. In fact, she met Samantha Lyn at one."

"I can't believe that poor girl is still with that Clark," Mom said, and shook her head. "Seriously, she is smart and young and pretty. What is she doing with the Fulcrum boy?"

"Their mothers are set on them getting married."

"No!" My mother put down her silverware to emphasize her disgust.

"Yes," I said, and nodded. "They have hired me to do the proposal and engagement party. I went to see Samantha Lyn. You know I do undercover interviews of all my clients, except Monica. I had to trust Laura that Monica would be good with the proposal."

"And she was?"

"She was," I said, and smiled. "It was great. Toby came and I set him up with Amelia. Remember Amelia?"

"Oh, yes," Mom said, and her eyes sparkled. "What a sweet girl. She's perfect for Toby. Aren't her parents members of the country club?"

"They are," I said. "And I think Amelia liked Toby."

"How was Toby with being set up?"

"I'm not sure," I said, and frowned. "I think he was good with it. I'm going to have to ask him if he's asked her out again since then. You know he isn't the quickest learner when it comes to human relationships. And Amelia is not the kind to call him and push." I tapped my chin. "I may need to step in and ensure they meet again."

"So now you're a matchmaker?"

"Oh, gosh no," I said. "If I were a matchmaker I'd tell Samantha Lyn to run—not walk—away from Clark Fulcrum. Like I said, I'm not a matchmaker, but I did tell her she should run away."

"And?"

"And she told me that she had run away crying at the wedding where she first met Ashley because of a fight with Clark. Ashley clocked out of her bartending and took Samantha Lyn home. Samantha told me that she confided in Ashley that she wasn't ready to marry anyone, let alone Clark."

"Then why is she still with him?"

"That's what I asked," I said. "Samantha told me it was complicated. I think she doesn't want to disappoint her mother. Mrs. Thomson is dead set on her one and only daughter making a good match, and she sees the Fulcrums as the perfect way to elevate the status of her family."

"That's terrible."

"Right?" I shook my head. "Mrs. Fulcrum and Mrs. Thomson are terrible together. All they talk about is how Ashley deserved what happened."

"What?"

"They are mad because Ashley made friends with Samantha Lyn and Ashley told Samantha to leave Clark."

"Do you think one or both of the moms killed Ashley?"

"That was my thought." I leaned forward. "Both of them have Xanax prescriptions, but Detective Murphy said that the idea that they would stoop to murder doesn't fit. After all, Samantha Lyn is still going along with their plan. In fact, the moms wanted me to set up the engagement ASAP. So, I've set it up for tomorrow."

"No!" Mom protested. "I thought you had a rule that only successful couples who meet your interview criteria would be able to use you. You already ignored that rule when you didn't interview Monica."

I sighed and put my elbow on the table and my chin in my hand. "I know, I know. This whole thing feels off. You know? But Monica was great and that worked out. And I hate to say it but the moms have given me this huge deposit. I was kind of hoping to use it to propel my business forward."

"Honey, you can't take it," Mom admonished. "You would never live with yourself should Samantha Lyn be stuck in a bad marriage."

"But they are determined whether I do it or someone else does it," I pointed out. "At the very least, I will be there as a voice of reason when he proposes. Maybe she'll look at me and say no."

"I think you're reaching," Mom said, and shook her head. "It sounds to me as if this little girl is trying to please her parents and you are making it happen. I'm disappointed in you, Pepper. I thought you had standards and principles."

"I do," I argued.

"If you do, then you should give those women their

deposit back. Take that poor little girl out for a nice lunch and be a friend to her."

"I tried, she won't listen."

"It's not Samantha Lyn who needs to listen," Mom said. "It's you, Pepper. You need to tell those moms no and you need to befriend that little girl. If as you say no one else in her life is listening to her, then you need to step up and do that."

"The last girl who did ended up dead," I pointed out.

Mom gasped. "They wouldn't hurt you, would they? Pepper, if you're doing this because you think they would hurt you, then that's even more of a reason not to do it."

I sighed. "Tomorrow's party isn't just for Samantha Lyn and Clark."

"No? But I thought you said it was."

"It's really a cover for another engagement. Do you remember Jennifer and Brad?"

"Who?"

"They were at Felicity's wedding. They were friends of Warren's mom. Anyway, Jen has decided that she wants this glitzy, over-the-top proposal, but it has to be a complete surprise."

"You specialize in surprise," Mom said. "Why are you nervous?"

"I'm not nervous."

"Pepper . . ." Mom said in the voice that said she knew I was lying.

"Fine. Because Jen is a complete control freak. She has been in on almost all of the meetings about it. She grills Brad about it every night. I can't tell Brad because if Jen is not surprised she won't say yes."

"That's ridiculous."

"I know. Brad has tried to propose six times and each time Jen has figured it out and then refused to say yes. Plus, he had to buy her a new ring each time because it has to all be a surprise."

"That is terrible."

"Brad seems to be okay with it. You know, he told me that if I thought Jen was a control freak, I should meet her parents." I sighed. "Brad says Jen's parents want them to move to California as soon as possible so they can live close by."

"What about the Brad's job? Isn't this Jennifer working?"

"It seems that Jen's parents are job hunting for Brad and Jen right now. Plus they have offered to buy them a house two blocks away."

"Well," Mom said, and sat back. "That is controlling."

"Anyway, Brad gave me the ring he recently purchased for Jen. It's a $100,000 Tiffany ring."

"Yikes!"

"I know," I said. "He says it's insured. I bumped up my insurance as well. I had to put it in my home safe overnight until I could get it to the bank and put it in my safe-deposit box. I plan on pulling it out just before their surprise engagement. That way the chances of losing it are small."

"Pepper, a ring like that might mean little to these people, but losing it could bankrupt you."

"It's okay, Mom. Brad and Jen's engagement is tomorrow.

I'm using Samantha Lyn's engagement as a cover for the real engagement of Brad and Jen."

"Well, that's confusing," Mom said with a frown. "So is Samantha Lyn getting engaged or not?"

"Yes, Clark is proposing," I said. "After Brad and Jen. It will make it appear more spontaneous. Anyway, I have told Jen that I need her to come and help it feel like another society event. Jen knows Mrs. Fulcrum. Mrs. Fulcrum sponsored Jen getting into her sorority at college . . . Wait!" I snapped my fingers. "That's where I know that fraternity name from. Mrs. Fulcrum is an active alumnus."

"What fraternity?" Mom asked.

"There's this mysterious cloth banner that Ashley's mom found in her things at school after the shooting. It has the Greek letters Xi Omicron Mu on it. I did some checking. Xi Omicron Mu is a coed fraternity. Mrs. Klein told me that she put it in the scrapbook of things that sometimes triggered memories for Ashley. I bet Mrs. Fulcrum knew Ashley through that fraternity."

"Did Ashley belong to the fraternity?"

"No," I said, "but I'm telling you there is something suspicious about those moms."

"You can't prove anything on suspicion," Mom said.

"Now you sound like Detective Murphy," I said, and frowned. "There's a connection between Ashley's memory of her shooting and her death. I'm going to find it."

"But first you have a double-engagement party to get through," Mom pointed out, and sipped her drink. "How are you getting them all to the same event again?"

"I sold it as a fund-raising event," I said.

"Fund-raising? For what?"

"We're supposed to be raising money for autism awareness."

"Oh, that's a good cause," Mom said.

"Yes, I've got flyers up and everything to make it appear as real as possible. It starts at eight P.M. with drinks and an ice buffet, then at nine P.M. there will be a fireworks show through the glass ceiling. I've got a big screen that will come down. I plan on positioning Brad behind it with the ring. Then we'll play music and light up the screen so all you see is his shadow as he gets down on one knee. He'll wear a microphone and his voice will play over the speakers as he asks Jen to marry him. Then I plan on lifting the screen enough for Brad to step out to hear Jen's answer. Meanwhile, behind them will be a display of pictures of their courtship and their childhoods."

"Wait, so no engagement dinner this time?"

"No," I said with a shake of my head. "The family and friends have been invited as part of the party crowd."

"And what about the kids? Won't their moms expect Clark to propose?"

"Yeah," I said. "I plan on fireworks to go off twenty minutes after Brad proposes and then Clark will get up on the ice stage and propose to Samantha Lyn. It won't be as dramatic as Brad and Jen, but it will be youthful and fun for the kids."

"So you'll get a two-for-one," Mom said.

"Yes, but this time Samantha and Clark's families and

friends will be there along with Jen and Brad's. They are all invited to the fund-raiser, and so I have an engagement reception planned for them following the proposal."

"That sounds like a lot of work," Mom said, and sipped her coffee.

"I'm up for it," I said.

"I know you are, dear, I know you are. Isn't it great that everyone involved runs in the same circles? I mean, they all belong to the country club. They all attend the same fund-raisers and they all know each other. It makes it helpful when planning two proposals in one night."

"Yes," I said. "Funny how small the world gets when you're at a certain income level."

"Well, we will make sure Felicity's world doesn't get too involved in all the rich people drama, won't we?"

I laughed. "Yes, I'll be happy to keep my baby sister's feet on the ground."

"Speaking of Felicity, your dad and I are planning a very small welcome-back dinner party at our house next Sunday night. It will be just you and Felicity and Warren and Gage. Can you come? We'd like to make a Sunday night tradition out of it."

I opened my mouth to say I wasn't so sure when she raised her palm to stop me.

"Before you say no, please think about it. We might live nearby, but you girls are building your own lives now. We really want to be a part of it, but we feel if we leave it to chance we'll never see you. Or you'll feel like we're invading your space because we randomly drop by. So we decided that a regular Sunday dinner was a great way to keep in touch and watch as your lives grow. Especially with Felicity married. We want our grandkids to visit once a week so that they grow up with us in their lives. We feel if we start the tradition now, it will more likely take root. Okay?"

I thought about Detective Murphy and how he wanted so much for his daughter to be a part of his life. I never thought I'd need to schedule visits to my parents, but with Felicity becoming part of high society, perhaps a Sunday night dinner tradition wouldn't be such a bad thing. "Okay," I said. "I'll be there."

"What about Gage?"

"I'll call and see if he can make it," I said. "Since I don't know where we stand on our dating yet . . ."

"This is the perfect time to have that conversation," Mom said, and looked pretty happy with herself. "Now, let's split a dessert. After all, you have a lot of party planning ahead and you're going to need your energy."

Chapter 18

Putting the fake fund-raiser posters up was easy. I sent out e-mails to everyone from the country club who was invited to my sister's wedding. That way the Fulcrums and Thomsons and Brad and Jen would see it as a society event.

My cell phone rang. I picked up. It was Mrs. Fulcrum.

"Hello, dear," Mrs. Fulcrum said. "I got the e-mail about the ice party fund-raiser. What a great idea."

"I agree that it's a good cover for a surprise proposal," I said. "I'm receiving RSVPs as we speak. People seem to be all for it even though it's last minute."

"It's because I made some phone calls," Mrs. Fulcrum said. "I want a full party when Clark proposes to Samantha Lyn. Now, you said there will be fireworks?"

"Sparklers inside," I said. "The roof is glass over the dance floor, so I've got a company to shoot off a short fifteen-minute color show. I'm so glad the Ice Pit is near the river."

"It's too cold to start any fires," Mrs. Fulcrum said. "I'm sure it will be fine. You mentioned costumes?"

"Yes, in the ad I mentioned costumes. I wanted people to know that costumes would be mandatory. They can wear their own, if they prefer. I thought it would be a good time to dust off some of the older furs the ladies have stored. But don't worry, Trinity Prop House will bring in racks of jazz-age costumes. They will be available for use for anyone who doesn't have their own. No one will be allowed entry without an appropriate costume."

"It sounds delightful," Mrs. Fulcrum said.

"I also promised the autism society a nice stipend for the use of their name and logo," I warned her. "That will be added to the bill."

"It's not a problem dear. In fact, Mr. Fulcrum will be happy to be able to write off any part of this event as a gift to charity."

"Perfect," I said. "Wait, one last thing."

"Make it quick, please."

"Yes, um, you mentioned that you are a contributing alumnus of Xi Omicron Mu."

"Yes, and?"

"And the bartender, Ashley, she had a banner with that fraternity's name on it from when she went to Morduray College."

"So?"

"So, I was wondering if you knew her before she was a bartender?"

"Was she a member of Xi Omicron Mu?" Mrs. Fulcrum asked.

"No—"

"Then no, I wouldn't have any reason to know her other than that she worked the bar at your sister's wedding—which, by the way, was lovely."

"Thank you," I said.

"Except for that creature ruining it by overdosing on the premises," Mrs. Fulcrum added. "Doing drugs and drinking while on duty. If she hadn't died, I would ensure she was fired and banned from bartending at any more events. My children and I should not be subjected to those kinds of people ever. What good is money if it can't keep you from the riffraff?"

"Right."

"If I were you, I'd ensure all the servers at tomorrow's party are drug tested tomorrow morning. I don't want anyone ruining Clark's proposal. Have I made myself clear?"

"Crystal clear," I said.

"Good, see you tomorrow," Mrs. Fulcrum said, and hung up.

I drummed my fingers on my desk. There had to be a link between those moms and Ashley's death. I was missing it. I sighed and thought about ordering drug tests for all the servers. That wasn't going to go over well. Maybe I was trying too hard. Two events in one would work for Jen, but would it work for Samantha Lyn? I cringed at the idea of that poor girl getting engaged to someone she clearly was not sure of . . . Maybe Jen and Brad's proposal would help Samantha Lyn see that she needed more time. It would put a kink in my perfect record of "Only a Yes!" but I would give that tagline up for Samantha Lyn's happiness.

I thought again about Ashley and what might have happened that fateful night that Kiera was killed and Ashley was left for dead. It happened near the college campus. I went over my notes. Morduray had a small private campus. It was coed with two dorms for men and two dorms for women. There was a sorority row where all the sororities had their homes. Two streets away was a fraternity row where all the frat houses were. The shooting took place in a part of campus that backed up to the sororities. Ashley and Kiera had participated in the homecoming parade and were at the bonfire after. According to Ashley's mother, the police interviewed witnesses who saw both girls leave the parade and head with the crowd toward the bonfire area. But then shortly after the bonfire party started the girls disappeared. They were found in the park near the sorority houses. It was assumed that they were ambushed in the park.

No one saw anything. I would have loved to see pictures of the crime scene but Detective Murphy wouldn't let me. All I had were pictures of the girls at the bonfire and that crowded picture Ashley's mom had shown me.

I wondered if there was some kind of feud between Ashley and Kiera and the fraternity. I decided to send an e-mail off to Ashley's mom to see if she knew why Ashley and Kiera weren't members. Then asked if she remembered any bad blood between the girls and that fraternity. Finally I ordered a yearbook from that year from a used-bookseller and of course was waiting for the pictures I ordered. Maybe there would be clues in there somewhere. I frowned. It felt like I was stretching.

So I let it go for now. Instead I called the pyrotechnician to make sure the fireworks show was ready and timed correctly. Then I packed up. A trip to the venue was in order. I needed to go over where Gage would set up his tents and his racks of clothes. The Ice Pit was installing a giant screen that would be backlit so that all you saw was Brad's shadow as he got down on one knee.

I arrived at the Ice Pit just as the sun was setting. I hated these long dark days of winter, but the good news was by the time Christmas came the days would start to grow long again. There was something so hopeful about the month of January when the light returned and there was the possibility of sporadic warm spells near the end of the month.

I met the event manager, Stephanie Howell, at the door. She opened it to me and handed me a thick, fake fur coat, hat, and gloves.

"It's kept at twenty degrees inside or the bar and the tables and chairs would melt," Stephanie explained as I bundled up.

The entire place was coated in ice. It dripped from the ceilings, making long icicles. The chairs were made of thick ice and the tall bar-height tables also were carved from ice. The glasses were ice carved in the shape of highball glasses, wineglasses, and shot glasses. It was the wineglasses that caught my attention. The bowl was perfect and the stem thin and tapering down to a balanced flat foot. "How do you make these?" I asked.

"They were made by Philip George. They do all the glasses. I think they create a mold and inject it with water— sometimes they add colors to the water like red or blue to accent the stems. Then they freeze them in a super cold freezer and ship them to us on dry ice."

"Wow," I said, "just wow." There were several tables scattered around the room. I did a quick count and realized they were more than adequate to meet the number of guests I was certain would show up.

"Let me show you the dance floor."

Stephanie led the way through the bar and table area to a glass-roofed area. "We have ice coolers under the floor here. That way if the sun gets too warm, it won't melt the floor. Really the glass top is so that people feel as if they are outside under the stars."

"That was a big selling point for me. My girl wants to have all the sparkle of the outdoors with all the glamour of the indoors."

"The band plays in the front on a small stage made out of twenty three-foot blocks of ice. Then the dance floor is eight inches of ice over the top of LED lights that change color in time with the music."

"Does anyone ever slip and fall?" I took a running step and slid to see how slick the dance floor was.

"No, generally everyone is happy with the ice and is very careful. We ask the girls to put mini chains on the toes of their stilettos to keep from falling."

"Mini chains?"

"Yes." She bent her right leg at the knee and showed me the bottom of her shoe. There was an elegant silver toe covering with what looked like tiny teeth. "It helps grip the ice."

"Nice."

"We also offer ice skate rentals," she said. "We don't allow skates on the dance floor but we have an outdoor rink for those who like to skate." She pointed at a door that led to a well-lit ice rink. A young woman in a red skater dress flew across the ice demonstrating flips and turns like those you see in the Olympics.

"Wow, she's good," I said as I watched the girl dance elegantly across the ice.

"Gayle is our resident skating expert. She offers lessons and tips to members who want to come in and skate but have never had a lesson."

"Great. Will she be working tomorrow night?"

"She most certainly will," the manager said. "Now, if you look up, you'll see the area where the fireworks will be. We can't fire off fireworks to demonstrate, so you'll have to trust me that it's going to be spectacular. We light the roof up with fairy lights before and after the fireworks." She flipped a switch and I could make out the undulation of the fairy lights in the roof.

"Good, now where are you hanging the big screen?"

"The big screen is right here in front of the band. A simple touch of a button and it will come down. Then the band will play the requested song and you can use our app on your phone to write something cool across the screen before your man gets down on one knee and proposes."

"Perfect," I said. "I've got a simple design with the words 'Jennifer, will you marry me?'" I showed her the script on my phone. It was bordered with scrolls and a diamond ring.

"That looks great," Stephanie said. "You can try it now, if you want." She waved and one of the guys hit a switch that lowered the screen. I put the script into the app and hit "Send." Within a second the words popped up on the screen, big and bold.

"Nice!"

"She'll be surprised, I'm certain of it."

"That's what I hope for."

She made a roll-it-up motion with her hands and the operator turned the projector off and the screen went back up into the ceiling. "Since you're raising money for autism, are you going to open the party to the general public?"

"I think so," I said. "I've got the go-ahead from Mrs. Fulcrum to do whatever I thought would make the night special."

"Just don't bring in a flash mob," Stephanie said. "Too many people all at once can overwhelm the cooling system and we might be dancing in a mud puddle."

"Got it," I said. "We'll cap it at two hundred attendees. Do you have room for that many?"

"It's a lot," she said, and tapped her chin with her long elegant nails. "One fifty would be best."

"I can up the price and make it feel very exclusive," I said.

"That might work," she agreed. "People like to know that they can give a substantial amount to the charity."

"Tickets will be purchased at the box office," I said. "That way they can turn anyone away over one fifty. I don't want to cause a scene."

"I think that's a good idea."

"It looks like everything is perfect," I said. "Do you have the tasting menu?"

"Sure, I'll bring it right out," Stephanie said, and walked away, leaving me to look closely at the venue to ensure it was the perfect fit for a romantic double proposal. Within five minutes, she and a waiter brought out giant trays of tasting foods. She gestured to the waiter to set the tray down on the table to my right. He did, then gave me a nod and walked back to the kitchen.

"These are all icy hors d'oeuvres," she said. "First, there is scafood on ice. Then there are vegetarian menu items and even gluten-free items. We want to be inclusive of everyone. Food and drink are so important. Go ahead, taste it."

The little bites were fantastic. All of them were chilled, but with bits of wasabi or chili or jalapeño to give it some heat. "Good."

"We'll serve them with ice-cold martinis—vodka and gin martinis."

"There will be kids here under twenty-one," I said.

"Yes, we have hot chocolate for them as well as virgin chocolate martinis if they want to feel like a grown up."

"Oh, good," I said, and my thoughts turned to Samantha

Lyn and Clark. Kids too young to drink alcohol should not be getting married. I sighed.

"Is something the matter?" she asked. "Is there something not to your liking?"

"Oh, no, everything here is perfect, especially on such short notice," I said. "It's the people at the party that I'm sighing over. One of my proposal couples is too young to drink alcohol. I think they are way too young to get married, but their mothers insist."

She leaned back and tsked with her tongue. "No, no, kids that young should be enjoying their lives, not settling down. I see it all the time. They have these big lavish weddings and then within six months are divorced. So sad. No one needs to do that to themselves."

"I agree," I said, and stood. "Listen, Trinity Prop House will be here in the afternoon to erect tents and set up dressing areas. We have told everyone that jazz-age costumes are necessary. If they don't have one, one will be provided for them. Can you have someone at the door to ensure that no one enters without a costume?"

"I can do that," she said. "Bruno is my guy at the door. I'll let him know that for this fund-raiser and proposal event, everyone must wear costumes."

"Perfect," I said. "Thanks. I think that gets us up to speed for tomorrow."

"Great," she said, and shook my hand. "Don't worry. This event will be spectacular."

"I'm counting on it."

Chapter 19

The next day was a complete madhouse. Snow had started in the wee morning hours and six inches were predicted by four P.M. I was biting my nails that people would come out. Most Chicagoans didn't let a little snow stop them, but it was a fund-raiser and it was a last-minute one to boot.

All I could do now was hope that the roads remained plowed and people actually showed up.

The driveway had to be shoveled before I could pull Old Blue out. I bundled up in my puffy jacket, snow boots, hat, and gloves, and got the shovel out of the garage. I noted that Mrs. C always kept an eye out that I didn't pile the snow against her house, but she never came to offer any assistance in the shoveling.

I was halfway done with the drive when I noticed the curtains in her dining room fluttering. Soon she had opened her door and stepped out into the cold morning air.

"They say we might get ten inches before it's over," Mrs. Crivitz said. People loved to be fatalistic when it came to snowfall. The worse it could be, the better. I, on the other hand, liked to be positive—especially when I had an event planned.

"Oh, I think it's only three inches," I said, and stuck the shovel perpendicular into the snow. "See? Not very deep at all."

"It's only just begun," Mrs. C predicted. "ABC7 says it's going to continue for the next eight hours. They are predicting snowpocalypse. I bet the kids come home early from school."

I looked at the half of the driveway I had done. It was slowly but surely being filled back in with fresh snow. I blew a stray strand of hair from my face. "I don't know, I think its stopping."

"You really should call Detective Murphy out to shovel your driveway. He's your landlord, right?" Mrs. Crivitz was wearing her hair in rollers with a bright turquoise scarf over them and tied around her chin. She had on a big old fur coat that showed the housedress she wore underneath it. She also had on thick socks and pink bunny slippers. Come to think of it, I'd never actually seen her off her porch or, for that matter, wearing anything but the housecoat. The curlers had to hurt.

"Detective Murphy is busy solving cases," I said. "I

knew when I rented the house that the yard work—including shoveling—would be my responsibility."

She leaned against her porch rail. "I have a nephew, Guido, who would come and plow you out for real cheap. In fact, if you flashed the girls a bit, he might even do it for free."

I sighed. I didn't really have much in the way of bosom to flash. "I like to shovel," I lied. "It's great acrobic exercise."

"Suit yourself," she said, and straightened. "It's really starting to come down now. You'll have to start over the minute you finish."

"Thanks for the encouragement," I said, and waved, then went back to work. Eventually she gave up and went back inside. I made it to the end of the drive and stood taking a moment of pride. Sure, there was now a new inch of snow on the drive, but at least the other four inches were shoveled. I headed up to the garage, running the shovel in front of me, when I heard the snow plow coming by. "No!"

Too late, the driver threw a nice, two-foot-wide section of snow across my driveway. It was at least six inches deep. I sighed and went back to work. At this rate I wasn't going to make it out to the Ice Pit until two P.M. All I could do was hope and pray that everyone else would make it as planned.

* * *

By two P.M. I was dressed in black slacks, flat-heeled booties, and a black turtleneck. My frizzy red hair was pulled into a messy bun. I had managed to get Old Blue down the slick streets to the Ice Pit. It was kind of ironic to have a cold party in the middle of a snowstorm. Too bad there wasn't a fire pit nearby. We could have made it fire and ice. I put Brad's ring in the Ice Pit's house safe for safekeeping, then went to work ensuring the centerpieces were set. The flower designer had gone all out with blue and crystal drops amid bare branches. White snowdrop blossoms and evergreens created drama. The centerpieces were kept small to decorate the standing bar tables.

The ice tables were draped in blue and white fairy lights so that they glowed. Stephanie, the Ice Pit event manager, sent two men up on the glass roof to sweep the snow off. It was five P.M. and luckily the snow had stopped falling.

Gage and his crew arrived and set up tents, then arranged the racks of costumes inside. I checked that the bar was well stocked and the hors d'oeuvres were ready.

My phone rang. It was Toby. "Hello?"

"Hey, Pepper," Toby said. "Are we still on? I'm supposed to meet Brad at the coffee shop at seven. The television says that some events for tonight are closed."

I glanced out the window. It was pitch black. "I think the snow stopped."

"It did."

"Then we're good to go," I said. "I'll send an e-mail around letting all the partygoers know it's still on. Hopefully they won't have a problem coming."

"What if Jen decides to stay home?"

I chewed on my bottom lip. "Well, that would put a kink in things, wouldn't it?"

"Yes," Toby said.

"I'll call Mrs. Thomson and ask her to ask Jen to drive her and Samantha Lyn to the party. That way she'll feel as if she has to go to help. Jen thinks this party is for Samantha Lyn's surprise proposal."

"That might work," Toby said. "Okay, I'll get Brad there by eight P.M."

"Thanks, Toby," I said, and hung up the phone. Gage walked in. He was dressed in a dark black zoot suit with a heavy watch chain. "Hi, handsome."

"You need to go get dressed," he said, and pulled out his pocket watch. "Time is ticking."

"I need to call Mrs. Thomson first. That was Toby. He was afraid that Jen might not come due to the weather. I'm going to call Mrs. Thomson and get her to call Jen and ask Jen to ensure she and Samantha Lyn get there."

"Will that work?" He asked. "The Thomsons have money and can get a chauffeur to drive them when the weather's bad."

"Oh," I said, and frowned. "How am I going to get Jen to come out in the weather?"

"You can still call Mrs. Thomson and ask her if they can pick up Jen and bring her instead."

"Oh, that's brilliant," I said. "She can tell Jen that Samantha Lyn is getting nervous and needs some company."

"What about Clark?" Gage asked.

"Mrs. Fulcrum is coming," I said. "I talked to her an hour ago. She has picked up the engagement ring and

Clark's costume. She'll make sure her boy gets to his engagement party on time."

"So, make the phone call and then go out to the dolls' tent and get dolled up," Gage said, and grinned at me. "I can't wait to see you all jazzed up."

"Okay," I said, and gave him a quick kiss. Then I phoned Mrs. Thomson, who assured me she would see that Jen showed up. Both Mrs. Thomson and Mrs. Fulcrum knew Jen and her parents and were aware of my dilemma of surprising the girl. Thankfully they didn't mind that I was using this one event for two proposals. I hadn't done two at once before. I was still half hoping that Samantha Lyn would say no.

My phone chimed, letting me know I had e-mail. I thumbed through to it as I entered the tent to change into my costume. Stopping short, I stared at the pictures in my hand. The college pictures from the time of Ashley's homecoming had come in. Suddenly it all became very clear in my mind. I dialed Detective Murphy.

"Murphy," he answered.

"Hi, it's Pepper. I think I know who killed Ashley and why," I said in a low whisper as I looked around. The tent was full of people who had arrived for the event and were having fun getting into costume. Luckily the place was filled with chatting and laughter and I knew that no one was paying me much attention.

"Pepper, where are you?"

I put a finger in my opposite ear and turned my back to the crowd. "I'm at the Ice Pit for an event. I need you to come and bring backup. I'm going to reveal Ashley's killer."

"Pepper, don't. Don't do anything stupid. Tell me what you know and I'll take care of the suspects."

"Pepper, darling!" Mrs. Fulcrum entered the tent wearing a full-length mink coat over a dazzling gold-beaded flapper dress. She had her arms out and smothered me in her embrace. "This is fantastic."

"Thanks," I muttered next to her ear as she gave me two air kisses. I kissed the air back and stepped away. "Hold on just a second." Then I put my phone back up to my ear. "I need you here ASAP," I said. Then I hung up.

"Who was that?" Mrs. Fulcrum asked. "One of your employees?"

"Sure," I said, and sent her a weak smile. "The weather has people all jumbled up."

"Terrible to have a snowstorm on the same day as this event, but I'm so excited. Clark is dressed and I sent him inside to get a beverage with a warning not to spill anything on his suit."

"Good," I said.

She locked her arm through mine and turned me to the happy, busy tent. "Tell me what's going on here."

"I got Trinity Prop House to donate jazz-age costumes and props," I said, and waved toward the three racks of clothes and the wall of accessories. "Then I hired a male stylist and a female stylist to help anyone who was having trouble putting together a look. That's Miranda in the corner helping those two young girls."

"Perfect," Mrs. Fulcrum gushed. She looked around. "I don't see our girls yet."

"I called Mrs. Thomson a few minutes ago. She is calling Jen and picking her up so that Samantha has a friend."

"Smart girl," Mrs. Fulcrum said. "Well, now, you need to get dressed and get inside the venue."

"Yes," I said with a nod. "I do. Why don't you go inside? There's a three-piece orchestra playing and there are cocktails. The hors d'oeuvres will be out in thirty minutes."

"And the courses?" she asked. "Are they still as we discussed in the proposal?"

"Yes, as discussed there will be six separate hors d'oeuvre courses," I said. "We start with a light shrimp cocktail, move through the courses, and end with wedding cake shots. Those will go around after the proposals."

"Yes, of course," she said with a nod. "Good, I'll see you inside."

"Have fun," I said, and waved her on. Then I rushed over to the rack with the blush pink flapper gown I had tried on earlier and asked Miranda to accessorize for me. She had set the outfit aside so that no one else would take it. Not that they could. It took a special type of dress to fit my beanpole figure. Flapper was a good look for me. The girls were meant to be boyishly thin with little bosom.

I yanked off my black turtleneck, then my black slacks, and slipped the gown over my head. Next I sat and rolled silk stockings up over my knees and held them in place with pink garters. Finally I went to one of five mirrored vanities at a long table on the far side of the tent and pinned my unruly carrot-red hair into a wavy faux bob. My makeup was cool neutrals with a Clara Bow lip. Then I slipped into silver twenties-inspired dance shoes, added chandelier earrings, and stepped up to one of the four full-length mirrors.

"You look fabulous," Miranda gushed as she walked over from where she had been helping an elderly woman find the right faux fur.

"Thanks," I said. "What coat do I have?" Coats and gloves were a must in the Ice Pit, as it was kept at twenty degrees to ensure nothing melted.

"I saved this faux silver fox." Miranda went over to her rack and pulled a three-quarter-length-sleeved swing coat in what appeared to be a silver fur.

"It's marvelous," I said, and put it on. It swung from the shoulders and was warm but lightweight.

"I thought you'd be warmer than most, running around ensuring everything went off without a hitch. Here is a pair of opera-length silver gloves."

She handed me the gloves and I put them on. "Not bad."

"Perfect," she said. "Now, go out there and be a success."

I smiled at her. "I'll do my best." But my spirit wasn't into tonight's proposals. My heart was beating fast as I hoped to goodness that Detective Murphy took me seriously and was on his way with backup. If I could get Ashley's killer to confess, then the event would certainly make the evening news as promised.

Chapter 20

I went into the Ice Pit and was stopped by the catering manager to ensure that the right courses were in the right order. I sent the miniature shrimp cocktails out first in tiny martini glasses along with sippers of pink champagne. They really pumped the icy air into the place as it filled up with guests. The atmosphere was one of excitement. Guests' breath puffed out as they talked, leaving a surreal feeling of fog and ice. The ice bar tables were lit softly. The décor was understated and yet sparkly and grand. The stars twinkled overhead.

"Pepper, everything is so divine," Jen said as she rushed up to me. She wore a lovely silver flapper gown that hit just above the knee with fringe that hung below so that when she walked the tops of her stockings and garters showed. It was the demure-yet-naughty-flapper look that had been all the rage in the twenties. She wore a mink stole and long opera gloves.

"Thank you," I said.

"These are my colors," she said.

"Oh, no, not exactly," I said. "Please note the cobalt blue accents and the starry night ceiling. Samantha wanted a pop of color. You were all silver and white. She also asked me to make it glittery and snowy and star-filled."

"Well, you certainly accomplished that," Jen said with a smile. She snagged a tiny champagne glass off a waiter's plate. "Samantha must be thrilled."

"I'm glad you came," I said. "Mrs. Thomson said that she wasn't sure if Samantha would feel comfortable without girlfriends."

"Well," Jen said, and winked at me, "I know you wanted me to see how your proposals go, and I was happy to see our little girl comfortable on her shining night."

I grabbed a drink as well and swallowed it straight down in one gulp. "Isn't it funny how you all know each other?"

"Oh, honey, it's the country club way. Samantha and I grew up in the same social circles. I might be five years older than her, but we've know each other forever, and once you're out of high school then it's all one big happy family."

"Except for the waitstaff," I said with a shake of my head. "Let's hope that nothing happens to anyone here."

"Oh, dear, that's right, your sister's event had that awful girl dying," Jen said. "I'm sure you learned to better interview your staff, right?"

"Right," I said, with a short shake of my head. "And I gave them all strict instructions not to drink while serving guests."

"Great idea," Jen said. "Do the same for my event."

"Oh, I plan on doing it for all my events from now on."

"Good," Jen said, and waved at a woman who passed by. "All right, I must go mingle or Samantha might get suspicious."

"Take a careful look around," I suggested. "You never know when it might be your last event."

"Will do," Jen said, winked, and walked off to say hello to Mrs. Fulcrum and Clark.

I texted Detective Murphy. "Please come and bring backup."

My phone dinged back. "Send me evidence."

I blew out a breath and sent him the e-mail with the pictures. Then I texted. "This won't make sense unless you know that Ashley's mom found a remnant with the Xi Omicron Mu symbol on it. She said it triggered Ashley."

There was a long pause.

"Pepper." Stephanie called my name. I looked up to see her motioning for me to come over to the bar. "Toby's here."

I nodded and followed her to the kitchen. Toby was in the back with Brad, who looked confused.

"Hi, Toby, thanks for this," I said, and greeted him with a kiss on the cheek.

"Pepper," Brad said, and greeted me with a hug. "You look awesome. Are you involved in the charity event Jen is attending?"

"It's a proposal party," Toby said.

"Oh, right, for Clark Fulcrum and Samantha Lyn Thomson," Brad said with a pointing gesture. "I remember Jen said she was coming to see one more of your proposals, this one really extravagant. More in keeping with what Jen was looking for in her proposal."

"That's right," I said. "It's fully in keeping with Jen's proposal." I waved for Stephanie to come forward. She did and I took the Tiffany box from her. "I planned on Jen being really surprised," I said. "Brad, here's the engagement ring. You're going to want it."

"What? Now? Before Clark?" Brad seemed confused and that made me happy. If he was caught off guard, here's hoping Jen would be as well.

"Yes, before Clark," I said. "It's a double proposal. Now, I need you two to go change into an appropriate jazz-age costume."

"A double proposal," Brad said, and broke out into a wide grin. "Yes, this might actually work."

"Please don't let anyone see you. Lacey will take you through the waiters' entrance to the costume tents. Text me when you're dressed and I'll have someone bring you back."

"Will do," Toby said. "Come on, Bradley. Let's do this thing right."

"Wait!" I said, and put my arm on Toby's. "Did you call Amelia?"

"Yes."

"And?"

"She's going meet me at the bookstore tomorrow for coffee."

I grinned and made a fist pump. "Yes!"

"We're going to talk books, music, and movies and see if we are compatible."

"Good," I said. Maybe something good would come out of this night. "Now scoot, you two. We have an announcement to make and you have to be in costume."

Lacey was the manager's assistant, and she took the guys out through the back to the tent where Gage would work his magic.

I looked down at my phone. There was no answering text from Detective Murphy. I frowned and shook my head. Then I went to find Cesar, who was recording the entire night. Cesar was near the ice dance floor and the big white screen shooting video of the crowd.

"Hi," I said.

"Wow, you look gorgeous," he said, and gave a low wolf whistle. I could feel the heat of a blush rush up from my chest to the top of my head. Even in an icy room I could turn beet red.

"Thanks," I said. "Listen, I'm going to be lowering the screen soon. I need you to pay special attention to that girl there." I pointed at Jen. "When the screen comes down, I want you to focus on her every word and emotion. Can you do that?"

"Sure."

"Don't start yet," I said. "It's supposed to be a big surprise and she'll figure it out if she sees the camera following her."

"Got it," he said. "Maybe if I go stand near her and

film the crowd from that angle, she won't think anything about it."

"Great," I said. "Thanks. She wants me to get every moment of the surprise and I can't disappoint her."

"Don't worry," Cesar said. "I'll get the footage."

"Thanks." I glanced down at my phone. Still nothing from Detective Murphy. I was beginning to wonder if he was deliberately ignoring me. I frowned. Maybe he thought my evidence wasn't enough. I chewed my bottom lip. Maybe it wasn't, but it felt like it was enough and I had to go with my gut on this. It was too important to me to not let something go. I scanned the room. Mrs. Fulcrum was talking to Mrs. Thomson and Samantha Lyn. Clark had been banished to the opposite end of the room to entertain himself among other guys his age. The guys were playing foosball on ice tables.

I looked at Samantha Lyn. She was gorgeous in a sparkling flapper costume. Her thick blond hair was curled, with baby's breath woven in like a tiara. Cesar went over to where Jen stood talking to an older couple I remembered from the country club. He kept his camera trained on Samantha Lyn as the girl tried to enjoy herself among the much older patrons of the event. After the third course of hors d'oeuvres, the orchestra cleared away for a swing band. As part of the band's performance, the screen was lowered and they were backlit so that they looked like a shadow band. People danced the Charleston and other dances. I was happy to see Samantha Lyn trying to dance and have fun. Her eyes sparkled and her skin was flushed.

I looked at my phone. Still nothing from Detective

Murphy. I chewed on my lip and looked around. If he didn't make it, what should I do? Keep moving forward, I guess. I used the phone app to quickly upload pictures into the projector that would be put on the screen behind Brad when he came out. The pictures were of him and Jen from the time they were in high school, through college and today. I made the last-minute decision to add a couple of pictures and change the headline.

Worrying the inside of my cheek, all I could do was hope that I was doing the right thing and that Detective Murphy and his squad would show up.

"Pepper, it's time," Stephanie called to me.

"Is everything in place?"

"Yes. Toby has Brad behind the screen now. The man-made snowflakes are ready."

"Let them fall," I said, and hit "Go" with my cell phone app. Fat snowflakes fell from the ceiling onto the dancers. I walked quickly over to Jen. Brad's silhouette showed on the back of the screen.

"Oh, is this it?" Jen asked me. Her gaze went to Samantha Lyn. "How gorgeous is this. I'm getting tears in my eyes."

"Just wait," I said, and pushed the next button. The screen lit up with the words I had just programmed into the computer.

"Wait, I don't understand," Jen said, her face shocked as she looked from the screen to me then back to the screen where I had typed "Jennifer McCutchen, why did you murder Kiera Smith and Ashley Klein?"

Everyone gasped and turned to me and Jen. "Jen," I

said. "I know you shot Kiera Smith that night at the homecoming bonfire. Why did you kill Ashley? Was it because she was remembering?"

Jen's face went from confusion to a brief moment of anger to fear to a mask of innocent outrage. "What are you talking about?"

"You went to Morduray College with Ashley and Kiera," I said, and pointed to the pictures from that homecoming day that played up on the big screen. There on the Xi Omicron Mu float was a smiling Jen waving to the crowd. The float was decorated with the white squares of fabric just like the fabric that Ashley's mom had put in the scrapbook. "You were up for homecoming queen, but you didn't make it, did you?"

"No, I didn't," she said, her nose up in the air. I noticed the fine tremble in her fingers. "Everyone knows that Kiera was homecoming queen the night she was shot."

I pressed forward, trying to get something on video before the entire evening went up in smoke. "Look at the pictures, Jennifer," I said. "That's you riding on the float for Xi Omicron Mu. Isn't it?"

"So?"

"Doesn't that sash identify you as the fraternity's president?" I pushed.

"Everyone knows this," Jennifer said. "What's your point? I thought maybe this might be my proposal night, but you've clearly ruined that, and if you're not careful you're going to ruin it for Samantha as well."

"What happened that night, Jennifer?" I asked when the

next picture flashed up. "This is you and Ashley and Kiera, isn't it?" The picture showed Ashley and Kiera laughing. Jennifer faced them holding a piece of Xi Omicron Mu fabric in the air—identical to the one in Ashley's mother's scrapbook. "It looks like you're shouting at them. They're laughing and you're shouting. You were very angry, weren't you, Jennifer?"

"Ashley and Kiera weren't nice girls," Jen said, her composure cracking at the sight of them laughing at her and her anger. "They were mean girls. Kiera didn't deserve to be homecoming queen. Ashley was the worst. She's the one who would pull horrible pranks. They did mean, terrible things."

"And you did mean things back, didn't you, Jennifer?" I asked, and noted that Detective Murphy had finally entered the Ice Pit with four uniformed police officers behind him. "Ashley's mother told me that pictures from this day and a sign from this fraternity are the only things that triggered Ashley's memory. They gave her severe headaches and spells just like the one she had when I met her at the country club. Something triggered her at my sister's reception. I bet that something was seeing you."

Jen started shaking from head to toe. I could see her freaking out at the evidence of her screaming at Kiera and Ashley the night they were shot. In the picture, her fists were balled up, the incriminating piece of banner in her hand. "I didn't do anything," she said. "This is crazy. You are crazy." She glanced over and saw the police. Then she took a step back. "You called the police? You can't call the police. This is my proposal. This is my time. You can't ruin it."

She raised her fisted hand and took a step toward me, shaking. Brad grabbed her. "It's okay, Jen, It's okay. She's crazy. Don't worry."

"I'm going to sue you for everything you've got," she said, and pointed a finger at me, poking me in the chest. "Everything you've got. You can't make accusations."

"You lied to me," I said. "That's not an accusation. You lied to the police as well. You said that you didn't know Ashley." I pointed at the screen. "You did know her, didn't you? Why, Jen? Why would you lie about knowing her unless you're the one who killed Kiera and you were worried because you thought Ashley saw something? When you saw her bartending at my sister's wedding, you got nervous. She kept looking your way. You figured she remembered what you did."

"I lied because I didn't want anyone to know that I actually went to school with that lowlife bartender, okay?" Jen screamed as people gathered around listening to my story, eyeing the pictures on the screen. "You saw her, Mrs. Fulcrum, Mrs. Thomson. She looked like a wasted drug addict. She should have never been allowed to tend bar anywhere near our social set."

"I heard that Ashley liked to play pranks in college," I said carefully. "Look at these pictures of you on the float. Look at the float skirt. Aren't those Ashley and Kiera's sorority's letters? They switched your letters with their own, didn't they?"

"Those two were horrid, mean girls. They laughed. They thought humiliating me was funny. They were nothing but lowlife girls who had to depend on scholarships and school loans to even get into the school. They had the gall to prank me. Me! My family has a pedigree that goes back seven generations."

"You'd had enough of their pranks that night, didn't you?" I asked, and flipped the picture back to the one where she was screaming with her fists raised. "You had a gun that night, didn't you?"

"Of course, I had a gun," Jen sneered. "My father insisted that I do. Michigan allows concealed carry. I wasn't breaking any laws. I had a permit."

"My guess is that you only meant to threaten them with it," I said softly. "Isn't that right? You were so mad you took it out and pointed it at Kiera." I flipped to another picture where she had her hand in the pocket of the jacket she wore over her parade gown. In the picture you could see the outline of a gun under the fabric. "That's all you meant to do, wasn't it?" I said, and stepped closer to put my hand on her arm. "You didn't mean to shoot Kiera, did you?"

I could feel her trembling under my touch. Her eyes were filled with anger and tears. "I didn't point it at Kiera, stupid," she said. "I pointed it at Ashley. She was not the nice person you seem to think she was. She had a vile tongue. She made fun of me. Me! She laughed and said I looked the fool in front of the entire campus and all the alumni waving and smiling as if I were some kind of float queen, and all the while my float had their letters on it. I took out the gun and shoved it in her laughing face. But she didn't stop laughing.

She saw my gun and laughed harder. She said it was a kid's toy. She couldn't be afraid of something so ridiculous."

"The gun went off," I said.

"The gun went off," she repeated softly. "Ashley fell to the ground." Jen looked at me pleadingly. "I didn't know what to do. Kiera started screaming. She was running away. She was going to tell."

"So you shot her."

"I raised my hand to make her stop. I told her to stop. Stop!" Jen said. Brad stepped back, letting her go with a stricken look on his face.

"She didn't stop, did she?"

"No," Jennifer said. "I shot her and she went down."

"And you left them both for dead."

"I . . . I got scared. I dropped the gun and fell to my knees."

"Why didn't you call 911?" I asked.

"I was in shock. I called my parents."

"You called your parents?" Detective Murphy said.

"Yes," she said, her gaze far-off and her shoulders slumped. "I called my father. I was hysterical. He told me to calm down. He asked me to look around. Was anyone nearby? Had anyone heard the shots?" She took a deep breath. "I figured that someone had to have heard. Two gunshots on campus. Someone had to have called the authorities."

"But no one came," I said.

"No, no one came. Then I realized that everyone was at the bonfire. There were firecrackers going off left and right. I told my father. He told me to leave. He told me to not go back to my dorm, but instead to get in my car and drive straight home to Chicago."

"So you drove," I said. "How were you able to drive?"

"I was in shock and it felt good to run away," she said. "I put the gun in a tote bag and put it in my trunk. When I got home, my parents met me at the curb. My mother got me inside and cleaned me up."

"What happened to the gun?" Detective Murphy asked.

"I don't know," she said, and shook her head. "Daddy took care of it. He had my car detailed. I spent the rest of the weekend with them. We came up with a story. I was to tell everyone, including Brad, that Aunt Millie had taken sick and I was called home right after the parade."

"You lied to me," Brad said, and took another step back. His face was filled with grief and disbelief. "Is that why your parents moved to California? Is that why they wanted you to move with them?"

"Don't you see?" she said, her expression pleading. "I stayed to be with you. I love you and I stayed. It was going okay. Really, it was . . . until I saw Ashley at the first wedding doing the bartender thing. She took off with Samantha Lyn and I had to know if she told Samantha anything."

"She didn't," Samantha said. "She never told me about any of this."

"I didn't know," Jen said. "I started waiting for her to remember. For the police to come." Jen shook she was so upset. "Then when I saw Ashley bartending at yet another event, I freaked out. I saw her watching. I swear she knew. She remembered. Then I saw her talking to Samantha Lyn and then you, Pepper. I knew she was telling you all my secrets. If she hadn't, she was about to . . ."

"So you slipped Xanax in her drink," I said.

"I just wanted her to leave, you know? I wanted her to forget even being at the wedding. I needed her to forget."

"Wait," Brad said. "Where did you get the Xanax?"

"I was in the bathroom with Mrs. Thomson and Samantha," Jen said. "I saw it in Mrs. Thomson's purse."

"You were in my purse?" Mrs. Thomson said, and put her hand to her mouth.

"You left your purse on the counter, remember? You asked me to watch it while you used the toilet," Jen said. "I took a couple of pills. I didn't think you would notice."

"I didn't," Mrs. Thomson said, her face going pale. "I trusted you, Jen."

"It wasn't supposed to kill her," Jen sobbed. "Just shut her up. I was going to speak to the hiring manager and make sure Ashley never worked another country club event." She turned to Brad. "Once we were engaged, Mom and Dad were going to move us to California, far from Ashley and anyone who knew about that night."

Tears formed in her eyes as she looked from Brad to me and back. "This was supposed to be our perfect night," she screamed. "You ruined it!" She advanced on me, hands raised like claws as if to gouge my eyes out. "You ruined everything."

Detective Murphy stepped in and took hold of Jennifer. "Come with me," he said, and pulled her away. "Don't make me handcuff you in front of your friends."

Brad stood in horror as he watched Detective Murphy haul his bride-to-be off. He shook his head and sent me a look of disgust. "I can't believe you did this. Jennifer only said that because you forced her to. I expect a full refund on my retainer. I can't believe this outrage." He stormed off and pulled out his phone. I assumed he was calling his lawyer.

I blew out a long breath and slumped into a nearby chair. "I'm so sorry, everyone," I said to the crowd. "That was not planned. Please enjoy your evening. We still have dancing and more food as well as a fireworks show." I turned to Mrs. Fulcrum and Mrs. Thomson. "We can reschedule Clark's proposal. I know this kind of put a damper on things."

"A damper?" Mrs. Thomson looked down her nose at me. "This is the worst evening of my life. That girl used my prescription to kill someone. I can't, no, I won't have Samantha Lyn involved in this spectacle. Come on, Samantha Lyn, let's go."

"Oh, no," Samantha Lyn piped up and pulled her arm out of her mother's hand. "We've just seen how bad choices can ruin lives. I'm not going to let you ruin mine. I won't marry Clark. Sorry, Clark."

"What? No," Mrs. Thomson said. "You've just had a scare, is all."

"I can't believe you pulled such a public stunt, Pepper," Mrs. Fulcrum said. "And now you've frightened poor

Samantha Lyn. Come child, you and Clark need to go home. You'll reconsider after the shock has worn off."

"No, I won't reconsider," Samantha Lyn said. "I'm finally listening to my heart. I don't care if you and Dad cut me off. I'm going to go back to college, somehow, and I'm going to decide my own life."

"Well, I never . . ." Mrs. Fulcrum said. "The audacity of some people. Come on, Clark, this disastrous night has made one thing abundantly clear. Samantha Lyn Thomson is not the girl for you. We can't have outbursts like that in our family." She looked Mrs. Thomson up and down. "We also can't be associated with people whose misjudgment can cause another person to die." She grabbed Clark by the arm and pulled him away. Clark didn't seem at all worried over losing Samantha. He merely shrugged and slouched his way out the door with his mother.

"Well," Mrs. Thomson said, and took a tissue out of her clutch to dab at her eyes. "I've never been so humiliated in my entire life. Samantha Lyn, how could you do this to me?"

"I didn't do this to you," Samantha said, and put her hand on her mother's arm. "I did this for me."

Mrs. Thomson shrugged away from her daughter. "I don't even know who you are anymore. You want to go to college so bad? You go ahead and pack your bags. You'll end up just as twisted as those girls. Maybe even dead," she sniffed.

"Lots of women go to college, Mother, and graduate just fine."

"You can expect your things to be put out of my house."

"Mom, please." Samantha Lyn looked at me as her mom stormed off.

"If you need a place to stay, I have a spare room," I said. "You're a smart and beautiful woman. Go to college. Live your life, you only have one."

Samantha blew out a long breath. "That's what Ashley said, too." She straightened her shoulders. "I'm going to do it, if for no other reason but to make Ashley proud."

"That's my girl," I said, and patted her shoulder.

She smiled at me. "Besides, I'm pretty sure Dad will talk Mom down. At the worst, I'll move into the carriage house apartment. It's not the Fulcrum mansion, but it will be a place of my own." She reached up and kissed my cheek. "Thanks, Pepper, for figuring out what really happened to Ashley and for helping me see that life is short. I need to live my life for me."

I watched her walk out as the fireworks started overhead. There were still a hundred people at the event. It might not have ended up being a proposal event, but it did raise money for autism awareness. I grabbed a glass of champagne off the waiter's tray and toasted the stars, then drank it down. I may have found a killer, but this night could ruin Perfect Proposals. I sighed. If I had to do it all over again, I wouldn't change a thing.

Toby came over to me with a glass of champagne in his hand. "Interesting party."

I laughed and put my hand to my forehead. "I hope that never happens again."

"I bet," he said. "This certainly didn't have the romance

you keep lecturing me about." He raised his right eyebrow. "Maybe my way of looking for a wife using background checks and learning all about her before we meet might be the smarter move after all."

"Really?" I asked. "You still think that even after meeting Amelia?"

"Oh, yes," he said, and his smile widened. "I did a background check on her the minute you told me about her."

"You did?" I frowned.

"Don't worry," he said, and winked. "She passed with flying colors."

"Of course she did," I said. "I wouldn't have introduced you if I didn't think she would."

"Also, she told me she had me checked out as well," he said, and sipped his drink.

"She did?"

"Yes," he said, and smiled. "I passed as well I was pleased to meet a girl who thought like me on the matter."

"When's your next date, again?"

"Tomorrow," he said. "I happen to know it's going to go a whole lot better than tonight."

I chuckled and clinked my glass on his. "Here's to new beginnings and better choices in love."

"Hear, hear."

Chapter 21

"So when all was said and done, you raised ten thousand dollars for autism," Mom said.

"Yes," I said. "The event was such a success as a fundraiser that Mr. Fulcrum insisted that his foundation pay for all the trappings even though I upset his wife. He said it was good press and good for his taxes as a write-off. In fact, he wants to plan another one for next year. He just asked that I not use it to catch another killer."

"I certainly hope not," Mom said.

"You won't be planning it, will you?" Felicity asked.

We sat around Mom and Dad's dining room table. Mom had made a roast with all the trimmings. Felicity and Warren looked tan and rested. They practically glowed with happiness. They held hands on the table for all to see.

"Oh, no," I said, and looked at Gage. "But Trinity Prop House has already been asked to do the costumes again next year. Isn't that right, Gage?"

"Yes," he said, and beamed at me. "Several members of the country club were impressed by what we had to offer and have set up meetings to discuss other events in the coming months."

Mom had the house decorated for Christmas. There was a fully decorated six-foot tree in the corner of the living room. Twinkle lights surrounded the dining room windows. Candles flickered on the beautifully done table. It was warm and cozy and I felt how full of love my parents' house was.

"What about Perfect Proposals?" Mom asked. "I heard Brad threatened to sue you over the accusation even though Jen confessed. Can he do that?"

"Perfect Proposals is fine," I said, and patted my mother's hand. "Warren's lawyer went over everything with me and promised me that there is no reason to worry. Any lawsuit brought against me or my company would be considered frivolous in the face of Jennifer's confession."

"I know she did horrible things," Felicity said, "but she must have been eaten up with guilt. In fact, you did her a huge favor. Imagine trying to live your life, knowing all the while that you were responsible for so much death."

"They'll plea bargain," Warren said, and sipped from his glass of pinot noir. "The McCutchens have money. They won't want this to go to trial. The press would devastate their reputation."

"What will happen to Jennifer?" I wondered.

"She will most likely spend the rest of her days in jail."

"Well, let's hope that I never have to do another proposal murder reveal ever again," I said, and raised my glass.

"Hear, hear," my family chimed in, and we all touched glasses to toast.

"You've come a long way since you first planned Felicity's proposal," Dad said. "I couldn't be more proud of both of my girls."

"Thanks, Dad."

"Love you, Daddy." Felicity blew him a kiss.

"Here's to family, friends, and perfect proposals." Warren lifted his glass.

I couldn't agree more. "Cheers."

Wedding Menu

THIS MENU IS AN AMERICAN VERSION OF THE BREAKFAST
MENU AT KATE AND WILLIAM'S ROYAL WEDDING

MARINATED PACIFIC SALMON

LIME CRAB

WILD LANGOUSTINES IN BUTTER SAUCE

FRESH HERB SALAD

MEURSAULT WINE

SADDLE OF LAMB

SEASONAL VEGETABLES

ASPARAGUS

SMALL POTATOES IN CREAM SAUCE

CHATEAU L'HOSPITALET WINE

TRIO OF HONEY ICE CREAM

SHERRY TRIFLE

CHOCOLATE PARFAIT

WEDDING CAKE SHOOTER

ROSÉ

————————

COFFEE

MINT TEA

Also from
Nancy J. Parra

Bodice of Evidence
A Perfect Proposals Mystery

Pepper's new wedding proposal planning business, Perfect Proposals, seems like a perfect fit. If only shopping for her sister Felicity's bridal gown could be so simple.

After a long day of lace, tulle, and tears, Pepper, Felicity, and their mother pull it together to try one last bridal boutique. Maybe they'll be surprised. And indeed they are—when they enter a deserted shop and soon discover the owner of the boutique slain in the alley out back.

Distressed by their proximity to the crime, Pepper vows to unveil the killer. As difficult as it is to draw a pattern from the clues, it's still easier than finding Felicity's perfect wedding gown. But as the killer begins to feel hemmed in, Pepper may be the one brought to her knees…

Also in the series:
Engaged in Murder

nancyjparra.com
facebook.com/nancyjparraauthor
penguin.com

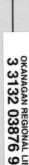